RUSTED SOULS

RUSTED SOULS

Chris Nickson

SEVERN HOUSE

First world edition published in Great Britain and the USA in 2023
by Severn House, an imprint of Canongate Books Ltd,
14 High Street, Edinburgh EH1 1TE.

severnhouse.com

British Library Cataloguing-in-Publication Data
A CIP catalogue record for this title is available from the British Library.

ISBN-13: 978-1-4483-1179-8 (cased)
ISBN-13: 978-1-4483-1209-2 (e-book)

All Severn House titles are printed on acid-free paper.

Typeset by Palimpsest Book Production Ltd.,
Falkirk, Stirlingshire, Scotland.
Printed and bound in Great Britain by
TJ Books, Padstow, Cornwall.

Praise for Chris Nickson

"Nickson . . . reinforces his place in the front rank of historical mystery authors"
Publishers Weekly Starred Review of *A Dark Steel Death*

"A good balance of historical ambience, details of police work in the early twentieth century, and heartwarming insights into Harper's family life . . . a sure bet"
Booklist on *A Dark Steel Death*

"A gritty police procedural with well-drawn characters"
Kirkus Reviews on *A Dark Steel Death*

"Stellar . . . James Ellroy fans will be enthralled"
Publishers Weekly Starred Review of *The Blood Covenant*

"A realistic, well-written historical procedural that will draw fans of Charles Todd's Ian Rutledge mysteries"
Booklist on *Brass Lives*

"Harper's ninth case is an excellent mystery buoyed by characters you care about"
Kirkus Reviews on *Brass Lives*

"A convincing portrait of pre-WWI Leeds. Historical procedural fans will be pleased"
Publishers Weekly on *Brass Lives*

"Superior . . . Nickson's consistent high quality across multiple series continues to impress"
Publishers Weekly Starred Review of *The Molten City*

About the author

Chris Nickson is the author of ten previous Tom Harper mysteries, seven highly acclaimed novels in the Richard Nottingham series, and five Simon Westow books. Born and raised in Leeds, he moved back there some years ago.

www.chrisnickson.co.uk

For all the forgotten Leeds dead

Leeds. Monday March 22, 1920

T
om Harper stood by the window and gazed down at the people walking along Great George Street. From his office in Leeds Town Hall he could pick out faces, some worried, some preoccupied, one or two smiling at a private joke. One or two still wore gauze masks, hoping to keep themselves safe from the Spanish influenza. The epidemic was receding; fewer and fewer were dying each week. But he was the chief constable, he saw the figures: the disease might be fading, but it hadn't vanished yet. The flu had killed too many, over two thousand in the city since it began, God alone knew how many millions across the globe, and all in the wake of the worst war man had ever known.

Miss Sharp coughed and broke his train of thought. He was grateful for the intrusion. Better than brooding on the people lost, or the men with broken lives he saw as he walked every day. He turned to face her.

'Have I forgotten something? Another meeting?' Half past ten, the week had barely begun, and Harper had already sat through two of them. He'd hoped that was it for the morning. But she was his secretary; she knew where he needed to be.

'Alderman Thompson rang. He'd like to talk to you.'

He gave a wry smile. 'Well, then, I suppose I'd better see what he wants.'

Thompson led the council, a man who lived and breathed Leeds. If he'd had his way, the city would extend from the Lancashire border all the way to the east coast. He was a cunning politician, relentless in his ambition. He'd also been the one who engineered Harper's permanent appointment as Chief Constable of Leeds City Police. For better or worse, Harper knew he owed the man.

He climbed the stairs, footsteps echoing. The whole town hall was grand, built to impress on a huge Victorian scale. Once it had awed him, but that was long ago. Now they were firmly in the twentieth century and it seemed ordinary, tired and dirty and in need of care.

As he moved, his body felt every one of the forty years he'd spent on the force, working his way up the ranks from constable to the top. Harper had hoped to retire after the armistice, but Thompson persuaded him to stay on and guide the city through the flu and the transition to peace.

Now it was set, though. Harper had turned sixty, and his final day as a copper would be at the end of April. Six more weeks, then retirement, when he could finally give his wife the attention she deserved.

Thompson's secretary waved him through.

'Close the door,' the alderman told him. 'Take a seat.'

'You wanted to see me?'

Thompson didn't reply, just gave a nod. Normally he was bluff, loud, rolling over everything in his path like one of the tanks the army had used in the war. Nothing stopped him. He was a big man, florid and hearty, with a large belly and quick, roaring laugh. But today he was hesitant, his body hunched in on itself.

'Can you keep your mouth shut?'

'I always have,' Harper replied. 'You ought to know that.'

Thompson fixed him with a glare. 'Then make sure it stays that way.'

'Why? What's happened?' Nothing good, that much was certain.

The alderman took a few breaths before he could bring himself to answer. 'I'm being blackmailed.'

Whatever Harper expected, it hadn't been that. Thompson had always seemed too shrewd to leave himself open to anything like blackmail. The kind who planned five or ten moves ahead and always made certain to cover himself. A man who left nothing to chance.

Humiliation showed on his face.

'We can arrest them, take them to court,' Harper said. 'It's a crime—'

'No.' The word came out harshly. 'No,' Thompson repeated more softly. 'Nothing public.'

'Then it's going to be difficult. You must realize that.'

'Of course I bloody do.' Fire flickered across his face. 'Why do you think I've come to you?'

He was furious at himself for being so stupid, Harper thought.

'What do you want me to do?'

'To stop it.'

That was a tall order. 'Do you expect me to do that all by myself?'

'You're supposed to be the best. That's why I helped you become the top dog here. Now it's time for you to earn it.'

Harper looked at him with curiosity. Thompson's face was flushed, the cheeks high, shining brick red with embarrassment. 'First of all you need to tell me about it.'

'I had a fit of madness,' the alderman admitted after a moment. 'Let myself be distracted by a lass.' He stared down at his desk, shook his head and snorted. 'Familiar story, isn't it? Old man allows himself to be flattered by someone younger. I thought I was too canny for that.'

'We're all human. Did you send her letters?'

He nodded. 'I was gushing like a twenty-year-old.'

'How many?'

'I don't remember.' He shook his head once again, as if he was stunned by his own idiocy. 'Five,' Thompson admitted after a moment. 'Too many, I know that.'

'Is she the one blackmailing you?'

'No. She telephoned me last week to say someone had stolen the letters. Then I received this yesterday.'

He unlocked the middle drawer of the desk, pulled out an envelope and pushed it across the blotter.

Everything typewritten, mistakes in the spelling and the punctuation.

> You sent some letters you should never have written. I have
> them. I will sell them back to you for £50. If you dont want
> to pay I will take them to the papers so they can publish.
> Tihnk about it. I will be in tuch

Unsigned, of course. He examined the envelope; sent from the Central Post Office. Nothing at all to help him.

'Don't bother telling me I'm pathetic, Harper. I already know.'

'Are you sure this woman's story is true, or is she in on it?'

'Ask me last week and I'd have said she was innocent. Now . . .' He shrugged.

'All I can do is ask a few questions.' He tapped the paper with a fingernail. 'This note doesn't tell me anything.'

Fifty pounds wouldn't mean much to someone like Thompson. He owned a big house on Chapeltown Road, never stinted himself. Married for years, children grown and off with their own lives, all manner of business interests. But if his love letters appeared in the papers, the man would lose everything. He'd be disgraced, forced to resign from the council. No more lucrative contracts from companies. His family might disown him. His reputation would disappear, the city would quietly forget him, and that would probably hurt him more than all the rest.

Not the first to be fooled by a pretty face, the man was right about that, and a long way from being the last. If it was someone else, Harper might have felt a little sympathy. But Ernest Thompson . . . the man was always convinced he was right, shouting down anyone who disagreed, overwhelming them. He possessed a certain ruthless charm, but few liked him. This was his own folly, nothing else.

Still, Harper knew he owed the man, and Thompson was finally calling in the debt.

'I'll need to talk to the woman.'

'I'll arrange it. Her name's Charlotte.'

'I'll start there, but I'll tell you this: I'm not going to be able to do much on my own.'

Thompson glared. 'I'm not having this spread from pillar to post.'

Harper shook his head. 'Then my hands are tied. I'm the chief constable, but all that means is I sit behind a desk and go to meetings. I don't do any real police work these days. I haven't for a long time. What you need is a proper detective.'

'You're what I've got.'

'For another few weeks,' Harper told him. 'Then I retire. And that's as well as my other responsibilities. I'm rusty; all my contacts are long gone.' He took a breath. 'I'll tell you the truth: I'm damn all use to you. I have absolutely no chance of solving this on my own. Before you say a word, I'm not trying to worm my way out of it; it's simply the way things are.'

Thompson said nothing for a full minute. Then: 'What would you need to make it all go away very quietly?'

'Very quietly?' Harper repeated the words. 'I'm not sure what you mean, but anything I do will be completely legal, Alderman.'

'No prosecutions.'

He nodded. 'If that's what you want.'

'Just find the bloody letters and bring them back to me. That's all I need.'

'I can't guarantee anything. Certainly not without help.'

'No. I don't want anyone else involved.'

Harper stood. 'Then I'll talk to this woman. Apart from that . . . I don't know.'

Thompson sighed. '*If* I agree, who would you bring in to help you?'

'Some men I've worked with for years. Before you say a word, I trust them completely. With my life.'

The alderman was silent. 'Let me think about it. I'll tell you in the morning. I don't suppose a few more hours will matter.'

'It's up to you,' Harper said. 'I won't say anything.'

ONE

Harper made out the voices at the back of the house. Even with his poor hearing, he could identify each one: Mary, his daughter; Julia, the nurse; and then deeper, with a rasping tone that stumbled over the words, his wife, Annabelle.

Still, speaking meant she was having a good day. Those had become rarer over the last year. Soon enough each one would be precious enough to treasure and remember. Seven years before, Annabelle had been diagnosed with early senility. No cure, no treatment. No hope it would go away. Just the knowledge that she would slowly drift off from them into some world inside her head.

The vibrant woman, the suffragist speaker – she'd vanished. With help, Annabelle had managed to keep on running the Victoria public house at the bottom of Roundhay Road. But bit by bit it became too much for her. After the Armistice was signed, the Palmaers, the Belgian refugee family who'd lived with them during the war, went home. Johanna, the wife, had looked after Annabelle. Without her, they were lost.

Harper did the only possible thing. He sold the pub to Tetley's Brewery; they'd been clamouring to buy it for years.

It had been more than a business. It was home; they'd lived upstairs. Their daughter, Mary, had never known anywhere else. Leaving had been hard, the breaking of some very solid bonds.

They'd moved out to the suburbs in May. A house on Hawthorn Road in Chapel Allerton. It was detached, but without any of the usual airs or graces; the front door opened directly on to the pavement, and the back garden was small. Still, it was far bigger than anywhere he'd ever lived, with a bay window on either side of the entrance, two floors and a basement with windows. Stone-fronted, the rest in cherry-red brick. Very solid, but so was he these days, he thought wryly. He'd filled out over the years, square-shouldered and thick-chested now. Hard to shift. Harper patted the door jamb. The place was a mansion compared to growing up in a terraced house on Noble Street, even to the rooms above the Victoria. Close to everything. A Co-op not fifty yards away, a fish and chip shop on the next street. Less than a minute from the shops on Harrogate Road. But it had needed plenty of work for Annabelle to live there comfortably.

He'd had the builders in, everything completed before they moved. Electricity installed, the ground floor changed around, a bathroom and toilet added. The basement had been opened up, lighter and brighter, for Julia the nurse. Mary had the whole top floor, her little kingdom.

Annabelle had found the change difficult. All the anchors of her life had been torn away. At first she couldn't understand it. She cried, she shouted at times, she was silent. It took months, but finally she settled, coming to some accommodation in her mind as she gradually became used to her surroundings. There was life all around them, a park just five minutes away. The air was clearer, healthier than Sheepscar. A different world. A fine place for a man to retire. And for a woman to fade to nothing, he thought.

Harper stood in the doorway, watching the women eat. Mary and Julia were chattering away and laughing. It was good to see his daughter happy; she'd lost her fiancé to the mud of the Somme back in 1916 and carried a widow's weight on her heart ever since.

Annabelle spotted him and gave a slow wink and a half-smile. Definitely one of her better days. He walked in and kissed her cheek as he sat beside her.

'Your plate's in the oven, Da,' Mary said. The way it had been so often over the years, never knowing when he'd be home from work. At least this time he wasn't too late. The mutton chop was still juicy and the potatoes hadn't dried out.

'What did you do today?' he asked Annabelle.

'We went for a walk.' She spoke haltingly these days. Every word became a small effort of concentration. He saw her glance at Julia, eyes imploring.

'To the park,' the nurse said. 'We sat and watched the men play bowls for a little while.'

'Boring,' Annabelle snorted and he laughed.

'It wasn't that bad,' Julia told her. 'The sun was out.'

The woman had been a real find. Replacing Johanna Palmaers had been difficult, but Julia had immediately taken to his wife, as if they'd known each other for years. She was a trained nurse who'd served at the Front during the war. Nothing made her panic; she took Annabelle's illness in her stride. The perfect companion. This position suited her, too, something that wasn't quite a return to full civilian life. Halfway to the world yet still able to hide.

He washed the pots with Mary, listening to her talk about the day. The secretarial agency and school she owned was booming. So good that she'd had to take on someone to run the training side.

'We're still inundated. These women all had a taste of freedom during the war and don't want to go back to being servants. You can't blame them.'

'Will there be jobs for them all?' he asked.

'Most, probably. As long as they're good at their work.'

They spent the evening talking and working on a jigsaw. Annabelle helped a little, said occasional words here and there. But she was becoming unmoored, sliding apart from them.

Age had caught up with her. Until the illness she'd always looked so young, filled with vigour. Now her hair was grey, coarse as wire when he brushed it for her. Deep lines all over her face. But he could look beyond that to the woman he'd married thirty years before, and he loved her more than he had then.

By the time he climbed into bed he hadn't given another thought to Alderman Thompson's problem. Tomorrow would be soon enough.

'Town hall, sir?' Bingham the driver asked as Harper slid into the car. A sunny morning but chilly, frost creeping across the roofs; at least the day held the promise of warmth later.

'Yes.'

He stared out of the window, seeing Thompson's big house as they sped down Chapeltown Road. A foolish man, but no worse than many others. No doubt this woman Charlotte had flattered him. Harper shook his head. Old men trying to recapture their virility.

The city centre was busy. But far fewer young men than before the war. Too many were buried in France and Belgium. Plenty had survived and come home, but they carried scars. Some were obvious, missing legs or arms, or copper masks to cover where part of a face used to be. For others, the damage stayed hidden inside.

These were the men who'd saved Britain. The prime minster had promised those old soldiers that the government would build habitations fit for the heroes who had won the war. Maybe they'd put some up in London, but in Leeds they were still waiting.

Miss Sharp had a cup of tea sitting on his desk, all the letters neatly opened and stacked. A written list of the day's meetings. Everything well ordered.

A chief constable's work. The only problem was that none of it felt like being a policeman. As he'd said to Thompson, he hadn't done any of that in almost three years, and being a copper was why he'd joined the force. He was going to end up retiring as an administrator, not a policeman.

Harper had been busy for an hour when the telephone rang, the bell loud and jarring. He pressed the receiver against his good ear.

'It's Walsh, sir.'

Harper had brought him into plain clothes when he was still superintendent of A division, over at Millgarth police station. Now Walsh had risen to become a superintendent himself and was running the place.

'Is there a problem?' Walsh wasn't one for idle chat.

'Do you remember how we were worried that after the war we'd have a lot of gun crime, all the soldiers bringing weapons home?'

'It never happened, though.' As he spoke, he felt a shiver ripple up his spine. 'Did it?'

'This morning.' He could hear the man's bitter sigh. 'Jeweller's shop on Commercial Street, about five minutes after it opened. A Model T Ford pulled up outside. Three men ran in. Gauze masks over their faces, caps, suits, all of them waving pistols. One fired a shot into the wall. They made the staff hand over rings and watches. Dashed back to the car and took off.'

'Anyone hurt?' That was the most important question.

'No, sir. I have two detectives and a couple of uniforms over there. They're taking statements and trying to find witnesses.'

'Three men,' Harper said thoughtfully. 'Another in the car to drive?'

'Sounds that way, but I don't have details yet. I wanted to let you know.'

'Thank you. If they're using guns, I want everyone you can spare on it.'

'Very good, sir.'

Pistols . . . Christ. This was going to be trouble. The robbers had certainly been in the army, taught how to use weapons. But a soldier was a machine, trained to kill. All it took was one small flash of temper or frustration and somebody would be dead. They needed to be in custody before anything more could happen.

Harper scribbled a few notes. Gauze masks. That was a clever touch; still enough people wearing them that it wouldn't attract attention. What about the number plate? Types of gun? He needed to have Carlton Barracks check to see if any pistols were missing. Somewhere to *start*.

He was tapping his pen against the blotter when Miss Sharp entered and leaned close to his good ear.

'Alderman Thompson's outside,' she whispered. 'He looks like the devil's been snapping at his heels.'

'Probably coming to claim his soul. You'd better send him in.'

She was right; the man had the harried air of someone who'd spent a sleepless night. Deep, dark circles under his eyes, and his jowls hung heavier than ever. The cigar between his fingers had gone out and he made a production of lighting it once he was seated. Anything to put off having to speak.

'Have you made up your mind?' Harper asked.

Thompson nodded. 'I thought it all through. What you said makes sense. But,' he added, giving heavy weight to the word, 'I need to know the men you choose are trustworthy.'

'I said yesterday—'

'I know you did. But this is my life, Chief Constable. My career.'

That seemed fair. 'I intend to use two men. Superintendent Sissons; he heads up the intelligence department.'

'I've met him.' Thompson nodded his approval. 'Bright lad.'

'The best researcher I know.' Sissons had been CID for more than two decades. During the war the man had worked for military intelligence. After he returned, he proposed a radical idea: set up a police intelligence unit. He'd made his case well; it could give them an advantage over criminals. Harper had promoted Sissons to Detective Superintendent and put him in charge of it. So far the experiment was paying off. But he was hardly a lad, he hadn't been for years.

'Who else?'

'Frederick Ash.'

He saw the alderman nod. Ash had been shot in 1917, forced to retire from the police. A man who seemed to know everyone. Gossip always flew to his ears, no matter how secret it was. He'd been so steady and vital; Harper still missed him. Ash had kept all his contacts; he'd relish the work and he'd be perfect for this job.

'Isn't he knocking on a bit?'

Ash was a year younger than Harper. 'He can do it and he'll keep quiet about it.'

'Very good. I'll have to rely on you, I suppose.' He opened his briefcase, took out a folder and set it on the desk. 'The girl's name and address are in there. Everything she told me about herself.' He gave a sad, wry smile. 'I assumed it was true. Now . . . we'll see. Still, it'll give your men somewhere to begin.'

'Did she write any letters to you?'

He shook his head. 'No. I never thought much about it. I suppose I was glad, me being married and all, but . . . well.'

'Who knows about her? Did you tell anyone?'

'Not a soul. There's nobody I'd trust. Round here they'd all stab me in the back, and it's hardly something I can admit to my wife, is it?'

He stood, weary and stooped. Thompson was the sort who'd hate to have his future in someone else's hands. At least he understood he didn't have any choice.

'We'll do what we can,' Harper said.

'Aye. Fair enough.'

'Busy?' Harper stood in the entrance to the small office. Sissons had two men working in his section, all three of them surrounded by papers. A copy of every police report came here, and the men behind the desks analyzed them for patterns or hints that might solve crimes, or better yet, prevent them.

It was set to run until the middle of the year. Three other chief constables had already asked about it, curious to set up similar units of their own.

'Always, sir.'

Sissons was older now, but he still had the same awkward, boyish air he'd carried around when he first joined Harper's squad. Marriage and fatherhood hadn't filled him out; he remained a beanpole, exactly the way he'd been when he began.

'I need you for a while. Something tricky.'

'Very good, sir.'

He didn't ask questions in the car, staring with interest out of the windows, assessing the faces of the people they passed. Everything was information to him, Harper realized.

In Burley, they pulled up in front of a terraced house. The tiny front garden was neatly kept, a clipped patch of grass, the border dug over. Harper knocked on the door and there was retired Superintendent Ash.

He'd lost weight, much thinner now, some colour in his cheeks, as if he'd been spending time outdoors.

'Sir,' he said with a smile. No hint of surprise, as if he'd been expecting them all along. 'What can I do for the two of you?'

'You could invite us in, for a start.'

Soon they were settled in the parlour. Ash's wife, Nancy, brought a tray with teapot, cups, and biscuits. As she closed the door behind her, Harper set the folder on the low table.

'Before I begin, I need to tell you that none of what we're going to discuss can be talked about outside this room. Understood?'

He explained what he knew and waited as they read through the information.

'Thompson wants everything kept quiet.'

'I can understand why,' Ash said. 'Retrieve the letters and warn off whoever's behind it?'

'More or less, and do it as quietly as possible. We'll definitely need to talk to the woman. I can do that, if you like. A chief

constable turning up on her doorstep might give her pause if
she's involved. Meanwhile, I could do with the pair of you digging
around.' He looked at Ash. 'If you're willing, of course.'

'And able,' he replied with a smile. 'It would do me good. I
still know one or two folk around town.'

Harper laughed. Ash was probably familiar with half the people
in Leeds.

'If I might suggest, sir, why not leave all the interviews to
us?' he continued. 'It would bring some continuity.'

'All right,' Harper agreed. He realized he was glad to evade
the responsibility. Time had left him far too out of practice at
questioning to be effective, and he didn't want his hands too
dirty in Thompson's business.

'What do you need me to do?' Sissons asked.

'A mix of records and old-fashioned policing. Whatever you
can dig up. I'll leave you and Ash to work out how you organize
it. There's a table in my office you can use. Anything you need,
ask me. We'll keep this between ourselves. As little as possible
in writing, please. None of this is completely official.'

He left them to work out their plans. At the front door, Ash
said quietly, 'We'll crack it, sir. Before you retire, too.'

'I sincerely hope so.'

'Bad business, these robbers with guns.'

It had only happened a couple of hours earlier. Ash was out
here, at home. No telephone, yet somehow he'd heard about it.
His own special magic.

'If you have any ideas, I'm sure Walsh would love to hear
them.'

'I wish I did, sir.'

TWO

'Let's go to Millgarth,' he told Bingham as the car turned
on to Burley Road. He wanted more details on the
robberies. They had to nip this in the bud.

'We're still piecing everything together, sir,' Walsh told him when they arrived. 'Inspector Jackson's leading the investigation. He's good, very clever and quick.'

'Is it three of them plus a driver?'

'Yes, sir. We got confirmation from witnesses. They look to be in their twenties, but with those caps and everything, it's impossible to come up with any worthwhile description. With the gauze, nobody gave them a second glance and once they were in the shop, the staff were too terrified to think after they saw the guns.'

Hardly surprising. Fear and obedience were exactly what they intended. 'And the shot would cow them completely.'

The superintendent nodded. 'The man deliberately aimed high on the wall.'

'This time he did,' Harper said. 'If they'd come across any resistance . . . I don't suppose we know what type of pistol?'

Walsh's face brightened. 'We did have a little luck there. A man was walking along Commercial Street with his wife. He saw it all happen. He'd been in the army during the war, wanted to try and stop them, but his wife held him back.'

'Sensible woman.'

'He said they were all carrying Webleys.'

He'd expected that; they were standard issue to British officers. But what did it mean? He glanced at Walsh. The man shrugged.

'Easy enough for anyone to get hold of a pistol, sir. And everybody who served knows how to shoot.'

'That's the part that worries me,' Harper told him. 'We were scared that something like this might happen. Now it has, we need to scramble and stop this lot before anyone else has the idea of copying them. Anything much on the car?'

He shrugged. 'A Model T Ford, nothing to distinguish it. No damage to the coachwork. The number plates had been covered in dirt, impossible to read.'

They'd been careful, right enough. A quick, precise raid, everything thought out in advance. The men were probably used to working together – maybe they'd been in the same squad. Very likely impossible to find out, but he'd check with the War Office.

'Ring Carlton Barracks,' Harper said. 'Have them take an inventory of their weapons. I doubt it'll turn up anything, but it's worth asking.'

'I've already spoken to the colonel there, sir. He's taking care of it. The men have the word out with all their snouts.'

He heard Walsh's doubtful tone. 'But?'

The superintendent frowned. 'Just a gut feeling. This lot don't seem like the usual criminals. They're using what they learned at the Front. They've planned this, they're disciplined. When we arrest them, my guess is we'll find they have no criminal records.'

No background. The thought made him shudder. 'I hope to God you're wrong. It'll make them impossible to find.'

'I hope I am, too, sir. I really do.'

Walsh would do a fine job, Harper was certain of that. He'd arrest the gang. But the weight of responsibility still pressed on his back as he sat through meetings and paperwork.

He could trust Thompson's problem to Ash and Sissons. Ash missed working; he'd be happy to be back to it. Whenever they met, he seemed eager for details of everything that was happening, as if he wanted to return to all the long hours and frustrations. Between the pair of them, they'd crack this.

It was late in the afternoon when Superintendent Walsh rang. The day was winding down, the light low through the windows.

'I wanted to bring you up to date, sir. We've interviewed every witness to the robbery that we could find.'

'Anything worthwhile?'

'Not really.' He sounded downhearted. 'Still no description worth a damn. The barracks has completed its inventory, no weapons missing.'

'Easy enough for them to smuggle one home after the fighting, or buy it here.'

'I could probably pop out tonight and come home with an entire arsenal, sir. We're going to need some luck on this.'

Lady Luck was a very coy mistress. Every copper prayed to her, but she didn't often smile back. 'Let's see if solid police work can help us catch them before they do it again.'

'Fingers crossed, but I'm not hopeful, sir. I suspect they already have their next job arranged.'

'Why?'

'They'd worked this one out to the last detail, like they'd rehearsed it. The other thing is, while they did reasonably well with what they took, it's not enough to last them long. They'll soon need more.'

'Do we have a list of the items they stole?'

'Yes, sir. Already gone out to every pawnshop and fence in the West Riding. We've let them know that we'll look favourably on them if they co-operate.'

'It sounds as if you're doing everything you can.'

'We are. It just feels like it's not going to be enough, sir.'

He understood. He'd had cases like that, where he felt he was constantly behind and struggling to catch up to events, rather than change them. When every day grew more frustrating, until something popped up and altered it all.

'Keep plugging away.'

He was ready to leave, tidying his desk, when Sissons appeared in the doorway with a folder under his arm.

'Do you have a minute, sir?'

'Something about the business we'd discussed?' No need to speak names.

The man frowned. 'No, sir. Completely different. I'd been intending to come and see you today, then you arrived with . . .'

'Yes. What is it?'

He took a deep breath. 'Some intelligence we've received about a gang of women, sir. As far as we can tell, they've come out of London and they're making their way around the country.'

'I don't follow. What are you talking about?' If he left it to Sissons to come to the point they'd be here all night.

'They go to different cities, spend a week or two shoplifting and picking pockets, then move on again. From what I've been informed, there are twenty or twenty-five of them. Get a group like that in a department store . . .'

It would be like a plague of locusts. 'Are you saying that they're coming here?'

'They're in Liverpool right now. Causing havoc, by all accounts, and they aim to hit Manchester, then on to us.'

God Almighty. This was the very last thing he needed right now. 'How good is your information? What do we know about them?'

'A couple of them have been arrested in Liverpool, sir. The force there has put together a list of names. I've requested it, and any files, from the Metropolitan Police.'

'How long before we can expect them?'

'Depends how soon they can get rid of them in Liverpool. Manchester's already preparing, so they probably won't stay long.' He shrugged. 'A week, probably. It could be a bit longer. Possibly two. It's hard to be exact.'

At least that gave them a breathing space. 'How do we stop them?'

'Circulate the information to all the large stores. Smaller shops, too. They hit those. Keep the constables who patrol the city centre on alert.'

'They will be already. You've heard about the armed gang?'

A nod. 'Dominic Walsh is going to have his hands full with them. These women, though, they could become a huge problem if we're not careful.'

'Then we'd better make sure we are. You're working this other case. Who do we put in charge of the women?'

'Sergeant Ricks has been putting all the information together, sir. He's probably the best one.'

Harper had met him, but he didn't know the man.

'Is he capable?'

Sissons grinned. 'Very, sir. An excellent man.'

'Right, it's his. But I want a plan for handling it, and daily reports, beginning tomorrow.'

The car was waiting on Calverley Street.

'Home,' he told Bingham. 'Then I need you to wait. I have to attend a do tonight. But I'm sure we can come up with something for you in the kitchen.'

'Thank you, sir. Penguin suit or white tie for you?'

'Dinner jacket and some half-hearted chicken. At least I don't have to make a speech.'

He wouldn't miss any of that. The dressing up, feeling on display, the evenings wasted on bad food and trying to show people that he was good company.

At home, Annabelle sat, pulled in tight, hunched over and trapped in silence. He kissed her cheek, but she didn't notice.

She was in her own world and he had no idea how to enter and draw her back.

'How long?' he asked Julia.

'It started about three,' the nurse replied. 'Everything was fine, she even managed a little dusting. I said she should sit herself down and I'd make a cup of tea. When I came back, she was like this.'

As if someone had turned a switch. Harper stroked his wife's hair, then opened up his pocket watch. Almost half past six. Her turn was nothing unusual; they'd happened before and lasted much longer. But after several good days, he always allowed himself to hope. Seven years on, he ought to know it was futile. There could be no reversal, only more declines.

'Leave her, I think. Be gentle if she's still like this at bedtime.'

A good excuse to cut the evening short, he thought as he mangled the knot on the bow tie. His wife was poorly, he needed to go home and check on her. He'd use that.

Plenty of people at the Liberal Club. The usual food. He took a few mouthfuls and pushed the plate aside. Lukewarm and taste-less. After the second speech, he wrote a short note, gave it to the waiter to pass to the organizer, and slid out of the room.

Bingham was waiting in the car, starting the motor as Harper settled in the back seat.

'Sorry to ruin your evening. At least it won't be for much longer.'

'I'll have the next chief, too, sir. It comes with the job.'

'Sooner you than me.'

The man grinned. 'It's not so bad, sir. Strange hours some-times, but easier on the feet than walking a beat.'

Harper laughed. He couldn't deny the truth of that.

'You're not Harry. Who are you? What are you doing here?'

Annabelle sat up in bed as he entered the room. Her eyes were filled with panic, her voice rising sharply.

'No, I'm Tom,' he told her gently. 'Don't you remember me?'

She shook her head like a child, exaggerated movements from side to side. 'I don't know anyone called Tom. Harry's my husband.'

He had been, but he'd died over thirty years before.

'I know. I'm sorry, I'll leave. Julia will look after you.'

The nurse had heard; she was waiting outside the door. Harper slumped in an easy chair, exhausted. She'd been somewhere far off and then she'd shifted to this; it was impossible to know what would happen from one minute to the next. He had help. What must it be like for the families who couldn't afford a nurse?

Ten minutes and Julia returned. 'All calmed down now. She'll know you.'

Maybe, but for how long?

As Harper entered his office, it gave him a jolt to see Ash working quietly at the small table in the corner. It took him back to their days together at Millgarth.

'Making any progress?'

'Early days yet, sir.' The habit of rank lingered. 'We have an appointment to see Miss Charlotte Radcliffe today. She's the alderman's . . . friend. Sissons has been digging into her history.'

'Has he come up with anything interesting?'

'A little murky, perhaps,' he answered with a grin. 'Never been charged or cautioned. A couple of dubious friendships. People who've tangled with us before.'

'Blackmailers, perhaps?'

Ash shook his head. 'No form for it. Nothing violent, either. Drunken fights, assaulting a police officer, that kind of thing.'

'She's not quite as pure as the driven snow, then.'

'A touch of soot on the surface. A lot younger than the alderman, too.'

'We already knew that. Don't be afraid to push her if you think it will help.' A thought struck him. 'That blackmail note was typed. See if you can spot a typewriter when you see her.'

'Very good, sir. We'll play it by ear.' He checked his watch and pushed himself up from the chair with a grunt, keeping a tight grip on his walking stick. He'd needed it since the gunshot invalided him out of the force. 'I have to go and meet Sissons. You'll hear from us later, sir. Nothing in writing, as you asked.'

'Very good.' He could trust the pair of them to do a thorough job. After he heard their report, he'd give his recommendation to Thompson. Whatever he said, the man probably wouldn't be happy.

Harper leafed through the daily reports from the divisions. Standard stuff, a few burglaries, drunken fights. Several broken windows along Armley Town Street; he assigned extra men to patrol. A couple of constables reported for coming to work with drink on their breath. Nothing to worry him. That was good. But there was still one urgent thing . . .

He picked up the telephone receiver and asked for Millgarth police station.

'Anything more?' he asked Walsh and even with his weak ear he could make out the man's drawn-out sigh.

'We're banging our heads against a brick wall, sir. The men have been asking round everywhere, but nobody seems to know these robbers, nobody's boasting about it, no word leaking. There's not even a rumour, and you know how scarce that is.'

He did. Criminals loved their gossip and speculation.

'Your idea about them being a small army squad is sounding more and more plausible,' Harper said. 'I'll contact the War Office.'

'I'd appreciate it, sir, but I don't know how they'd find something like that. Not with the war this far behind us.'

He didn't, either, but he'd still ask the question. Maybe he'd strike a piece of luck.

THREE

A morning with flickers of sunshine through the clouds and the promise of something warmer in the day ahead. Harper breathed in some fresh air, relishing it after an hour of being frustrated by the clerks at the War Office. At least he hadn't set his hopes too high; they definitely wouldn't be able to help him find information about these robbers.

Sergeant Ricks had reported to his office. Smartly dressed, hair carefully combed to present himself to the chief constable.

The man definitely seemed on top of things. Had his information ready, and arrangements for passing it out to everyone who needed it.

'Not too early, sir,' he said. 'We want it fresh in everyone's mind when these women arrive.'

As Sissons had said, very capable. In his middle twenties, old enough to have seen service in the war.

'I was in intelligence, sir,' he answered when Harper asked. 'Served under Mr Sissons. He's the one who recruited me to the police. A few weeks on the beat, then into his unit.'

This would be the young man's first big test, Harper thought as he settled on a bench in the middle of Park Square. Bundled in his overcoat and hat and eating a sandwich, he felt curiously content. The branches were heavy with fat buds, blossoms brought colour to the bushes, and the grass all around was a vibrant green. He was tempted to close his eyes. Just forty winks . . . but he knew if that happened, he'd still be here at three o'clock, snoring his head off.

Reluctantly, Harper stirred himself and ambled back across the Headrow to the town hall.

'Superintendent Walsh rang five minutes ago,' Miss Sharp said. 'It sounded urgent.'

Had they managed to catch them? It would be a miracle if they had. There'd been nothing in the way of clues.

'Harper,' he said as Walsh picked up.

'They struck again, sir. Just after noon, when everyone was out and about.'

Christ. Flaunting themselves. These robbers were brazen and fearless.

'Where? Was anyone hurt?'

'No, sir.' Thank God, he thought, pressing the receiver against his ear. 'Same MO as last time,' Walsh went on. 'That jeweller's shop on the Headrow, just below the corner with Briggate.'

He didn't know the name, but he could picture it in his mind's eye. Poky windows, all the wood painted a bilious green with gold lettering.

'A single shot into the wall, just like before, everyone terrified. In and out in half a minute, jumped into the car and took off along the Headrow. Model T, a man driving, number plates covered in mud. People on the street saw them, but with the gauze masks and caps . . .'

'And the guns,' Harper added.

'Yes, sir. Too dangerous for most.'

'It looks as if you were right; they had this one planned. How much did they take?'

'More than last time, by the sound of it. The owner is putting together descriptions and values for us. We'll circulate it later.'

'No one's tried to sell anything from Monday's robbery?'

'No report of it yet, sir. That's surprised me. I thought they'd be eager to have some money in their pockets.'

'Strange,' he agreed. 'One more little mystery involving these men. Try sending the descriptions of the jewellery to forces all over the country.'

'I will, sir. We'll keep pressing,' Walsh said. 'They're bound to make a mistake. They always do.'

Not every time, and the superintendent knew it as well as he did. But some wishful thinking couldn't hurt. It kept up the spirits.

The day was almost over when Ash and Sissons arrived. Ash looked grateful to take the strain from his leg, grunting with pleasure as he sat.

'Well, gentlemen?' Harper asked.

'We had a long talk to Miss Radcliffe, sir,' Sissons began. 'She says she's beside herself about what's happening to the alderman. Claims someone must have stolen the letters from her bureau, but she has no idea who did it. People visit her often, it must have happened when she was out of the room.'

'I see,' he said slowly. 'Did she give you any names?'

'Several, sir.' The superintendent smiled.

'What do you make of her?'

'She comes across as charming. You know the type, sir. All fresh, butter wouldn't melt,' Ash replied. 'But strip that away and she's calculating, hard as diamonds. A few times she let the mask drop and it was right there in her eyes.' He pressed his lips together. 'For what it's worth, I don't believe a thing she told us and I wouldn't trust her an inch.'

This was why he wanted experienced men for this. They could read a person, and they were very rarely wrong.

'Is she involved in it all?'

The moustache hid his smile. 'Oh, I'm certain of it. No typewriter that I could see. But she could have had one in another room.'

'What do you think?' He turned to Sissons.

'I agree, sir. As best I can tell from the documents I've found, she must be twenty-six or seven. She told us she was twenty-one.'

Twenty-one. Of legal age, and a good forty years younger than Thompson.

'I can see why he was beguiled,' Ash continued. 'She has something about her, if a man's looking for that.'

'I suppose we can't really press her, not without any hard evidence.' Harper glanced from one face to the other. 'Is there a chance of that?'

'Not as things stand, sir.' Ash told him.

'Then where do we go from here?'

'Those names she gave us. We can talk to them,' Sissons said. 'It's quite possible she's involving others to try and push suspicion away from herself.'

'Go ahead and do that. Remember, it's better for the alderman if there are no records.'

Ash stood wearily, leaning heavily on his walking stick.

'Would you like a lift home?' Harper asked. 'My car's downstairs.'

'That would be very much appreciated. It's not been a good day for the leg.'

'Do you think you'll be able to retrieve the letters?' Harper asked as the car weaved through traffic.

'I daresay we'll get there in the end,' Ash replied. Tiredness coloured his voice. 'I've a feeling it might take a while, though. I tell you, sir: that Miss Radcliffe is quite a piece of work. I've seen steel with a softer core than her.'

Thompson must rue the day he'd met her, Harper thought.

'What else are you going to need?'

'We could use one or two more men, sir,' Ash said. 'Not full time, but a little more help would be good. Sissons still has his department to run and I'm not as active as I used to be.' He tapped his bad leg.

'We need to keep this very close,' Harper said. 'That's the alderman's worry, rumours spreading.'

'The pair I have in mind can keep their mouths shut, even after a few drinks. Retired constables.'

'Do I know them?' Harper asked.

'Probably not,' Ash answered with an easy, knowing smile. 'They worked hard, kept their noses clean. Not the type to be noticed.'

'But you trust them?'

'I do, sir.'

'That's good enough for me. You tell them what you need and take care of it. I'll arrange some payment.'

'Thank you, sir.'

'Keep me up to date on your progress,' Harper said as Ash climbed out of the car. Perhaps they'd have a better chance of solving this than the armed robberies.

Annabelle was having another silent evening. Harper attempted to feed her, but each time she turned her head away like an obstinate infant. Finally, he gave up. Julia had tried earlier, with no more luck. Better to let her be.

He read the newspaper aloud, but Annabelle didn't notice. Mary had gone to a suffragette meeting. Some women over thirty had been given the vote at the end of the war, but most remained without. She was still two years away from being old enough and that rankled. The suffragettes had supported the war and held off on their activities. Their reward hadn't been enough and she was determined to change things.

At ten, he and Julia washed Annabelle and put her in a night-gown. She still hadn't said a word. Not even a sound. In bed she stared at the ceiling, her eyes only gradually closing.

On occasions she'd slip through time, talking to him as if she was convinced he was her father or her first husband. She'd mistake Mary for her mother. At first it broke his heart; now he'd become used to it. That was awful in itself. The silences, though . . . they always terrified him in case she never spoke again.

*   *   *

Annabelle slept on when he woke in the morning. Quietly, he slid out of bed, washed, dressed, and ate. It had taken time, but finally he could find his way around this new house without having to think about it.

As he stood outside, waiting for the car, the front door opened and Mary joined him.

'Any chance of a lift?'

'It's early for you to be going to work, isn't it?' A little after seven and still dark.

'I'm meeting a couple of possible new clients. I want to go over everything first.'

'I'm sure you'll come away with their business.'

She frowned. 'Careful, don't jinx it.' Her secretarial agency had already grown into one of the largest in Leeds, bigger than even she could have hoped.

'At this rate you'll end up a millionaire. Keep your parents in the way they want.' Her mouth smiled, but it didn't reach her eyes. Too much on her mind, perhaps.

'What are you doing for your dinner, Da?'

'Nothing planned,' he said. 'Why?'

'Do you fancy the Kardomah? My treat.'

If she was offering to pay, it had to be important. Impossible to refuse.

'Half past twelve?'

'Perfect.' Her smile was full of relief. 'Here's the car.'

It was a morning full of nothing. No new information on the robbers. They'd struck and vanished. No names, no answers, nothing at all. They held the whip hand. All the police could do was grasp at air.

Harper sat through a meeting with the education committee on truancy and another with the health people, talking about the influenza epidemic. He had the latest figures waiting. Deaths were much lower and falling, but the Spanish flu was still killing people. Last year and during 1918 they'd buried so many. An enemy nobody could see. The gauze masks helped a little, but there was no protection. Coming on top of the war, it often felt like God's final, brutal blow. Now, as it tailed off, people wanted to forget. Few tied on masks any longer, and he was guilty of that. He'd grown lax, glad to be without one, to sense some return to normality and start anew.

The health department wanted the message to remain loud and clear. The flu was still deadly. How could the police help?

It was a fair question. He wished he had an answer. The force had no power to make people wear masks. Encouragement? It would never work. Not any longer.

She was in the restaurant before him, sitting at the table, scribbling something in a notebook then putting it in her handbag, a cup of coffee in front of her. He untied his mask and pushed it into his pocket.

'Cautious?' she asked. 'Is there something I should know?'

'Reminded about them,' Harper said. 'I thought I'd better set an example. How were your morning meetings? Did you come away with the accounts?'

'They're going to let me know. I think they went well.' She sipped her drink, silent for a moment; gathering her thoughts, he decided. 'Tell me something: do you remember last November, the Great Silence?'

The question caught him off guard. Of course he remembered. Everybody did; it was impossible to forget. On the anniversary of the armistice, the eleventh of November, a two-minute silence at eleven o'clock in the morning, the time the guns had stopped firing. Across the country, everything came to a standstill. Leeds was hushed. The only sound came from weeping women. It was very powerful, more moving than he could have anticipated, sparking memories that resonated through him for a long time.

'What about it?'

'It set me thinking. About remembering. About life and death. About Len.'

She held out a carefully folded copy of the *Yorkshire Post*, an advertisement circled in pencil. He read it and raised his eyebrows.

'Are you considering going?'

She offered a small, bashful smile. 'I've already booked, Da. Travelling in July.'

Thomas Cook and Son. Trips to the battlefields of Belgium and France, with prices from eight pounds, eleven shillings and sixpence. It was a huge step. She'd never travelled that far before. Never to a foreign country, and definitely not alone.

'I need to see it,' she continued. 'I want to know . . .'

Of course. The news that her fiancé Len had been killed on the Somme in autumn 1916 had ripped her apart. At first he'd been listed as missing in action, everything hanging by a tiny thread of hope. Then the confirmation that he was dead. She tried to hide it, but Harper knew the sorrow was always there, a constant in her life. Like so many young women all over the country, she still dressed in mourning black. Maybe this was the first sign that she was ready to emerge from the past.

'If you think it will help.' Harper wanted to sound enthusiastic, but he couldn't stop the doubts creeping into his voice.

'It will.' She had nothing but certainty. 'I'm going with Len's mam. We both have to look.'

Len's father had died two years before, one more victim of the flu epidemic. The pair of them going together. It was a surprise, but he was relieved; they'd help one another through it all.

'It's a big trip,' he warned.

Mary nodded. 'We know that. We're not expecting any kind of luxury. We want to . . . understand, I suppose.'

As much as anyone could make sense of the thousands of deaths, he thought. Still, if it was a way for Mary to start closing the door on it all, that had to be worthwhile.

'When in July are you going?'

'We leave on the nineteenth and come back a week later. I wanted to wait until you retired, so you'd be at home with me mam.' She hesitated. 'I hope you don't mind.'

'Mind?' He wasn't sure what she meant. 'Why would I mind?' If it helped to fill that chasm in her heart, he'd be over the moon. 'Why don't the pair of you take a day or two longer? Go and see Paris. People say it's beautiful.'

More than that, it would cleanse some of those horrors of the battlefield from her mind.

'We talked about that, but it felt wrong, as if it would end up making light of it. Doing this seems like enough.'

Probably more than enough. Seeing where someone you loved had died . . . 'I imagine it is.'

'Are you sure you'll be fine with me going, Da? Me mam and that.'

He squeezed her hand. 'We'll manage, don't you worry. I'll have Julia.'

'And you'll be at home then.'

Retired, with every single day on his hands. 'I'm going to spend a lot of time with your mother.'

While he could. Who knew how long they'd have together?

'There's something else.'

Harper laughed; he couldn't help himself. More? What else did she have planned? A trip to New York on an ocean liner? Opening a branch of her business in London?

'Go on, you might as well spill the lot.'

'I've decided to buy a motor car.'

'Well,' he said. 'Well.' Another revelation, but after the trip it seemed trivial. 'What's brought this on?'

'It seemed to make sense. I end up going to so many places for work. This way I won't spend half my life queueing for trams. I can afford it, and I can go out on Sundays and discover places.' Her eyes twinkled, brimming with ideas. 'I can take us all on trips once the weather's warmer.'

'After you've learned to drive,' he said.

'Oh, I already know,' she told him. 'Jeannie Carson's been giving me lessons. I've been planning this for a while.'

Typical of her. Arrange everything, take care of every detail, then tell him.

'I'm picking it up on Saturday,' she continued. 'Do you remember the one me mam had?'

Oh yes. The big Rex tourer she kept parked on Manor Street, behind the Victoria. The only motor car in Sheepscar, a thing of wonder to every child in the neighbourhood. They'd sold it before the war, not long after Annabelle's diagnosis.

'You do right,' he told her. 'You've earned it.'

'Do you know,' she admitted cautiously, 'I believe I have.'

'Nothing else up your sleeve?'

She looked at him and her mouth curled into the same mischievous grin she used to wear when she was a girl. 'You mean that isn't enough for one day, Da?'

FOUR

'Alderman Thompson has rung four times while you were out,' Miss Sharp said when he returned. She managed to make it sound like Harper had been in the wrong for leaving.

'Then I'd better go and see him.' He hung up the coat and hat, straightened his tie and strode to Thompson's office. A tap on the polished door and he entered, wearing his mask. The alderman sat, back straight, glowering.

'Where were you?'

'Out,' Harper replied. The man didn't need to know his business. 'Has something happened?'

'What progress have those men of yours made?'

'They've talked to Miss Radcliffe. She's given them a few names, and they'll be interviewing them.'

'How long will it take?'

'I don't know. I trust them, I'm leaving them to work at their pace.'

'I want it all done, Harper. Over, finished. This came in the second post.' He brought the envelope from his inside pocket and tossed it across the desk. Addressed to the alderman, marked Personal and Confidential. Once again, sent from the Central Post Office. Harper pulled out the note.

> You have had time to think. I now you can afford £50. If you want these letters back, have it in notes on Tuesday and be ready. You will heer from me.

'He's making his move,' Harper said. Thursday today; the police still had ample time. The misspellings were deliberate; he felt absolutely certain of that. A trick that didn't work.

'What are you going to do?'

'If he takes money from you, I'm going to arrest him. All very quietly,' he added before Thompson could object. 'Nothing in the records, and he won't go through the system.'

Harper thought about his words. He? Could they be certain the blackmailer wasn't a woman? It could very easily be Charlotte herself.

The man nodded. 'What about the letters?'

'I don't expect the blackmailer will be carrying them.' Harper held up the paper. 'This would just be the beginning. Pay and there could be more demands. You've probably heard the kind of story.'

'I have,' he replied with a sigh. 'I've been a bloody fool, haven't I?'

'Not for me to say.'

He rubbed the back of his neck. 'No need. I'm going to be on edge until I hear from him again.'

That was the price he'd have to pay and if it was the worst of things, he'd end up with a light punishment. Nobody escaped scot-free.

'I'll pass this on to the men investigating,' Harper said, 'and we'll sit down with you on Monday evening.'

'I don't suppose there's much more you can do before then.'

'They'll be talking to the names your friend gave them. Any more contact, let me know immediately.'

On the way back, he stopped at the intelligence office, took Sissons aside and passed him the note. 'See what you think. Could Miss Radcliffe be organizing this? Talk to Ash, then see me.'

'Very good, sir.'

Now he needed a quiet afternoon. Maybe some good news. Or was that too much to hope for?

By five, Harper had laboured through most of the papers on his desk and dictated replies to the letters. His voice was scratchy from talking, and he looked forward to going home and a mug of tea.

He was packing his briefcase when the phone rang, the bell loud and shrill.

'Chief Constable Harper.'

'It's Walsh, sir.' From the man's tone, he knew his day was nowhere near over. 'The robbers again.'

Again? That made three times in less than a week. 'Where?'

'Boar Lane. Not far from City Square. It's worse this time.'

Harper shuddered, unable to stop the chill rising through his body. 'Go on.'

'They shot someone who tried to stop them. A bystander.'

Christ, that was as bad as it could get.

'How is he?'

'At the infirmary now, sir, but it doesn't look good. It's probably going to be a murder charge.'

He pinched the bridge of his nose. 'I'm on my way.'

'Inspector Jackson's already there.'

At least murders were very rare. Thank God. Perhaps this wouldn't end up as one. Maybe the man would survive, he thought as the car nudged through traffic.

Jackson looked calm as he directed the constables and detectives who were bustling about the scene. He had an air of calmness and ability, with a broad, open face and shrewd, pale eyes under a bowler hat.

'Sir,' he said with a nod, directing a copper towards a witness. There was a frantic, urgent sense to everyone. Except him. He was in control.

'How did it happen?'

'Exactly the same as the other two times, sir. Pulled up outside the jeweller's there' – he pointed to the shop across the street – 'a shot into the wall as they entered, took what they could and left. It would have gone smoothly, except this time a man tried to grab the last of the robbers as he was heading for the car. Tugged on his arm, attempted to drag him down, according to witnesses. The robber knocked him to the ground, then shot him before he joined the others and they left.'

'Cold blood,' Harper said. Why? There'd been no need for it. Just a soldier's urge for violence that boiled over.

'Completely, sir. The wounded man's name is Walter Pass. My sergeant has gone over to his house. No idea yet if there's a wife or family.'

'Nothing new to help us identify the robbers?'

Jackson shook his head. 'Not a thing: caps and gauze masks, mud over the number plates. About the only thing is the shop

assistant is sure that they're local, the accent when the man in
the lead said: "Don't give us no trouble."'

'I think we'd assumed that, hadn't we?'

A nod. 'Yes, sir. But always good to have it confirmed. At
least it's one new scrap of information. They've been few and
far between on this case.'

'Do you need any more men?'

'Not at the moment, sir. If Mr Pass dies, that will change
everything.'

Even with his poor hearing, he could pick out the undercurrent of anger in the man's words. 'Of course.' He glanced around.
There was nothing he could do to help here; he was just another
old man cluttering up the pavement and stopping the inspector
doing his job.

'We need this gang in the cells.'

Jackson looked back towards the shop and the blood on the
cobbles. 'We'll have them, sir. We'll have them.'

'Keep me informed.'

'Home. sir?' Bingham asked as Harper closed the car door.

'Not yet,' he answered after a moment. 'The infirmary first.'

Pass was still in the operating theatre. Nobody paced in the
waiting room, offering up prayers for him. Here, everyone was
wearing masks. He found a nurse, walking with her arms full of
clean sheets, and begged her to try and find out what was
happening. Five minutes passed before she returned.

'The surgeon said to tell you that he's doing his best to keep
the man alive. Beyond that, he's not willing to predict.' She
blushed. 'I'm sorry, sir, but that's what he told me.'

'Thank you.'

This time she was a young woman. All too often she was a child,
with her mother still alive. Sometimes older, still married to her
first husband, a man thirty years her senior. Seven years since
this illness began and he'd never come across this particular
memory before.

'Do you remember we were standing down by the river?'
Annabelle said. 'It was dead quiet with all the men on strike.
You said you'd never seen it like that before.'

'Yes,' he answered, with no idea who she believed he was. 'Very eerie.'

The strike on the wharves. He recalled that. It had happened just a few months before he joined the force, over forty years before. She'd have been eighteen, perhaps nineteen.

'I had everything I owned tied up in a sheet, scared to go home and tell my da I'd been given the heave-ho.'

Now he could place it among the patchwork of things Annabelle had told him about her past. She and her best friend Mary had been maids at a big house, sacked for not doing their work properly.

'I thought my da would belt me into next week when I told him. Yours did.'

'I know,' he said. He was Mary. Now he was getting his bearings.

'Never raised his hand. Told me I had a week to find something or he'd pitch me on to the street. He meant it, too. That's why I've been out so much every day, you see. I'm looking.'

'Having any luck?' He knew he had to say something. He wanted to see where this led. At least she was speaking.

'I have to pop over to Sheepscar later. Mrs Green at number nine said some pub there is looking for a lass to live in and skivvy. I'm not like you, I can't go back to the mills. It killed me ma, all that dust in the air.'

'I hope you get the job.'

'Something will turn up. I have two days yet. What's this I've heard about you and one of the foremen, anyway? Walking out together already. You could do a lot worse than that.'

'You never know,' Harper said. He had no idea what had happened to Mary. Annabelle had never seen her during their marriage, rarely even mentioned her. But it didn't matter now. Her eyes closed and she began to sleep.

'You knew what she was talking about, Da.' Mary kept her voice so low he had to strain to make out what she said.

'Some of it was guesswork,' he said, looking at his wife. 'That Mary she mentioned, your mother named you for her.'

'I wondered about that. The time, was it just before she started at the Victoria?'

'Yes.' He shook his head. Strange to hear her talk about it like she had no idea how her life would unfold. 'Not long after your mother began there, the landlord's wife was diagnosed with cancer. Your mother took over more of the work while he looked after her. Harry Atkinson, his name was. Not too long after she died, your mam became Annabelle Atkinson. He was a lot older than her. Died of a heart attack in his sleep.'

'I've heard her talk about it.'

'Harry Atkinson seems like he was a good man.'

'Were they happy?' Mary asked.

'Oh yes.' He glanced at Annabelle and smiled. 'They were.'

'We should put her to bed. She's spark out.'

Once Annabelle was settled under the blanket and eiderdown, he stood with Mary in the kitchen, sipping a cup of tea.

'Don't tell my mam about this trip to the Somme yet,' she said.

'All right,' he agreed. 'Any particular reason?'

'I need to do it in my own way. On a day she's really here and can understand.'

He nodded. Mary was an adult, twenty-eight now. No more little girl. He knew his daughter would never forget Len, the way her mother had never forgotten Harry. But just like Annabelle, perhaps she could keep that sorrow close and still have other joys ahead.

It seemed as if he'd barely fallen asleep when the clamour of the phone woke him. He stumbled into the hall and lifted the receiver.

'Walsh, sir,' the voice on the other end of the line said.

No good news ever arrived in the middle of the night. The fog vanished from his head.

'Go on.'

'Mr Pass died. The surgeon thought he might survive, but he wasn't strong enough.'

Harper closed his eyes and gave a long sigh. Christ, a killing, and all because someone tried to be a good man. 'Did he have any family?'

'A married sister in Doncaster. No wife, parents both dead. Fought right through the war, came home without a scratch.'

And then this, Harper thought. Poor devil.

'Right, it's a murder inquiry now. Let's pour men into this and catch this lot quickly.'

'I could use three more in plain clothes,' Walsh told him. 'I think that should be enough.'

'Are you sure?' he asked, surprised. 'I can let you have more.'

'For right now.'

'I'll arrange it first thing. What else?'

'I don't know yet, sir.' He sounded worried. 'I've never run one quite like this before.'

'Be grateful for that. But you know what to do, you've been through it. Remember, anything at all, let me know. This is going to be all over the papers, national as well as local, so you'd better be prepared for the reporters.'

'There's nothing I can tell them. We don't have a bloody clue on the killers.'

Killers. That's who they were now. Not robbers any longer.

He gave his instructions as if he could see everything lined up in front of him. 'If the papers are going to be running stories, use them. Ask people to report Model Ts with mud over the number plates. Pass the word to every bobby on the beat. We need information on any groups of four young men.'

'We've already done some of that, sir.'

'Do it again. It's nowhere near perfect, but it's somewhere to start. It means we're taking action.' He had the experience. He'd done it all; he knew it never became any easier. 'Get cracking and I'll see you in the morning.'

Harper expected to be plagued by the murder all through the night, but tonight it barely grazed his pillow; to his surprise, he slept and woke refreshed.

'Millgarth police station,' he told Bingham as he slid into the back seat of the car.

Everything in the building smelled familiar. He'd spent so many years working here that the place still fitted him like a skin. The air, the shape, everything was ingrained in his mind. He took the mask from his pocket, then replaced it. Stupid, he knew, but easier to be without.

'Any more news?' he asked Walsh. Men were moving around, talking in low voices. There was a sense of urgency and fury in the room. In the centre of it all, Inspector Jackson sat calmly at his desk, rumpled and weary, studying a pile of papers and smoking. A pile of cigarette ends tottered in his ashtray.

'We're going back over all the statements in case there's some little thing we missed.' Walsh's face was drawn and grey with the strain. He looked like a man who hadn't slept, someone whose heart was beating dangerously fast. 'Nothing so far. The death happened too late for the morning papers, but I've had reporters contacting me all night.'

'Let's see what today brings. Someone has to know them.' He placed a hand on the superintendent's shoulder. 'We'll get there.'

'It needs to be soon, sir.'

'Yes, it does,' Harper agreed. 'Very soon. Please, God.'

The usual correspondence and meetings, the sense of being hemmed into his office by the work. It felt like a relief to walk down the front steps of the town hall in the noon sun, patting one of the stone lions for luck.

The air was sooty, tasting of grit, but a light breeze was blowing as he walked to the market. He'd better enjoy the old places while there was still time, Harper thought as he climbed the iron stairs next to the stalls, up to the small café.

The shepherd's pie was still tasty and filling; after he finished he strolled along the flagstone paths, listening to the traders cry their wares, then across George Street to Millgarth.

'We'll be in all the afternoon editions,' Walsh told him. He seemed a little less frantic now things were moving. 'Headline in the *Evening Post*. People won't be able to miss it.'

'It should stir some information. Let's make these men pariahs, turn the city against them.'

'I was very careful to point out that the gang killed when there was no need.'

Harper nodded. They both knew the formula: most murders were solved quickly. The longer an investigation dragged out, the harder it became to trace a killer. Speed was vital.

'You'll start receiving tips soon. All the extra men will be with you tomorrow.'

'They should be enough for now.'

*   *   *

The urge kept clawing at him. To take charge himself. He had ample experience of murder cases. It would be his final chance to be a real copper. But he'd promoted Walsh for a reason. The man was excellent at his job, as good as Harper had ever been. He had to let him run things. Offer a little advice if it was asked for. Otherwise, stand back and allow him to do the job.

But the itch was there, growing stronger every hour.

He'd been dozing in the chair, eyes closing then fluttering open again, but too comfortable to go to bed. Just half past nine in the evening. God, not even retired yet and he was turning into an old man.

The phone rang. Harper stood and stretched.

'Sorry to disturb you at home, sir.' Walsh's voice was taut as wire, like someone in shock. But he was a copper, that hardly seemed likely.

'What have you found?'

'You're not going to believe this.' He paused for a moment, composing himself, more in control when he continued. 'The man walking the beat on Pontefract Road spotted something on the embankment that goes down to the railway.'

'What was it?' Important enough to make Walsh ring him at home, that was certain.

'A body. A man. He'd been shot in the head, like an execution.'

'What?' The word exploded out of him. This couldn't be real. Not in Leeds. Two men murdered in two days?

'There was a note tucked into the breast pocket of his jacket, sir. I have it right here.' He made out the faint rustle of paper, then Walsh cleared his throat. '"We don't approve of anyone killing an innocent man. We're sorry it happened. He did it and now he has paid the price." Looks like the paper was torn from a notebook. Scribbled in pencil. Very erratic writing.'

'Christ.' Harper exhaled slowly. His heart was thumping in his chest. Any chance of rest had disappeared. Nobody could have anticipated this.

'You'd better send a car for me.'

FIVE

Small circles of torchlight illuminated the scene as Harper arrived. Inspector Jackson stood on the pavement, staring down the slope. A thin, wet mist hung in the air.

'The body's gone to the morgue, sir,' he said. 'Nothing it can tell us lying here, anyway.'

Harper gazed around. There was little to see in the darkness. 'What's your take on things?'

He let out a long, weary breath. 'It sounds like something out of those American gangster stories, doesn't it? But it's a given that he's the one who shot Pass.'

'Agreed.'

'Maybe the leader made the decision to kill him, or the others all voted on it. Take a glance around, sir.'

The railway line below, a glint of light on the rails at the bottom of the cutting. A factory across the road, dark, closed for the night. The closest house was a hundred yards away. An ideal spot to kill.

'I see what you mean.'

'Can't really tell until it's light, but it looks as if there might be a little blood just over there' – he pointed – 'and you can make out where the grass has been flattened as they rolled him down the hill.'

Jackson shone his lamp on the spot. The man had keen eyes, Harper thought; it barely looked disturbed. But his theory felt right.

'The superintendent read me the note.'

Jackson frowned. 'Curious, isn't it, sir? They're carrying guns, we're as sure as we can be that they served in the army, now they're acting as judge and jury over one of their own for killing.'

'You sound like you have some ideas.'

The inspector hesitated before answering. 'Seems to me it's their way of saying they're good men, they don't murder people,

and this is how they treat anyone who does. Trying to show
themselves as principled.' He pressed his lips together. 'At the
same time, this is very Old Testament, an eye for an eye and
that.'

Perfectly possible. What they'd done to Pass was in all the
papers. They must realize that people would turn against them.
Someone had to know who they were and be ready to inform.
Was this their way of trying to blunt that anger, to claim they
were men of morals?

'I don't suppose he had any identification?'

Jackson snorted. 'We should be so lucky. They'd emptied his
pockets, not even any coins. Only that note. The leader must
have written it after he shot him.'

'Definitely.' He breathed in, feeling the damp chill of the air
seeping down into his bones. 'What can I do to help?'

'I won't really know until daybreak, sir. I'll tell the super.'

'You seem on top of things. Now we just need to find them.'
Harper looked down towards the tracks. 'It's out of hand.'

He dozed on the way home and settled into bed. He could
feel sleep tugging at him, but something kept him awake, nibbling
at him, leaving him worried in case he'd seen something and
not realized its importance.

'Pontefract Road,' he told Bingham as he climbed into the car.

The scene still looked bleak in the grey morning light. A pair
of constables huddled in their capes as they stood guard on the
scene.

Harper walked slowly around the area, lingering as he peered
down the hill where the body had rolled, before moving along
the street. He tried to let his mind drift and allow the place to
offer its suggestions.

A quarter of an hour and he'd found nothing. Harper gave up
and went back to his vehicle. It must have all been in his imagination. Old, he thought, you're getting old.

'Millgarth, please.'

Jackson looked drained, the skin on his face pale and taut.

'Have you come up with anything else?'

'Not yet, sir.' His voice was empty. 'Feels like a brick wall
every way I turn.'

'The post-mortem's this morning?'

'Top of Dr Amersham's list.' Amersham had taken over from Lumb as the police surgeon shortly after the war. Good and sharp, with experience in a field hospital in France. 'I'm not sure what he can say that we don't already know.'

'Did anyone take fingerprints from the body?'

'I took care of it myself, sir. They're with our people, gone down to Central Records and the War Office in London on the express.'

Jackson was on top of everything. Walsh had put the right man in charge.

'Go home for a few hours. Rest.'

A wan, hopeless smile. 'I don't think I could sleep, sir.'

Harper knew that feeling. 'Try. That's an order. The super can take over for now.'

He sat with Walsh, arranging for more men to pack out a murder squad.

'After last night's execution, the whole country's going to be looking at us,' Harper said. 'We can't afford to put a foot wrong.'

It had everything to grab public attention and put the police squarely in the spotlight.

'I know, sir.' He looked nervous and who could blame him? It was more responsibility than anyone would want.

'More than that, we have to wrap this up sharpish. You can handle this. I wouldn't have promoted you otherwise.'

But the man's smile was fleeting, unsure.

In his own office at the town hall, he paced. Miss Sharp had finished her week at lunchtime, off to join the Saturday afternoon crowds on the street.

Sergeant Ricks appeared with news of the group of shoplifters. 'They're playing merry heck in Liverpool, sir. The coppers can't keep up with them. They've arrested four, but the others are running riot.' He frowned. 'There's a new wrinkle, too. One of the women in custody gave it away. I hate to admit it, but they've come up with a good idea.'

'What are they doing?'

'After a week, the ones in a city are replaced by a fresh crew.

Makes it almost impossible to keep track of them. We'll have to catch them in the act.'

'A plague of locusts,' Harper said.

'And it's coming this way, sir.'

Harper pushed a hand through his thinning hair. One more bloody thing ahead of them.

Finally, a little after three, the phone rang.

'Jackson, sir.' He sounded refreshed, some vigour in his voice. 'We've heard back from records. Whoever this man was, he's never been arrested in England.'

Damn, they could have used some luck. But he wasn't surprised. 'What did the War Office say?'

'They don't fingerprint recruits, and he was never up on charges if he was in the forces.'

They were absolutely nowhere. Not one single idea who the man was. They weren't even trudging along; they were marching on the spot. 'It was worth trying.'

'Dr Amersham confirmed what we knew. Shot in the back of the head from a few feet away.'

Harper thought. 'How badly damaged was his face?'

'The forehead was a mess, sir,' the inspector answered after a little thought. 'But you can make out most of his features.'

'Why don't you contact Superintendent Sissons in intelligence? They sometimes use an artist to give an impression of how a person looked when they were alive. We don't have anything else to identify him, so let's try a sketch. An impression.'

He could almost see the inspector's approving nod. 'Not a bad idea, sir.'

'If we get it done today, we can give it to the papers for Monday.'

'Yes, sir.'

No sooner had he replaced the receiver than it rang again.

'I wasn't sure if you'd still be there, Da,' Mary said.

'Needs must. Are you working, too?'

'Catching up with the books.'

'I thought you were picking up your new car today.'

'I am, but . . . could I cadge a ride up there? It's Roland Winn's up by the university.'

He laughed. 'Go on, then. I suppose you'd like to be picked up at your office, too.'

'Well, if you're offering . . .'

'Quarter of an hour, and you'd better be outside, ready and waiting.'

It was a little longer. He'd just placed his hat on his head when the phone rang for a third time.

'I haven't heard anything from you.' Alderman Thompson. He had fire in his voice. 'I expected regular reports.'

'You know Ash and Sissons are working on it. We'll have word when they have something to say. The police are dealing with two murders.'

'Aye, I know. But you're paid to handle everything that's thrown at you. You promised me results, Harper. I'm still waiting.'

'You'll have them.'

'When?' He barked out the word. 'You told me you'd take care of this.'

'We will. It's not straightforward.' He knew he sounded like a man making excuses. 'You want this done quietly, don't you?'

'You know I do.' A grudging admission.

'Then we're already working with one hand tied behind our back, Alderman.' He wasn't about to bow and scrape for doing exactly what the man had demanded. 'We're conducting a criminal investigation in secret. That takes time. I'm not even sure it's legal. It has to be done very carefully.'

'Maybe,' the man allowed.

'No maybe about it. I trust Ash and Sissons. They'll come up with an answer. Have you heard anything more from the blackmailer?'

'No,' Thompson replied. 'But that deadline's coming.'

'I'm aware of that. Let's see what it brings.'

Mary was standing on Albion Place, talking to Gladys Naylor, the woman who ran the secretarial school for her.

He rolled down the window. 'Hop in.'

Bingham pulled into traffic, slipping smoothly between the

trams and carts. A few lorries on the road, one or two motor cars. Mary reached into her bag and waved a piece of paper with an official stamp. 'See, I even have my driving licence.'

He smiled. 'I'm glad I won't have to arrest you.'

Outside Roland Winn's Ford agency, the driver stopped by the kerb. Mary opened the door.

'Good luck.' He watched the confident way his daughter marched into the showroom. God help any salesman who tried to divert her.

'Home, sir?'

'I think we'll take a small detour first,' he answered after a second. He needed something to lift his mood, to send this deep headache packing. 'Why don't we stop at Cantor's on Chapeltown Road? I fancy fish and chips. I'll buy you some.'

A Model T Ford . . . Harper stood by the window, gazing at the black coachwork of Mary's new car as it shone under the sodium lights. Early in the morning and still dark.

When she arrived home she'd been beaming, eager to show off her new purchase. They'd each taken one of Annabelle's arms, steadying her as Mary pointed at the vehicle parked on the street. Harper watched his wife's face. It had been a quiet day again; only a few words, Julia said. Even that was better than complete silence. For a tiny moment he believed he saw a glimmer of something in her eye as she looked at the vehicle. A memory of driving, maybe. But if it was ever there, it vanished before he could blink.

A Model T . . . the killers had one. Then again, it seemed as if half the motor cars on the road were made by Ford. Still, maybe there was something in that they could use.

'I know your witnesses said the number plate of the car was too muddy to read.'

'That and the fact it's a Model T seem to be the only consistent things we have about the vehicle, sir.' The sound on the telephone line fluttered as Walsh replied. Sunday morning, growing lighter outside, a pale blue sky and a faint promise of warmth in the air, a tease of spring.

'I read in a report that there are about a million cars in the entire country. That's every single make. There can't be too many Model Ts in Leeds.'

The superintendent snorted. 'You'd hardly know it by walking around, sir. They're everywhere.'

'My daughter just bought one. That's what made me wonder if there's any way we can find out about Ford owners locally.'

'I suppose it's possible,' Walsh answered very slowly, trying to work things through. 'Every vehicle has to be registered. I'd never thought about it. But there are still going to be hundreds round here, maybe a few thousand. And without knowing any names or what's on the number plate, I don't see how it will help us.'

'It might be something to consider if you can't make any other headway.'

'I've made a note of it. It's scraping the barrel. Still, the rate we're going, I could be trying it soon.'

'No progress?'

'Nothing at all. The artist made a sketch of the dead man. We hit lucky – it's in the national Sunday papers. We'll have it locally tomorrow, too. That should bring some decent tips. God knows we need them.'

'Let me know what happens.'

Annabelle was wrapped in a warm coat, a scarf around her neck and a hat over her hair as she stood in the back garden. She gripped two sticks for balance and stared around the small plot.

'It's lovely.' Her voice was a soft, happy rasp. 'I've never had a garden before.' It was a good day, one of the best she'd had in a long time. Her eyes were lively, mouth smiling. A high wall sheltered them from the breeze, caught in a pool of warm sunlight.

'It's not much now, but tell me what you want out here, and I'll plant it,' he said. 'You'll be able to sit by the window and see it all.'

She laughed, enjoying herself. 'You're going to plant flowers, Tom Harper? Going to take a spade and dig?'

He patted the handle of the shovel. 'I am.'

'That should be better than the music hall.' Annabelle looked around. 'Why don't we have flowers against the back there?

Something colourful. And I'd like a rose bush under the window. I've always fancied one of them.'

'You'll have it,' he promised. With luck, she'd live long enough to see it flower.

They moved her chair close so she could watch him work and still be warm inside the house. The ground was tough going; soon he'd sweated through his shirt, glancing over his shoulder to see his wife and daughter together, talking and giddy with pleasure as they watched. At least he was entertaining them.

He was grateful when Julia appeared to say there was a telephone call.

Harper wiped his face with a handkerchief as he lifted the receiver.

'It's Ash, sir. I hope you don't mind me ringing on your day off.'

'Not at all. I'm glad to hear from you. I had the alderman trying to raise hell with me yesterday. How have you and Sissons been moving along?'

'We've managed to talk to some of the names Miss Radcliffe gave us.'

'What do you make of them?'

'They all come from money. Most of them managed to use connections to avoid the fighting. Only one of them put on a uniform. Hardly any of them work, they have monthly allowances from their parents. By all accounts, the one who went to the Front drinks like tomorrow will never come.' He paused. 'Not exactly a lovable bunch, sir.'

'Doesn't sound like it. Are they blackmailers?'

'Honestly, sir? Sissons and I discussed it, and we don't think so. Not among the ones we've interviewed. We're not ruling them out, but we'll be seeing the other gentlemen in the next few days. After that we can take stock. Of course,' he added, 'it might not be any of them at all. There's her brother. She said he visited her often, but he's in London, due back this afternoon.'

'When he returns . . .'

'We'll be ready. Safe to say she doesn't have good taste in friends, though.'

'Which means there's one big question, isn't there?'

'Very much so, sir.' He could sense Ash's smile, hidden under the thick moustache. 'It would be obvious for her to be running the blackmail. It still seems very possible. She doesn't need the money; she and her brother inherited a good-sized fortune when their parents died. If she's involved, it's just for the thrill of it. Boredom.'

He'd come across people like that, but he'd never understood them. In his world, people committed crimes for money or revenge. Lust, sometimes. But never because they simply wanted something to do.

'They're supposed to contact Thompson tomorrow to give him instructions for paying them on Tuesday. It doesn't give us much time.'

'I think we'll manage.' He paused. 'You know, it's a very strange business with these robbers Walsh is chasing.'

An abrupt change of topic. 'It is. Any ideas?'

'Not really. I don't envy him with that one. Sorry, sir. And those shoplifters won't be easy, either. You'll have your hands full, sir.'

In the afternoon he sat Annabelle in the wheelchair and pushed her to the park. Five minutes along Regent Street and Woodland Lane, then through the tall stone gateposts. No crown green bowling today; a band was playing, and she nodded her head and tried to sing along with a few tunes. A quarter of an hour later she put her hand on his wrist.

'Would you mind if we went home, Tom? I'm feeling jiggered.'

'Of course not.'

She dozed in front of the fire. He sipped from a mug of tea and watched her. Maybe they'd have many more days like this once he retired. But he knew the truth. He should have left the force after the war, when he originally intended. *That* would have given them proper time together. But he'd allowed himself to be persuaded and flattered, told that he was needed when someone else could have done the job just as well.

Too late for anything but regrets now.

SIX

'I think we have a breakthrough on the robbers, sir.' Walsh was beaming as he took the chief constable aside before the meeting of all the division heads. He looked ready to burst with hope.

Harper felt the hard, urgent knot in his belly. 'What is it?'

'A tip, sir. Someone saw the drawing in the newspaper and telephoned from Dewsbury. He thinks the dead man might be someone who served under him during the war.'

It would fit, it could be exactly what they needed. He felt his pulse quicken. The first lead. 'Part of a section? That's what they call them in the army, isn't it?'

The superintendent gave a thin smile. 'Yes, sir. He gave us a name: Trevor Curtis. Even remembered the rest of them. Said there'd been eight to start, and four of them survived. All from Leeds, he thinks.'

Harper was stunned; he'd never had luck like this from a drawing. For one small moment he wondered if someone was playing a joke on them, then belief began to surge through his body again. Maybe they could close this case quickly . . . 'Sounds like we might have our men.'

'Jackson is on his way to interview him, and Sergeant Clough is talking to the War Office, seeing if we can get the files on these men sent up here today.'

'I trust we're already trying to locate the men he named?'

'Yes, sir. I gave Sissons the information, too. This is right up his lot's street.'

The word spread among the superintendents. He could sense the crackle of electricity all through the meeting and the undercurrent of urgency. As soon as they finished, Walsh hurried off.

'Mr Ash is in your office,' Miss Sharp told him. 'Since he has that table in there, I knew you wouldn't mind.'

'It's fine,' Harper said. 'Any chance of some tea? I'm parched.'

'I took a pot through not two minutes ago. Another cup, too.'

He'd miss having someone as organized as her around. But after retirement, what would need to be arranged in his life?

Ash was pacing, hands clasped behind his back, face in a deep frown.

'What is it?'

'I went to see Miss Radcliffe's brother this morning, sir.'

'What did he have to say for himself?'

'Not a word.' He let the pause stretch out. 'He's scarpered. Rooms in Headingley, all very pleasant. The landlady said he came back from London yesterday afternoon; she heard him moving around first thing this morning, taking stuff down the stairs, several trips and placing it all in a motor car. I persuaded her to let me in. All his personal things have gone: clothes, papers, the lot.'

'Paid up on rent?'

'For the next three months.'

Not a midnight flit, then, but that never seemed likely. 'No job?'

Ash shook his head. 'A gentleman of leisure.'

'Did he know you were coming?'

'No, sir. I popped over to see Miss Radcliffe; I wondered if she could shed any light on it. After all, she's his sister. She seemed surprised by the news.'

'Seemed?' Harper jumped on the word.

Ash gave a quick smile. 'Exactly, sir. She's good, I'll give her that. For a few seconds, I believed her. But she's not quite good enough. Not when you've spent a lifetime listening to lies.'

'I'm sure she said she has no idea where he is.'

The man grinned. 'More or less her precise words, sir, but she'll let us know as soon as he's in touch. She's worried about him . . . fill in whatever sentiment you like.'

'What about the others?'

'Sissons and I have one of them lined up for today.' He pinched his lips together and shook his head. 'I'm honestly not sure what's going on with this blackmail payment idea. I know fifty pounds is a fortune to you and me, but the truth is it won't make a difference to the lives of this lot. My gut feeling is that Miss Radcliffe is the one behind all this. She's sly, a schemer. The brother's along as an accomplice. The other men might be, too. We don't know enough to say yet. They probably thought the alderman would pay up and that would be it.'

'Instead they have the police hunting them.'

'And a former policeman,' Ash added with a grin. 'Don't forget that.'

'They've bitten off more than they can chew.'

'Much more. I think they're starting to panic.'

'Good. Let's pile the pressure on them,' Harper said. 'Have Sissons spread the word about the brother. He'll probably be petrified if we pull him in.'

'I'm banking on it, sir. Just a pity we can't bring any charges.'

'As long as we can retrieve the letters. Enjoy the chase.'

Ash's face lit up. 'Believe me, I am. I haven't had this much fun since I retired.'

'I'll talk to the alderman. He's supposed to hear from them today. Tomorrow is when they want their money.'

Things were moving. Slowly, but he could feel them beginning to shift. Harper glanced out of the window. A day with high, pale clouds.

'Do I have any more meetings this morning?'

'Nothing until half past two,' Miss Sharp told him.

He opened his pocket watch. Not long after eleven. Plenty of time to go down to Millgarth and become a part of the investigation for a few minutes. First, though, a visit to Thompson.

But he wasn't in his office. He'd been there earlier, his secretary said, then announced he'd be away for the rest of the day; he hadn't mentioned where he was going.

Nothing to be done, Harper thought. It niggled at him that the alderman would vanish like that with all that was happening. The timing was curious. But there was nothing he could do, he decided as he walked down Eastgate.

'Jackson's still out in Dewsbury, talking to that man who gave us the tip.' Walsh was speaking rapidly, the words tripping over themselves. His eyes were alive with excitement. 'Sergeant Clough has been on the blower to the War Office again. All the files are on their way here.'

'We'll have everything, then. Tell me exactly what we know so far.'

'*If* the information is correct, the body belongs to someone named Trevor Curtis. I told you that. Grew up in Beeston, joined up as soon as he was of age in 1917. Spent plenty of time up on the line, according to the man who telephoned us.'

Harper nodded. 'How sure are you that it's our man?'

'Very, sir.' The superintendent's voice held no doubt. 'It feels right. Local, part of a section. They were a very close-knit bunch, the officer said.'

'Do we have an address for his parents?' Harper asked.

Walsh shook his head. 'Not yet. The War Office refused to tell us over the phone. As soon as we have the file, Jackson will go and see them.'

The mood was infectious; Harper could feel it creeping through his body. Walsh had summed it up: it *felt* right. God knew he wanted it to be. But he'd had all the pieces in place in the past, only for everything to collapse at the last moment. Belief was fine; he needed to temper it with fact.

Gazing around the faces of the murder squad, he saw the smiles, the sense of pushing ahead. It had given them heart.

'When's the train due?'

Walsh's gaze flickered to the clock. 'Quarter to three, sir.'

Not long until they'd know.

'Ring me as soon as you have the information.'

But by late afternoon he'd heard nothing. Harper tried to distract himself by reading papers after an exhausting meeting about truancy. Ricks had appeared; the shoplifters and pickpockets were still causing havoc in Liverpool; more were being arrested every day. Very likely they'd soon pull out and a fresh crew would descend on Manchester.

'And after that, it's us?' Harper asked. It sounded like a bleak prospect.

'If our intelligence is right, sir.'

For once he hoped it might be wrong.

Still no word from Thompson. He rang the alderman again.
No reply.

At five Harper called for his car, wished Miss Sharp goodnight,
and strode down the steps in front of the town hall.

'Millgarth,' he told Bingham, and the car swept out into traffic.

'It wasn't on the express, sir.' Walsh was frantic, pushing his
hands into his trouser pockets then taking them out again as he
strode around the room. 'It was supposed to be left with the
guard, but he swears up and down that nobody gave him anything.
I've had my men go through the whole train with a nit comb
and there's no sign of it.'

'What does the War Office have to say?'

'They're searching for the messenger who delivered it to the
station. It was his last job of the day before he went off duty.
Nobody seems to know where he is.'

A mess. A complete bloody mess. A cock-up in London, damn
all they could do about it in Leeds. Meanwhile, they were sitting
on their hands . . . or maybe not completely.

'This officer Jackson talked to, he offered the names of all
four men, didn't he?' he asked.

'Yes, sir.'

'Here's what we'll do until we have those files. We're going
to put the word out to every copper on the beat,' Harper ordered.
'I mean that, every single one of them, and I want it done tonight.
They can pass it to the shopkeepers and busybodies. These men
are in Leeds, and someone has to know them.'

'Very good, sir.' He saw Walsh's flash of anger for not thinking
of it himself.

'You're stuck in the middle of the problem,' Harper told him.
'I'm standing outside it. Maybe I can see things more clearly,
that's all.'

A quick nod. 'I'll get on it.'

Very strange about the files and the missing messenger, he
thought as the car took him home. The same with Thompson
suddenly taking off just as the blackmailers were due to be in
touch with him about making the payment. Was he running
from that?

Nothing he could do about either one of them.

In the gardens the trees were coming into leaf, shades of brilliant greens to brighten everything. This coming weekend he'd do more digging and try to give Annabelle the colourful flower beds she wanted. He'd need to learn about it all; he'd never had a garden in his life. There should be a book in the public library.

All evening he expected the telephone to ring, but it stayed silent. A broken night – Annabelle kept thrashing around in her sleep, flailing under the covers and lashing out wildly. He'd calm her and she'd settle; fine for an hour, then it would begin again.

By the time he'd shaved and dressed, he felt as if he'd already lived an entire week.

'Town hall or Millgarth, sir?' Bingham asked as they started towards town.

He thought for a moment; it was a toss-up. 'Millgarth.' He needed to know what was happening.

'The files are on their way,' Walsh told him. Relief in his voice, but the strain still showed in his face. 'Finally.'

'What happened to them?'

The superintendent snorted his disgust. 'Turns out the bloody messenger sloped off early to meet a girl when she finished her shift. They had the police out looking, caught up with him about ten o'clock. The package went on the first train this morning. No doubt about it this time.'

At least the day was beginning with some good news.

'Any luck with that idea of spreading the word?'

'Too early to tell yet, sir. Between that and these files, we'll be able to make real headway.' He crossed his fingers. 'Assuming they actually show up, of course.'

'Have faith.'

Walsh chuckled. 'I gave that up a long time ago, sir.'

Before his meetings, he telephoned Thompson.

'You were gone yesterday.'

'Personal business, Harper. Nothing to do with this. I had to go and see my daughter in York. It was important.'

'I wondered if you were trying to avoid the blackmailers.'

'They haven't tried to get in touch yet,' Thompson replied, and Harper could hear the man's uncertainty. 'I have the money right here, but there's been nothing. I already checked the post. How close are you to catching them?'

'It's become more complicated.' Harper explained about Charles Radcliffe's disappearance and Ash's belief that his sister was behind it all.

The alderman sighed. 'You don't need to say it. My own bloody fault. Can you clear up my mess, Harper?'

'I hope we can.'

'Thank you.' Rare to hear him contrite and grateful. 'If anything arrives in the second post, I'll let you know.'

'The files are here, sir.' Walsh sounded as if he could weep for joy.

'On all four of them?'

'Yes, sir. We have addresses for the families. Jackson's sending men out to talk to them.'

'What about Curtis, the one they executed?'

'He's going to see the parents himself. Tactfully. He won't go barging in.'

'I'm sure he won't.' The inspector seemed like a sensible copper; he'd know how to approach it. 'If the dead man really is Curtis, they should be able to tell us quite a bit.'

'I'm banking on it, sir.' Sorrow, anger . . . They'd both seen it.

'If it all goes well, and you have a following wind, this could all be wrapped up by this evening.'

Walsh snorted. 'Not a chance of that. Breathing down their necks, maybe. Hang on a moment, sir.' Someone was shouting, followed by silence as the superintendent covered the mouthpiece. Then he was back, his voice loud and urgent. 'The bastards have done it again. Jeweller's at the bottom of Albion Street. Just been called in. I'm on my way there.'

'Cancel my meetings,' Harper told Miss Sharp as he rushed through her office. Breathless, he hurried through the streets, dodging between people, following the short cuts through to Albion Street. Breathless as he arrived.

From elation to misery: Walsh stood with his shoulders slumped as he listened to a report. Sergeant Clough was ordering constables around.

'Was anyone hurt?'

The superintendent turned, surprised by the voice behind him. 'Evidently not, sir,' he said. At least there was that. 'They shot into the wall, same as always, but that was it. Just two of them went in this time.'

'Doesn't need more than that. The third must have been driving the car.'

'Has to be.' He gestured at the coppers talking to the crowd. 'We're interviewing witnesses.'

Nobody dead or wounded. That was the most important fact. The jewellery would be insured, plaster and paint would cover a bullet hole in the wall. The robbers didn't know it yet, but the police were closing in on them. He started to turn away, then a thought jolted him.

'Still nothing showing up with the fences or pawnbrokers?'

Walsh shook his head. 'Not that we've heard about, and we've been keeping an eye out. I know, it doesn't make sense to me, either, sir. They've acquired a fair bit by now.'

The coppers would find out once they arrested them. Harper turned away and began to walk back to the town hall. At least his heart was beating at the normal rate now.

A little after nine. Mary and Julia had given Annabelle a bath. He could just make out the faint mutterings of conversation from the other end of house as they dried her and put her in her nightgown.

He'd been glancing at the *Evening Post*, a cup of tea growing cold at his side as he read through the letters page. A few bloody idiots were trying to build the killers up as heroes because they'd executed the one who did it. It left him furious, and it would only stop when they were behind bars.

The telephone disturbed his thoughts. It was going to be bad news.

'Duty sergeant here, sir. The shift inspector thought you ought to know: Alderman Thompson was attacked outside his house. He's been taken to the infirmary.'

Harper drew in a breath. Sweet Christ. 'How bad is it?'

'The details are sketchy, sir, but he was able to walk to the ambulance.'

One tiny piece of good news, at least. He sighed. 'You'd better send a car for me.'

SEVEN

L ying in the hospital bed, Thompson looked like an old man. Deflated, smaller and weaker, all the pride and defiance gone from his face.

He grunted. 'Come to gloat?'

'Not at all. How do you feel?'

'It looks worse than it is.'

'Just as well,' Harper told him. 'You're a mess.'

Cuts to his face and hands, the start of a pair of black eyes. But nothing that would need stitches. It had been a light beating. A mild warning.

Thompson tried to chuckle; it became a painful cough. 'At least I can depend on you to be honest.'

'What happened?'

'I was walking up the steps from the garden to the front door. They must have been waiting around the corner of the house, I suppose. I never even heard them.'

'They? How many?'

'Two.' He grimaced at the memory. 'One was behind me. He pinned my arms while the other hit me. Seemed like an hour, but it was probably less than a minute.'

'It's surprising how much you can do in that time.' Harper studied the alderman's face. 'He must have had some boxing lessons. Did he say anything?'

'Oh yes. Word for word: "I told you I'd contact you. But you went to the police."' He drew in a breath. 'I'm not likely to forget. Kept punching me as he spoke. Body as well as face.'

'What did they look like?'

'I never caught a glimpse of the one behind me. Didn't have

chance. The other one had one of those, what do you call them
. . . balaclavas. All I could see was his eyes. Full of anger.'

'What about the voice?'

'Not common,' Thompson answered after a moment. 'Is that
what you mean? He'd had an education.'

'Did you know it at all? Was it familiar?'

The alderman paused, thinking before he answered. 'No, I've
never heard him before. I'm sure of that.'

Charlotte Radcliffe's brother and a friend? Even without a
shred of proof, he'd put good money on it. Copper's instinct.

Harper worked his way through all the possibilities. 'We won't
be able to hush up what's happened tonight. It's news, the papers
are going to want to know. But we'll keep the letters and the
blackmail out of it.'

'How?'

'Simple. You were attacked on your doorstep. You have no
idea why. The police are investigating.'

'All right,' Thompson agreed after a moment. 'It sounds plausible. God knows, I've made a few enemies in my time.'

'We'll look into it on that basis.' An idea came to him. 'I'll
put Superintendent Sissons in charge. He's already working on
the blackmail. Two birds with one stone.'

'Did you just come up with that, Harper?'

'I did,' he replied, surprised by the question. 'Why?'

Another grunt. 'I knew there was a reason I put you up for
the top job. Go on now, let me get a good night's sleep. I'll be
out of here tomorrow. Send your boys round to talk to me at
home.'

A short, thoughtful stroll across to the town hall, his footsteps
echoing through the empty building as he climbed the stairs. In
his office, he telephoned Sissons at home, running quickly through
what had happened.

'Will this investigation run in parallel with the blackmail one,
sir, or be separate?'

'A bit of both,' Harper answered after a moment. 'Use Ash,
and keep him in charge of that pair of ex-coppers he's brought
in. Let them handle the blackmail side. That stays quiet. I want
you to put together a small squad and dig into this assault. Given

Thompson's position, people will expect it. The blackmailer has to be the one who hurt him. Radcliffe's brother seems the obvious suspect, since he's gone missing.'

'Racing certainty, sir. What do you want us to do when we find him?'

He smiled. Nothing like a bit of optimism. 'Let's think about that when it happens. I'll tell Ash in the morning. He's bound to have heard about it all, anyway; he always does.'

Ash was already sitting at his small table when Harper arrived the next morning.

'Good morning, sir,' he said. He had a cup of tea in front of him, even a small plate of biscuits, a sure sign of Miss Sharp's approval.

Harper glanced at his calendar. The last day of the month, April Fool's Day tomorrow. Where had March gone? His time in the job was growing short.

'You know about Thompson, then? When did you find out?'

'Someone stopped by and told me last night. How bad is he?'

'He's looked better, but the beating was fairly light. I think his pride's taken more of a battering than anything else. Thompson will be going home today.'

'I have feelers out for Radcliffe's brother. His friends all claim they haven't heard from him. Same with the sister.'

'Do you believe them?'

Ash gave a broad grin under his moustache. 'Not a word. But it'll help if this squad Sissons assembles tightens the screws on them. The usual thing: if they don't tell the truth, they'll be accessories. We all know how it works.'

Oh yes, they did. Sometimes the threat was a charm. Especially with inexperienced criminals.

'You work that out with him.'

'Am I still unofficial, sir?'

'Very,' Harper told him and they both chuckled.

'The men have visited all the parents,' Walsh said. 'I'm convinced this section is the gang.'

Harper nodded to himself. That feeling of iron certainty. 'Did any of them have an address where we can find the men?'

'No, sir. They've been very careful, not even given that away to their families.'

Of course they hadn't; that would have been too easy. 'Then we'll have to rely on the beat bobbies and neighbours. Any joy from them yet?'

'A couple of possibilities, but they turned out to be nothing.'

'Pass their names to the papers,' Harper said. 'Let them know we're nipping at their heels.'

'Are you sure that's the best way, sir?'

It would tip their hand and give away how much they knew. If it made the gang cautious, that might not be bad; it could keep them quiet for a while.

'Go ahead and do it. Just leave out the one they executed.'

'Curtis. Yes, sir.'

'How about *his* parents? What did they have to say?'

'Jackson talked to them. I think he mostly listened. It's what you'd expect. The men were all together in the war. Grew closer as the others in the section died. Old comrades by the end, couldn't believe they'd survived. Curtis's parents had no idea what he was up to. He came for his dinner a week ago Sunday and told them he'd found a good job. They had no reason not to believe him.'

'Jackson seems to know what he's doing.'

'He's become my right arm, sir.'

Harper smiled. Exactly the way he'd been when he was a superintendent and Ash his inspector. The same before that, back when he was an inspector himself and Billy Reed was his sergeant. That was another age, but one thing didn't change: you needed someone utterly reliable.

'None of the loot turned up yet?'

'Nothing. It's baffling, sir.'

Very. One more thing to worry about.

It was a day that didn't want to end. Meetings, telephone calls, papers to read and sign; everything crept by sluggishly. Harper wondered how the detectives were moving along in their investigations, forcing down the urge to walk away from his desk and join them. But he knew the hard truth: he'd be more of a liability than an asset. Too many years had passed since he'd been out there. A new generation of criminals had grown up, toughened and bitter from fighting in a war, and he didn't know a single one of them.

Like the killers in the Model T. They tried to give themselves a gloss of honour with the execution, but it was pure survival. They'd lost members of the section before; chances were they'd keep going until they were all dead or behind bars. Even if they didn't realize it, that was the pact they'd made with each other.

Nothing by five o'clock. He stopped his hand from reaching for the phone and ringing Walsh at Millgarth. Leave the man to do his job. The same with Sissons. No word. A note from Ricks. The group of women remained in Liverpool.

He believed in the men he'd put in charge, but it didn't stop him fretting in the car on the way home.

'Inspector Walsh has telephoned twice,' Miss Sharp announced as soon as he walked into the office. A dull morning, warm, close enough to put a film of sweat on his forehead.

Harper felt the shiver of excitement. They'd caught the killers. They must have.

'You wanted me.'

'Yes, sir.' The superintendent's voice was faint on the line; he pressed the receiver against his ear.

'Do you have them?'

The silence stretched out until Walsh said, 'No, sir. We don't. They've pulled something on us.'

'Another job? The shops haven't even opened yet.'

He snorted. 'I wish it was that simple. Right about the time it started getting light, we began receiving reports from people who'd found paper bags on their doorsteps. They told the men on the beat and handed them over.'

'Bags?' His mouth was dry, skin tingling, not sure what was coming.

'They contained watches and rings. A few little bits and pieces from the robberies in each one.'

'That's . . .' He couldn't find the words. Beyond belief. Why? 'How many of them?'

'Five so far, sir. Those are the ones we know about. I have people searching high and low. God only knows how many have been found and not turned in. Could even be our lot keeping some, too. They're only human. The word's already spread; people are out hunting.'

Free jewellery? It was the same as someone standing on the corner and handing out fivers. People would be scrambling and fighting over it.

'Where did the killers leave them?'

A long, heartfelt sigh. 'Not a scrap of rhyme or reason to it, sir. About the only thing is they were all in poorer areas. We've recovered one from Bramley, another from Armley. Two by the Bank and the last one in Holbeck.'

Those were the ones the police knew about. There could be dozens of them around town.

'How much in each bag?'

'Only two or three things. I did a few quick sums; they'd need to fill at least eighty bags to give away everything they've stolen.'

Harper ran a hand through his hair; not too much of it left these days. 'For all we know, they might have done that.' His voice was bleak. How could anyone predict these men? 'Any notes with them?'

'Nothing. But people are going to guess. It's not difficult.'

'True enough.' Overnight, they'd turned the tables, going from murderers to Robin Hoods, distributing the riches they stole to the poor. They were clever bastards. Quick, too, he had to give them that. His head was throbbing and it wasn't eight o'clock yet. April bloody fool. 'I'll come over to Millgarth at nine. They've put us on the back foot. You and I and Inspector Jackson are going to sit down and decide what to do about it.'

'I'll expect you, sir.'

'Do you have any of those headache powders?' he called out to Miss Sharp. 'I could do with one.'

EIGHT

Walsh's desk had been Harper's once, years before when he ran this division. Every gouge and scratch in the wood was familiar.

'Have we recovered any more of these packages?' he asked.

'Two, sir,' Jackson replied. 'Seven in total. But we've no idea how many people might have found and kept.'

Harper nodded. 'And we never will. Let's take that as understood and write the jewellery off. Log everything and compare it to the list of what the killers stole.'

'I've been going through their files,' Walsh said. He had a dazed, defeated air. 'One of them is a little older than the others. Twenty-four. Left his job very suddenly a week before the first robbery and moved out of his parents' house. He was being trained as a foreman at the sewage plant, so he must have something about him.'

'You think he's the leader?'

'That's my guess. His name's Will Hobson. Lance-corporal when he was in the army. All the others were privates.'

'They'll be used to obeying him,' Jackson said. 'It becomes a habit.'

'Catch him and we'll cut off the head,' Harper said. 'The gang will fall apart.'

'The car is his, too,' Walsh added. 'His parents told the sergeant who talked to them. It had belonged to his older brother. He was killed in the trenches and left it to Will.'

'Do we have the number plate now?'

'For what it's worth,' the superintendent answered with a snort. 'We also discovered the others all moved from home at the same time as Hobson.'

'We'd guessed that, hadn't we? What are their names?'

'John Booth and David Templeton. Both twenty-two.'

Harper stared at the others. 'All this is fine, it's ammunition. But how do we catch them? So far we're stumbling along in their wake.'

'I've been racking my brain, sir,' Walsh answered. 'They always seem prepared for a job. More than that, they can adapt.'

'Think on their feet,' Jackson agreed. 'We've just seen that. All of Leeds should be against them for killing someone. Even the execution wouldn't stop that. Now people are going to be scrambling everywhere and hoping to find a package of jewellery. Times are hard.'

'I know,' Harper agreed. It was there in the bleak faces of the men, the worn-down looks of their wives, the hunger that kept the children thin. The wounded ex-servicemen reduced to begging on the streets. Things hadn't changed much from when he was young. Britain had won the war but forgotten its own people. Jobs had gone, the empire wasn't buying English goods any longer; they'd developed their own industries.

He tried to imagine the men, what was making them do this. 'These others in the section, were they employed?'

'Booth was,' Jackson told him. 'Not Templeton. He couldn't settle after he came back. Kept moving from job to job, his parents said, then gave up altogether. Spent time with the others from the old section whenever he could.'

'How about friends?' Harper asked. 'They must have some. Girlfriends?'

Jackson shook his head. 'The parents don't know of any, sir. We've checked with the old soldiers' associations, and they don't know the names. Looks as if it was just the four of them. Very self-contained. They probably learned to survive like that over there, only trusting each other, and that's carried on.'

'Except there was one they couldn't trust.'

'I wonder how much division that caused,' Walsh said quietly.

'They probably deferred to Hobson.'

Harper exhaled slowly. 'Tell me what we have on Booth.'

'Baptist parents, brought up religious, but he lost all that in the war.' Jackson shrugged. It had been a time to shatter all manner of beliefs and illusions. 'Parents said they didn't know him when he returned. Familiar story.'

Harper stared at the wall for a minute. 'We can't put a constable in every jeweller's. By the time a robbery's reported, they've already gone. What can we do to stop them?'

'Do you remember you said we might be able to use the idea of a car, sir?' Walsh asked.

'That was just a wild thought,' Harper said.

'There might be more to it than you imagined. After we found out the number plate, I checked the registration address. It wasn't where Hobson's parents live. He'd changed it to a place in Cross Green. When I talked to the man on the beat, he said the house belonged to a widow, but it has a garage she sometimes rents out.'

'It can't still be there, or we'd have him,' Harper said.

Walsh shook his head. 'Hobson was sly enough to shift it before they pulled their first job. But it's another angle to try, especially now we have the number plate. The beat men are asking around, everyone who has a garage or small workshop for rent. Like you said, there aren't too many cars around, even Model Ts. Nobble the car and they'll be helpless.' His eyes glittered with hope.

It was the only possible lead they had, he thought as he walked back to the town hall. Slim, but they had to push it. Anything that could break this gang and take them off the streets. Hobson and his gang had changed their game. They'd managed to upend everything.

Why had they held on to all their loot in the first place? Certainly not to give it all away later.

The answer struck him as he walked up the steps, towards the stone lions. The gang didn't know any fences. They had no contacts, no idea how to dispose of all the jewellery. They were organized, but they were amateurs.

But he had little time to think about it. He rang Walsh to suggest it to him, then he was plunged into a series of meetings and telephone calls, followed by time with the deputy chief constable, Albert Dickinson. He'd been gone for three weeks, compassionate leave to look after his sick mother in Carlisle. She had died while he was there and he'd stayed on to arrange the funeral.

Dickinson would take over as acting chief when Harper retired. The solid, reliable type the city needed while they decided on someone new.

'I'm very sorry about your mother,' Harper began.

Dickinson settled heavily into the chair, a squat, thick man just shy of fifty years old, with hair the colour of wet sand. 'Sounds like an awful thing to say, but it was for the best, really. She was in pain.'

'Even so . . .'

'I know.' He nodded slowly. 'Thank you. Looks like we've had quite a bit happening with these robberies and killings.'

'We're making progress.' He brought the man up to speed, watching as he methodically filled and lit his pipe.

'Sounds like a matter of time before we nab them.'

'It is,' Harper agreed. 'The problem is time is something we don't really have. They've probably already lined up the next shop to hit, and scattering those packages around means people are going to be on their side. Then there's this group of women, the shoplifters. They'll probably be here soon.'

'What can I do to help?'

'Well . . .' Dickinson had made the offer. 'Are you sure?'

'Positive. I've come back to a clean desk.'

'You could take over most of the meetings and the correspondence. They'll all be yours from next month, anyway.'

Dickinson chuckled. 'Hand over the boring stuff?' He cocked his head. 'You want to be involved with catching this gang? Last chance?'

Harper thought about Thompson and the blackmail. 'Something like that. Do you mind, Albert?'

'Not at all. It makes sense, really,' he agreed. 'I'll be familiar with it when I take over. I was reading about Alderman Thompson. Strange business, isn't it?'

For a moment, Harper froze, wondering how much the man knew. Then he realized: the attack.

'Very. I've put Sissons on the investigation. Thompson's made plenty of enemies over the years.'

'Looks like you have everything in hand, sir.'

'I'll tell Miss Sharp to forward everything to you.'

She appeared a few minutes later with a cup of tea and a single biscuit.

He raised his eyebrows. 'Just one?'

'You've been putting on weight,' she told him. 'Your daughter said I should ration you.'

God save him; the women were conspiring against him. 'I thought rationing ended after the war.'

'She says she'll keep an eye on things once you're at home all the time.'

'I've no doubt she will.'

'Now you've cleared the decks, I suppose you'll be haring off to help catch this gang.'

'I'd like to finish my career with some proper police work.'

'It's always been hard enough to keep you in the office.'

'I'll still come here every day, and I'm available if anything important crops up.'

She sniffed. 'I suppose that's something.'

'What about you?' he asked. 'What will you be doing after I leave?'

'Working for the next deputy chief. Try to teach him the proper way to do things.' Another little sniff of frustration. 'I never quite managed it with you. You arrived with too many bad habits.'

He held out until early afternoon before striding over to Millgarth. Walsh was in his office, but the detectives' room was empty.

'They're all following up on leads, sir.'

'What can I do to help?'

'Sir?' He stared in astonishment.

'I've handed over most of my paperwork and meetings. I'm determined to have this lot arrested, everything done and dusted before I leave. So, if there's anything I can do . . .'

Walsh ran a hand through his hair. 'Right now, I'm not sure, sir. Jackson's running it all, and he seems to have the men under control. I'm hoping we might have information on where they're keeping the car by tomorrow.'

'Fingers crossed.'

'That thought of yours about them having no contacts. It makes sense.'

'Except it doesn't tell us what they hope to achieve by robbing these places.'

'True.' The superintendent hesitated. 'I don't think the inspector's going to be back until late.'

Harper chuckled. 'Come back tomorrow and see if there's a job for me? Is that it?'

'Sorry, sir, but . . .'

'It doesn't matter. I'll be here in the morning.'

As he walked up the Headrow, Harper had to smile to himself. Rejected by his own men. That had probably never happened to a chief constable before. He stepped aside to avoid a drunk fumbling his way out of the Three Legs public house.

A man passed, dressed in a suit and tie, his right leg gone, concentrating as he used a crutch to move along the street. Not too long ago, a sight like that would have made people stare. Now it didn't warrant a second glance. All the wounds of war had come home. Maybe they were the lucky ones. So many, like Mary's fiancé Len, had never made it back.

At the town hall, Harper went to the small room housing the intelligence section. The men were there, but no Sissons. He'd received a telephone call and told them he needed to go and see somebody. No name. All very mysterious; to do with the Thompson case, they believed. They didn't know where he'd gone or when he'd be back.

Ricks took him aside with a report that the women had all left Liverpool. Very sudden. No word of them in Manchester; nobody knew what was happening.

Harper felt stuck in limbo. No luck at all today. If he returned to his own office, it would be an admission of defeat. Instead, he wandered like a lost lamb, back along the Headrow, then down to Albion Place, climbing the stairs to Mary's office.

She looked flustered as she came out to meet him. Harper stood completely still, staring at her. He was speechless, stunned into silence. For a moment he didn't recognize his daughter. She was wearing a cotton frock that came halfway down her calves in gentle, pastel colours. Harper had seen a few like it in shop windows, proclaimed as the new fashion. Softer, more feminine. No more heavy corsets. But he'd never imagined Mary in one of them. He'd become used to the harsh black she'd worn since Len died. This made her look young. The transformation shook him. It made her seem . . . alive.

'I wasn't expecting you, Da.' Mary blushed. 'I was . . .' She waved her hand as an explanation.

Harper finally found his voice. 'I'm sorry. Just popped by on the off chance. I can go if I'm interrupting something.'

'No, I was caught up in figures. They always drive me mad.' She smiled. 'Asking me out for afternoon tea?'

'A quick cup and a piece of cake, if you have the time.'

'Don't be daft, Da. You caught me on the hop, that's all.' Mary's eyes glittered with laughter. 'We can go round to the Kardomah. If you're not afraid to be seen with me, of course.'

'Give over.'

Out in the thick air of Leeds, walking up Briggate, she put her arm through his.

'Go on, you might as well say it,' she teased him. 'You looked like your eyes were about to explode from their sockets back there.'

He laughed. 'You have to admit, it's quite a change.' He was aware of people staring at her, turning their heads as they passed. Mary didn't seem to care.

'I know.' She began to laugh. 'You should have heard the girls when I came in this morning. The way they carried on, you'd have thought the sky was falling. But it feels comfortable, it's so light.' She turned silent for a full minute. 'I'll always love Len, but I realized I couldn't stay the way I had been.'

'The trip,' he said with a nod. 'Closing the book.'

Mary gave a quick shake of her head. 'No, it's not like that. Still the same book, but a new chapter. It felt time.'

'And the car?'

'That really is practical, Da, just like I said. But I suppose it's part of everything, too. Time to . . . not to leave it all behind, but to know I can live a little and it will all be fine. I've worn those heavy dresses and corsets all my life. They've always felt like a cage. I saw these in the shops and yesterday I screwed up my courage and bought a couple of them.' She cocked her head to look at him. 'Can you understand that? Is it bad?'

'Of course it's not,' he told her. 'Len's still there in your heart. You're young, you need to spread your wings and fly a little. You're not sullying his memory, you're making some changes in your life.'

Mary nodded. 'Quite a few of them,' she agreed, stopped and twirled. 'Anyway, what do *you* think of the dress, Da?'

She was putting him on the spot, and the mischievous gleam showed how much she relished it.

'I don't know.' He was going to give her an honest answer. 'It's very feminine. It's just so . . . different, I suppose.'

'It is,' she agreed. 'Freer. Maybe that's part of the appeal.'

'It's going to take me a while to get used to it. I've had a lifetime of the old style.' He glanced at her again. Clothes like this didn't hide her; they put her on display. 'I'm not sure what your mother will make of it, though.'

'She saw me this morning. It was during a good moment. She looked me up and down and said, "You're a right bobby dazzler in that. You should have done it before."'

He threw his head back, roaring with laughter. He could easily hear Annabelle speaking those words.

'You have the seal of approval.'

'I know,' she said. 'About the best way I can put it is this feels like the right time.' That was enough.

People kept looking at her in the restaurant, their eyes shifting away again quickly.

'Shouldn't you be working?' she asked. 'Or have you decided to start your retirement early?'

He told her, feeling foolish and old. 'On top of everything, I hear you've been telling Miss Sharp to cut down on my biscuits.'

Mary eyed him. 'Take a look at yourself, Da. You're podgy.'

'That'll soon go once I start walking more.' He stopped as the waitress placed a slice of cake in front of him. A smile played across Mary's mouth.

'Whatever you say.'

After they parted, he found himself drifting around the streets. For the first time in years, nobody was expecting him, no meetings to attend, he had no responsibilities for the rest of the day.

He saw one other woman dressed in the same new style as Mary, looking self-conscious as she hurried up Briggate. Never mind; give it a month and they'd probably all be in clothes like that. His daughter was right, it was time for something new after so much war and death. Something with plenty of life and colour to it.

No car waiting to drive him home. He queued and rode the tram out to Chapel Allerton. Another month and this would be how he travelled; might as well get used to it.

The telephone was ringing as he unlocked the front door. He lifted the receiver just as Julia rushed out of the kitchen.

'Harper.'

'It's Sissons, sir.' He picked out the quiet urgency in the man's voice and pressed the receiver close to his ear.

'I missed you in the office earlier today.'

'I was out following up on a tip. A sergeant told me about a suspicious suicide.'

'Does it tie into the Thompson case?'

'Very much, sir. A man jumped in front of an express train as it passed through Garforth station.'

He shuddered at the idea. 'God, that's a horrible way to go.'

'It was a mess, sir. I saw the body.'

'How's it suspicious, though?'

'Nothing to identify him.'

'Is that rare?' He had no idea.

'Not always, sir. But the sergeant wanted to alert me to something after he talked to the engine driver.'

Typical Sissons, taking the long route to the heart of the matter. 'When did this happen?'

'Yesterday. It was a small story in today's papers, sir.'

He hadn't paid attention. Even if he'd read it, he'd only have seen another sad, gruesome tale. But he was still wondering how it was relevant.

'Go on.'

'I talked to the engine driver myself. As I said, it was an express, coming through from the coast and Selby, not stopping at Garforth. He wasn't really watching; didn't even realize he'd hit anything until he heard the thump. But he thought he saw something from the corner of his eye, a man running from the platform. He's not sure, it was only a fleeting glimpse.'

Harper felt the first wrinkles of doubt creeping through him. 'Did anyone else see him?'

'The station master was out, and the signalman was looking at the lines. No passengers waiting that we know about. Since everyone assumed it was a suicide, there wasn't much questioning. No need.'

'You still haven't explained how it connects to our case.'

'They fingerprinted the corpse. The results came through late this afternoon. It's Charlotte Radcliffe's brother, the one who vanished a few days ago. Charles Radcliffe.'

Harper exhaled slowly, trying to make sense of it all. 'What now?'

'We're going to find out what really happened, where he's been since he vanished.'

'Have you told the family yet?' He had no idea what it all meant. The case was spiralling out of control and turning into a twisted monster.

'There's only the sister; both parents are dead.' Of course; he'd forgotten that. 'I sent a constable round to inform her, but she was out.'

'Don't go back today,' Harper ordered.

'Are you sure, sir?'

'Positive. First thing tomorrow, you and I are going to see her. I want to watch how she reacts to the news.' It would give him the chance to meet her, talk to her and form an opinion.

'Very good, sir.'

'After that, we'll collect Ash and talk to the alderman again.'

'What else do you want me to do today, sir?'

'Gather everything you can on Charles Radcliffe.'

'I started that a few days ago, sir. People he knocks about with, things like that. There's family money, he receives a good allowance, the same as his sister. Like most of that group, he's never needed to work. Managed to avoid the war.'

But that hadn't saved him from death. That faint possibility of someone else on the platform intrigued him, too. The idea of murder, not suicide.

'What did Dr Amersham say at the post-mortem?'

'He hasn't done it yet.'

'I want a thorough job.' He paused. 'What do you really think about this? You had enough doubts to ring me.'

'None of it feels right,' Sissons answered after a long gap. 'That's about the best way I can put it, sir.'

'Good enough for me.' The man's hunches were usually sound. He felt something stirring. Simple blackmail had suddenly become very complicated. 'We're going to need to question everyone on that train and living near that station. We'll need to make sure we press a few people, as well.'

'Including the sister, sir?'

'Especially her. Gently at first, but I'm sure she has some answers.'

Annabelle's day had turned sour, Julia told him. After the fine morning with Mary, she'd raged for a while, screaming, then started crying about nothing in particular; nothing that made sense. Finally she'd exhausted herself, not long before Harper arrived. The nurse had put her to bed.

He sat in the parlour and read the paper. The suicide was there, three lines at the very bottom of the front page. He'd be back to it all tomorrow, not that his day of respite had felt like relief in the end.

His thoughts drifted towards Mary. She was shedding her old skin and coming back to life, able to finally leave behind the weight of mourning. He was glad; it was certainly time. She was only twenty-eight, still a young woman, she deserved a good life.

Another few years and the war that killed Len and all those others would be relegated to the history books. People would forget all the deaths of the Spanish influenza. And no one would remember him, just another obscure name on a town hall plaque.

NINE

Harper watched Charlotte Radcliffe as Sissons delivered the news. All the colour fled from her face and her fingers clutched the chair arms tightly, as if they might stop her from falling.

She wasn't acting. No one could be that good. Miss Radcliffe hadn't known about her brother.

'Suicide?' The word stumbled from her mouth. 'I don't understand.'

Sissons told her. No more than a sentence or two, sparing the details. She was shaken to her soul.

'He'd been missing, I believe,' Harper said.

She turned to face him, shaking her head as if she was trying to clear the mist inside.

'Yes. I wasn't worried. Charles and I often went a week or two without seeing each other, you see. More, sometimes.' She blinked, as if speaking surprised her.

'I'm very sorry,' Sissons said. 'Forgive me, I know this must be awful, but can you think of any reason your brother might kill himself? Please understand, we have to ask.'

As they'd agreed outside, the superintendent was playing his part, the earnest, honest policeman.

'No.' She frowned. 'No. Of course not. He'd never do that.' She looked from one face to the other, imploring them. 'Why would he? He didn't have any reason.'

Harper rubbed his chin. 'We believe your brother might have been involved in the beating Alderman Thompson received the other night.'

'What?' Her voice was full of disbelief, but this time he could tell that she knew the truth. 'I read about that. It's awful. But Charles . . . he wasn't physical at all.'

'We feel he was part of the blackmail, Miss Radcliffe.'

She was a small woman. Her naturally pale complexion had turned ghostly white. A face to turn heads, delicate, with intelligent eyes. The type a man would want to protect. But there was something else about her, too. A sensuality, a challenge. The right man would make a fool of himself trying to win her. Someone like Alderman Thompson. Harper could understand what had attracted the man.

He kept watching her. The first wave of shock had passed. She was beginning to make calculations. Her mind was working, deciding what would suit her best.

'No,' she answered. 'I can't believe Charles would be involved in anything like that.'

'You said he was over here regularly, that he could have stolen the letters,' Sissons said.

'I suppose it's possible, but—'

'We'd been looking for him when he vanished down to London, Miss Radcliffe.' Harper paused for a moment and stared down at the thick rug that covered most of the floor. 'Do you know if he had any enemies?'

'Enemies?' She sounded as if she'd never heard the term before, trying to feel her way around it. 'Why would he? He hasn't . . .'

Time to take her by surprise again, he thought. Keep her shocked. 'We're trying to establish the truth of it, but the engine driver thinks he might have spotted someone with Mr Radcliffe on the platform before it happened.'

He watched the emotions cross her face; she wasn't skilful enough to keep them hidden. Horror, pain, not wanting to believe. Then she realized the truth, even as she scrambled to hide it. She knew exactly what had happened.

'What? You believe someone killed him?' Charlotte Radcliffe asked. 'Is that what you're trying to say?'

'We don't know,' Harper told her with a dip of his head. 'Why, do you think it could have happened?'

She frowned and pursed her lips. 'No. It's impossible. It doesn't make any sense. Why would anyone want to kill Charles?'

'We're hoping you can give us a hint, Miss Radcliffe,' Sissons said. His tone had changed, turning dry and business-like.

'I can't. I'm sorry. Everything you're saying . . . Charles would never take his own life. That's just not like him. He's my brother. I'd *know*. And no one would murder him. I'm sure of that. It must have been some sort of accident.' She stood, pushing herself up from the chair. 'I'm going to have to ask you to leave. The news . . . it's . . .' She shook her head and stared at Sissons, then asked, 'Are you absolutely sure it's him?'

'I'm afraid there's no doubt,' he replied. 'I'm sorry. As his next of kin, I'm afraid we'll need you to officially identify his body.'

They didn't speak again until the car had pulled into traffic, heading towards Burley.

'What did you make of that, sir?' Sissons asked finally.

'She definitely didn't know about her brother. It knocked her sideways. But she recovered swiftly enough. Did you notice that? You could practically hear the gears turning in her head, trying to work out what to say and how to use it. She's involved, I'm positive of it.'

'She's cunning, no doubt about that.'

'Oh, yes.'

'I think she has a suspicion who might have killed her brother, too.'

Harper nodded. 'I'm sure she knows who's responsible.' He

gave a sigh. 'The question is, how are we going to drag the truth out of her?'

No answer, not even when Ash joined them and the car sped along Chapeltown Road to Alderman Thompson's house.

He moved like an old man, more a shuffle than a walk. The bruises on his face were in full bloom and the cuts had scabbed over. Not a pretty sight; no wonder he was staying away from the town hall until he was fully healed.

As they settled in the front room his wife fussed around, a prissy woman with a frosty glare beneath her smile. Finally she left, and Thompson said, 'Right, what do you have to tell me?'

Harper sat back in the chair and listened as Sissons ran through it all, the suicide that could be murder, the belief that Charles Radcliffe had been involved in the assault. Then it was Ash's turn, his slow voice telling everything they'd discovered about Charlotte, her brother and his friends.

A dissolute bunch. He saw the alderman flinch and his face harden as he learned more and more.

'I've been a right damned fool, haven't I?' he said at the end.

'We all make mistakes,' Harper told him.

'I've made a bloody whopper. Now someone's dead. Because of all this, do you think?' he asked Sissons.

'It's very likely, sir.' A judicious answer.

Harper stepped in. 'Don't go thinking that's your fault. If the blackmail really is the cause, remember, they're the ones who chose to start it. Have you heard anything more? Another demand?' The alderman hadn't mentioned anything.

Thompson shook his head. 'They've been bringing my post out here, but I've not had any more letters and it's well past their deadline.'

Tuesday. That was the day they'd set for handing over the money. Friday now and so much had happened in between that the demand for money felt like ancient history.

'Until we find any proper evidence to the contrary, Mr Radcliffe's death will remain a suicide,' Sissons said.

'Do you think you'll come up with any?'

'I don't know, Alderman. We have constables talking to possible witnesses.'

He nodded slowly, weighing the knowledge. 'What now? Someone's dead, and I know this probably sounds callous, but how do we get my letters back?'

Harper smiled inside at the word *we*. Another man's death was unfortunate, nothing more. He saw it in Thompson's eyes; he was desperate to feel safe.

'You have to understand that this changes everything,' Ash said. 'We've had a constable guarding Mr Radcliffe's rooms overnight. The superintendent and I are going to search them this morning.'

'So there's still hope.' Thompson gave a wan smile.

'Yes, sir.'

'You don't really expect to find them, do you?' Harper ask once they were back in the car.

'No, sir,' Ash replied. 'I don't know if they were ever there. But if they were, my money is on Radcliffe taking them when we bolted.

'We only have Miss Radcliffe's word that they were taken from her flat, don't we?'

'Yes, sir.' It was Sissons's turn to answer. 'Of course, we didn't have any reason to doubt her at the beginning.'

'If we find some more evidence, let's see if we can obtain a warrant to search her place somehow.'

A very big if, certainly at the moment. Still, with the right reason and some bending of the truth, it might be possible, especially with a chief constable's backing.

Harper told Bingham to drop him at Millgarth, then take Ash and Sissons to Charles Radcliffe's rooms.

He'd been so hopeful for a break of some kind with the Model T killers, but there was nothing. No more bags of jewellery turned in to the police. How many had they set out, Harper wondered? Quite a few more than had been handed in, that was certain.

'Has anybody tried to pawn any of it yet?'

'Not that I've heard,' Walsh replied, then looked at Inspector Jackson.

'No, sir. But it would probably be just one or two things from a few houses, spread around the city.' He shrugged. 'We might never find out.'

The way of the world. Hard times and everybody was struggling to survive.

'For you, sir,' Walsh said, handing Harper the telephone. 'It's Mr Ash.'

'Any luck?'

'Not so you'd notice, sir. We've been right through Mr Radcliffe's flat. But his landlady did say he'd cleared out quickly when he came back from London, so it's hardly a surprise. We were already trying to find out where he went; now we'll make it urgent.'

'Very good.'

He opened the front door, ready to step out and wait for his car. Saturday was going to be sunny, barely a cloud in the sky; Harper could already feel the welcome warmth against his face. Real spring; after work he'd take Annabelle out in her chair for a stroll around Chapel Allerton and up to the park.

His foot came down on the stone step and something hard crunched under the sole of his shoe. He bent and picked up a small brown paper bag, the top folded over. Very carefully, he opened it.

Four rings, the gold glittering. One with a ruby, another with an emerald.

Harper glanced up and down the street. Not a soul around. His front door faced the gable ends of the villa houses across the road; with only frosted widows in the landing, no one could have seen anything.

Not a gift. The bastards had sent him a message. A direct challenge.

Catch us if you can.

At Millgarth, he strode through the detectives' room and through to Walsh's office, waving for Jackson to join them.

'Close the door,' Harper ordered, then took the bag from his pocket and dropped it on the desk.

'This was outside my house this morning.' He stared at the superintendent, then the inspector. 'My house.'

He let the words hang. For years it had been common knowledge that he lived above the Victoria pub on Roundhay Road. People had come to see him there; a couple of times, men had tried to kill him outside the place. A very public house. But the move to Chapel Allerton had been done quietly. Hardly anyone knew where to find him now.

Jackson tipped the contents on to the blotter. 'Brazen. They're giving us two fingers.'

'No, they're giving them to *me*.' He could feel the anger alive in his belly, hard and solid and hot.

'If they're running scared, they're hiding it well,' Walsh said.

'We need to stamp on them damned fast.' He knew he was close to shouting, but he didn't care. 'I want to know how they found my address.'

His home. His wife and daughter were there. He saw Walsh's eyes flicker towards Jackson.

'It's hardly a state secret, sir,' the man said slowly.

Harper sighed and nodded. The man was right; the information probably wouldn't have been too difficult to find. It felt like . . . a violation. One more reason to be glad that retirement was coming.

'Let's find that bloody car and take them off the road.'

The desk sergeant hurried in, his face riddled with worry. 'They've done it again.'

'Where?' Walsh asked. Harper felt a cold hand on his spine. The bag, now this. They weren't running, they were stepping it up.

'Bottom of Lower Basinghall Street, sir. Just up from Boar Lane.'

'Anyone hurt?' Jackson asked. The urgent question.

'Not that I've been told.' The sergeant placed a scrap of paper on the desk and left.

'What are we waiting for?' Harper asked.

TEN

People were standing around on the pavement gawking as the car pulled up. Jackson jumped out, issuing orders before his shoes hit the pavement. Harper took his time, gazing around, watching faces.

One constable was trying to keep order, pushing the spectators back, while two more were starting to interview witnesses. Only English reserve kept it all from chaos.

Harper stared at the shop, a poky little jeweller's less than five yards from the junction of the two roads. The men had picked their target well. Easy to pull up, then a straight path to get away.

Inside, he saw the bullet hole in the wall and smelled the cordite from the shot. Jackson was talking to the owner, a nervous, stammering man who kept looking down at his shaking hands in disbelief.

A pale, terrified assistant was attempting to return some order to things. Her hands were trembling too, her skin so white that for a second he believed he could see right through it.

'It's over,' he told her gently. 'They won't be back again.'

A brittle, wary smile arrived, then vanished again in an instant.

'I . . .' she began, before she looked up at him. The tears were ready to roll down her cheeks. Harper took out his handkerchief and passed it to her.

'Can you tell me what happened?' he asked as she dabbed at her eyes. 'I'm Chief Constable Harper. That's Inspector Jackson, talking to your boss.'

'I'm Miss Lowther, sir. Kate Lowther. I only started here last month.' She pursed her lips and breathed slowly, forcing the Leeds accent back under the cultivated voice she used for customers.

'I'm sure you never expected anything like this. You look like you're in shock.' He offered her a reassuring smile. 'What you need is a cup of tea. Wait here.'

There was a café two doors down. Tea slopped from the mug as he carried it back, but it was strong, just a splash of milk and thickly laced with sugar. Miss Lowther raised it and sipped.

'Thank you.'

It took time but the colour returned to her face. Harper talked about inconsequential things: the weather, the feel of spring. After a couple of minutes she seemed more at ease, the memory of fear beginning to ebb away.

'Right, guide me through it, please, Miss Lowther.'

Her words came in fragments, disjointed, but he began to build up a picture. She was the first witness he'd interviewed on this case. It had a different feel from reading words on a page. This was real and immediate. He could sense the men in the shop, smell their sweat, almost see them.

'That's all,' she finished. 'I'm sorry, it's not much.'

'It is,' he told her. 'Believe me.'

Maybe she hadn't provided any new facts, but now Harper had a clearer sense of the men, and that was without price.

'Your handkerchief,' she said, extending her hand as he began to turn away.

He joined Jackson back on the pavement. The inspector was listening to the constables give their reports.

'Nothing we haven't heard before, sir.'

Later, they sat in the café, watching the street through the window. People had moved along, and now everyone passed as if nothing had ever happened. The first they'd know would be a story in the paper.

'They have their routine, and they've honed it,' Harper said. 'In and out of the place in less than thirty seconds.'

'Did the young lady have much to add?'

He shook his head. 'Not in a way that'll help us catch them. But I feel I know them better.'

And he intended to repay them for the insult on his doorstep. That had made this into something very personal.

'Now tell me what I can do to help you,' Harper said.

Going through all the witness statements, hunting for any small thing they might have missed. One small clue to make the hunt easier. He spent the morning reading, making a note of anything odd, any inconsistencies. By noon, he could feel the first tendrils of a headache.

Being outside helped, even in the smoke and rank air of Leeds. As he reached the town hall, the throbbing in his skull had passed.

'The prodigal chief,' Miss Sharp said. 'Had enough of real work and come home?'

'I popped by to see if there was anything urgent.'

'Mr Ash is in your office. Superintendent Sissons left a few minutes ago. I've been supplying tea and biscuits.' She rolled her eyes. 'I feel like a waitress.'

'You're undervalued,' he told her.

Ash sat at the small table, chin cupped in his hand.

'Stymied?' Harper asked.

'Maybe a little, sir,' he admitted. 'We're still trying to piece together what happened to Mr Radcliffe between the time he vanished and he turned up dead.'

'What did Dr Amersham find at the post-mortem?'

Ash's gaze soured. 'Exactly what you'd expect on a body that was hit by an express train. Too badly damaged to see much.'

He felt a cold hand on his back. The picture wasn't one that anyone would choose to imagine. 'Have we found any witnesses?'

'Actually, yes.' He brightened for a moment. 'A passenger on the train was gazing out of the window. He swears he saw a man sprint off just as he felt the engine strike the body.'

'You didn't prompt him? No encouragement?'

Ash gazed at him, disappointed. 'You ought to know me better than that, sir.'

Harper felt ashamed. The man was always scrupulous with witnesses. 'Sorry. Anybody else see it?'

'Just the one so far. We're following up with the other passengers.'

'So it's far from convincing, and we still have a big question mark over Mr Radcliffe's end.'

'Between this one and the driver, we've decided to work on the theory it was murder. But we're going to keep the investigation very quiet, as if we accept the suicide.'

'Hoping someone makes a mistake?' It was a dangerous tactic. The evidence of murder was sketchy as best. Not enough to begin a full-blown investigation and certainly nothing they'd ever dare take to court. The whole thing was far from legal, yet on balance it was the right decision. At least it kept Alderman Thompson's name well out of things.

'What have you come up with on Radcliffe's movements?'

'That's where we've run into the problem. None of our snouts know him. He's never spent any time around criminals. It's all his own, what do you call them . . . set.'

'And they keep very much to themselves?'

'They're quite social, but they're hardly likely to tell us anything about one of their own.'

'Closing ranks on outsiders?'

'Completely. No time at all for the police. We don't have a hope with them.'

Far more money, upper class, but they weren't much different from the Model T killers. Just another gang, tight-knit and wary of outsiders.

'How do we find the truth, then?'

Ash sighed. 'That's what we've been trying to come up with, sir. So far we can't see a way inside.'

'What about the sister? I saw the shock on her face when we told her about Charles; that was genuine.'

'It's possible,' the man agreed. 'But she's had too much time to compose herself since then. The closer we look, the more I'm convinced she's the one behind it. She'll have found out what happened and why. I don't think we'll be able to get under her skin again.'

'Worth a try?'

'Only if we're desperate.' He smiled. 'It's not that bad yet. And the alderman hasn't had another demand.'

'No.' That was something. He didn't believe they'd try after Charles Radcliffe's death. It would only turn the spotlight on them, and they needed the shadows. Thompson might have been lucky. But someone else had paid a heavy price.

'Do whatever you think will work,' Harper said. 'There's a murderer out there who believes he's going to walk away scot-free.'

'We'll make sure he sees the error of his way, sir.'

*   *   *

One more visitor: Sergeant Ricks.

'My information is that a crew of women has arrived in Manchester, sir. Piled off the London train like they were going on their holidays, according to my source.'

He grimaced at the image. 'That doesn't bode well for us.'

'The coppers arrested half of them before they were even out of the station.'

An interesting tactic, he thought. 'What charges?'

Ricks began to grin. 'Anything and everything, sir. Vagrancy, begging, you name it; they were making it up as they went along. Gave them the choice, the next train back to London or they'd sling them in jail. Most of them knew they were beaten and decided to go home.'

'Most?'

He shrugged. 'Always a few defiant ones, sir. The gang will probably send more tomorrow.'

'Can we use the Manchester idea here?'

'I don't see why not. We won't catch them all, but if we arrest most of them . . .'

'It removes a lot of the problem. You'd better make sure I stay informed on this.'

He woke with a start and turned his head to look at the luminous hands of the clock. The usual time. For a moment, guilt almost tore him from bed and down to Millgarth. The men were going to work, why shouldn't he? But Harper was the chief constable; he'd spent too many years starting early and staying late, working every day that God sent. He'd earned his Sundays off.

Another hour and a half of sleep, then up, feeling refreshed. While Julia washed and dressed Annabelle, he made the breakfast, their routine for Sunday. He was no cook, but he'd mastered frying bacon and eggs.

'You're improving.' Annabelle's eyes were twinkling with pleasure as she ate. A better day and he felt the relief. She was still with them. 'Another few months and you might be able to get a job in a big house. I'll give you a reference if you behave.'

'I'll keep it in mind.' He gave her a wry grin.

'Don't worry, I've not forgotten you're retiring at the end of the month.'

Definitely a good day. A very good day.

Mary bustled in, wearing one of her new dresses. After seeing her hidden in black for so long, it still came as a shock. But she seemed lighter, happier, as if she'd shed the weight she'd been carrying.

Time to take advantage of Annabelle's brightness and the fine spring weather. By nine they'd helped her settle in the back seat of the car, and Mary was driving them into the country. Harper sat next to his wife, pointing out the small things – cows gathered under a tree, young lambs gambolling around their mother. She was attentive and curious, talkative.

Knaresborough. A ruin of a castle looking over a steep hill to the river. Harper watched as Mary held her breath and navigated the tiny streets until she parked by the remains of an old tower, no more than a few yards to walk to take in the view.

Sun sparkled on the water below and lent warm colours to the stone arches of the tall railway bridge: everything felt close to perfect. A picnic on the bench, fish paste sandwiches, cakes from the baker, the three of them sharing a bottle of Vimto.

He sat back and closed his eyes for a moment. Relishing the peace of Sunday and the heat on his face.

'Look at those people on the water,' Annabelle said. 'I wish we could do that.'

Couples and families, in punts and rowing boats out on the Nidd. But it would be impossible to manoeuvre her in and out of one of them. The slow longing in her voice meant she knew it, too. He squeezed her hand.

'Maybe next time.'

'Do you remember the steamboat on the big lake at Roundhay Park?' she asked. 'I wonder if it's still there. What did they call it?'

'The *Mary Gordon*,' he replied. 'I don't know if it's running these days.'

'Have you ever been out to Knaresborough before, Da?'

He shook his head. 'I know about it. All those tall tales about Mother Shipton were around when I was a lad. But I never had any reason to come out this way. I suppose we could have taken a train.' He looked over at the crumbling stone of the tower. 'I didn't even have any idea there was a castle.'

'Len and I cycled out here, about a month before the war began,' Mary said. She pointed. 'We sat on the wall over there and ate our lunch.' She stared, as if she could see the young lovers. 'Feels like another life.'

It was, but he stopped himself from saying it. Days of innocence, before all the slaughter of the war and then the influenza coming to tear the world apart. Back when Len was still alive and the pair of them were engaged to be married.

'Being here makes me feel closer to him for a little while,' she said with an awkward smile. 'Does that make sense?'

'Yes,' he replied. She was collecting the memories. Not to wish them farewell, but to hold them close again and tuck them away somewhere safe as she changed. He turned his head. From the corner of his eye, he'd noticed the shift in Annabelle's expression. Her eyes had dulled and he could pick out the start of a low, keening wail. Like a storm whipping up from nothing. 'We'd better get your mother back to the car.'

By the time they had her inside, she was howling. No words, just cries and sobs. People turned to stare at them. It had happened before. No warning; often it stopped as suddenly as it began.

Harper rubbed her hands, some physical contact, and spoke softly into her ear as Mary drove. His heart was thumping; he could feel a vein pounding in his temple. It wasn't Annabelle's fault; she couldn't control any of it. But there were times when his impotence overwhelmed him and the frustration rose. That was when he wanted to shout at her. Except she wasn't doing anything. He knew that. It was this illness he hated, the one that was killing her so slowly. So he kept it all inside, saying nothing to a living soul, filled with shame and guilt for feeling that way at all.

They were halfway home before his wife's face relaxed and the noise abruptly ended. Annabelle put her head back and closed her eyes. At least she'd have some peace for a while. He felt the tension drain from his body and saw Mary soften a little. Still concentrating fiercely on the road, but she lowered her shoulders.

'She's asleep now,' he said.

ELEVEN

Another bright start to the day, as if summer was putting in an early appearance to mock the workers on a Monday morning. Dust motes floated through the air in the detectives' room at Millgarth. The place stank of stale tobacco; the ceiling was stained golden brown.

'What progress did you make yesterday?' Harper asked.

Walsh and Jackson glanced at each other. 'We didn't, sir. The constables are asking about the gang all over Leeds, but they haven't turned up anything definite yet. It's like this bunch can just vanish.'

He snorted. 'A very useful trick for criminals. Probably just as well for us it's not possible. No more bags of jewellery?'

'No,' Jackson said, then corrected himself. 'None we know about, anyway. The pawn shops haven't told us about anyone trying to sell them stuff.'

Of course not. In such small quantities, why would they? It was business.

'What else can we do?' Harper asked. 'We're banging our heads against a brick wall. They're still two paces ahead of us and we look like a bunch of bloody fools. Three of them and they're running all of Leeds City Police ragged.' That bit into his pride nearly as much as the personal insult of the bag on his doorstep. They were making his force look like the Keystone Cops.

'That's just it, sir,' Jackson said quietly. 'There are just three of them and they have a car. They're quick and organized and they can be in and out before we have chance to react.'

'Fine. But they still need somewhere to live, a place to keep that damned Model T. They have to buy food. We're hunting high and low. Why can't we find them?'

'I really don't know,' Walsh told him. His face was drawn, almost grey with weariness. 'I told you, sir, we've tried everything.'

'Then we'd better go back and try it all again.' Harper pursed his lips. 'They're human. They make mistakes. That happened when—' He tried to think of the man's name.

'Curtis.'

'Curtis shot the bystander. They're disciplined, but they're not machines.'

'We haven't had a scrap of luck, either,' Jackson said.

Harper felt anger flash across his face. 'I hope to God we're not relying on that to solve this.'

The telephone rang in Walsh's office and for a moment they all froze. Not another robbery?

'Sissons, sir,' he said after he replaced the receiver, and Harper felt a wave of relief. 'Asks if you can go over to the town hall. He and Mr Ash need to speak to you.'

Could they have found Alderman Thompson's letters? Where? He hurried through the streets. The sun was warm against his face, but he was in too much of a rush to enjoy it, questions skittering through his mind.

'Are they in my office?' he asked Miss Sharp.

'The pair of them.'

'Good news?' Harper asked as he settled behind his desk. His body was tense, throat tight.

It was Ash who spoke, his voice grave. 'I wish it was.'

He sighed. Damnation. 'Why? What's happened?'

'You know copies of all the reports come through the intelligence department now, sir,' Sissons said.

'Of course.' He was the one who'd instigated it.

'I was glancing at the ones that came in overnight, and something caught my eye. A traffic accident. Looks like the driver veered off the road and hit a tree. He died at the scene.'

'Go on.' Something must tie it to their case.

'It was out past Shadwell, towards Wike. By the time any constables arrived, the body had gone to the morgue. But from the skid marks, they believe it's possible he was forced off the road. There was damage to the side of the car, too. I have a man out there now.'

'Who was the dead man?'

'That's the thing,' Ash said. 'One of the crowd around Charlotte

Radcliffe, sir. His name's Ben Rogers. He was her brother's closest friend.'

'I see.' He couldn't buy that as a coincidence. But what were they to make of it?

'We'll know more once the details come in, but something in my gut tells me it's murder,' Ash said.

'Why?' The man might be right, but he wanted to know his reasons.

'It's just . . .'

Copper's instinct. Harper nodded. His first thought had been exactly the same.

'Has anyone informed the family?'

'A uniformed inspector,' Sissons told him.

'Let's give them today to digest it all. Had you already talked to this man?'

'Yes, sir,' Sissons replied. 'There was nothing to single him out for suspicion.'

'Tell Dr Amersham I'd like the post-mortem carried out, today, please.' Harper was thinking, trying to make sense of the information. 'Make sure there's a complete examination of the car. See if you can find out what he was doing yesterday evening. You both know what to do.' He thought for a moment. 'Let's find out where Rogers was when the alderman was attacked, too.'

'Very good, sir,' Ash said. 'I know an excellent mechanic. I'd like him to give everything a once-over.'

'Arrange it.' He jotted a few notes on a piece of paper and took out his watch from his waistcoat pocket. 'We'll meet here at four.'

'There are some things that need your attention.' The pair had barely left before Miss Sharp arrived with a sheaf of papers.

Harper sat and groaned. 'Can't Mr Dickinson take care of them?'

She shook her head. 'These are definitely for the chief. Want me to bring you a cup of tea?'

'And two biscuits,' he told her. 'I don't care what my daughter says.'

He worked steadily until half past eleven, going through the pile. At the bottom, an envelope addressed to Chief Constable Harper and marked *Personal and Confidential*. Miss Sharp had left it unopened; that was the rule with private correspondence.

The writing wasn't familiar. He sliced it open. A single sheet of cheap white writing paper, so thin it was almost transparent.

> I hope you liked the bag we left on your doorstep. You could keep it; nobody would ever know except you and us.
> You and your coppers think you can stop us, don't you?
> We can run rings round you and there's not a thing you can do.
> Watch out for Thursday.

Harper took a deep breath and studied the postmark. Sent on Saturday. He read it through again, then slid it back into the envelope and placed it in his jacket pocket.

'I'll be back later,' he told Miss Sharp.

The envelope fluttered on to the desk. Walsh glanced up, curious.

'Take a look.'

'They're getting very cocky.' The superintendent gave a frustrated sigh when he'd finished reading.

'Too bloody cocky by half.' The anger had been building as he walked. These bastards thought they could lord it over him and his men.

Walsh hesitated, took a breath then said, 'The problem is it's true. They *are* running rings around us, sir.'

The killers were winning, and all the police could do was flail around helplessly in their wake.

'Thursday.'

'They're taunting us, sir. Look at it: this is when we're going to strike next. Try and stop us.'

'If we can.' He exhaled. 'We'd better make damned sure we do. We have time to plan. Is Jackson out chasing leads?'

'Yes, sir.'

'Then you and I are going to make a start on this. First of all, we need to know the location of all the jewellery shops in the city centre. Every single bloody one of them.'

*   *   *

Five to four, and Harper paced around his office in the town hall. Clouds had blown in off the Pennines, whisking the early spring warmth from the air.

He heard voices, then the door opened.

'Right, gentlemen, what have you managed to discover?'

'The car that Mr Rogers drove took a beating after it left the road,' Ash said, then paused for a brief moment. 'Went into some woods. However, while the mechanic who looked at it wouldn't swear to it on the Bible, he's reasonably certain it was forced off the road. We took him out to look at the scene.'

An unknown car that might have forced another off the road, a mystery man who might have pushed someone in front of a train. Ghosts flickered across the deaths here.

'What about Rogers's friends? What do they have to say?'

'They were all shocked. Very sad,' Sissons answered. 'They have no idea what could have happened, none of them saw him the day of the accident.'

'All very convenient. How much do you believe?'

'Could be true, sir.'

'Could be?'

'Yes,' the superintendent said. 'I wouldn't go any further than that.'

'Did you examine their motor cars?'

'Quick glances. No damage to any of them.'

All it meant was they weren't stupid. 'Fine. How do we break them?'

'If we can find something on one and get him away from the others, we can squeeze him and threaten a little,' Ash said. 'He'll crumble.'

'Which one?' Harper asked.

Sissons looked at Ash. 'Let us have a think on that, sir. Today or tomorrow, it's not going to make any difference. In the meantime, we'll go through Rogers's rooms in the morning. I have a constable guarding them.'

Alderman Thompson was back at work but keeping close to his office.

Most of the bruising had faded, and the cuts were healing. But something was missing. The fire that had roared through him was dimmed. Thompson had always surrounded himself with bluster, making his voice fill every silence. Now he was quiet and thoughtful as he listened to Harper's report.

'This has turned into something awful, hasn't it?' He shook his head.

'Two in the morgue, and that's just so far. It's all spiralled out of control for them.'

'Poor devils. I never . . .' He waved his hands and let the words drift away.

'I doubt they did when they started, either. It was just a bit of excitement. Some fun to liven up the boredom. No more contact about the letters?'

He shook his head. 'Not a word.'

That was one blessing. All of that had passed. But now there were two suspicious deaths, and a beating that the police couldn't let go.

'What do you intend to do?' Thompson asked.

'We're going to find some truth,' Harper told him. 'Ash is excellent at that. He'll dig right down to the bottom of things.'

The alderman hesitated before his next question. 'What about Charlotte? Do you still think she's involved?'

'No need to think. She's right at the centre of it. We all believe the same.'

It didn't seem to jolt him. Just a sad nod of acceptance. Maybe his experience had shifted something inside.

'Can you get those letters back, Harper?'

'I'll say the same as I did before: I think there's a very good chance. These deaths make everything more complicated, though.'

'I understand that.' He pressed his lips together. 'And can you manage to keep my name out of it?'

Some things hadn't changed. There might be concern in his words, but underneath he was pushed by self-preservation.

'We'll do everything we can.' He wasn't foolish enough to offer a complete guarantee.

'I trust you will, Harper.'

In the car, he let out a long, weary sigh.

'Long day, sir?' Bingham asked as he pulled into traffic.

'You don't know the half of it.' How could it still only be
Monday? He felt as if he'd already lived through an entire
week. At least there wouldn't be many more before it would
all be over. But he needed to leave with these two cases closed.
Had to.

His stomach lurched for a second as he stared out of the
window and saw two men with gauze masks over their faces
emerge from a shop. Ordinary people, he realized after a moment,
trying to keep themselves safe. He patted his jacket. His own
mask was still there. He knew he should wear it. The influenza
deaths were tailing away, but people were still dying.

He leaned his head back and closed his eyes until the car
stopped and Bingham turned off the motor.

'Usual time in the morning, sir?'

'Yes, thank you.'

He stood on Hawthorn Road and stretched his back, staring
up at the house. A long way from the shabby terrace on Noble
Street to this. His parents would never have believed it. He still
wasn't sure it was real himself, that it belonged to him, even if
it was there in black and white on the legal papers.

'She's been quiet all day,' Julia told him. 'She'll eat if I feed
her, but she hasn't said a word.'

He sat and gently stroked Annabelle's cheek. It was happening
more and more. She didn't notice, never turned her head. Her
body was here, but her mind . . . nobody could tell, not even the
experts he'd consulted. They didn't have answers.

Each time it happened he stayed on edge, terrified that this
might be the time she stayed lost inside her mind. Locked away
from him forever.

It hurt, a sharp, physical pain, and the worst thing was that
he was powerless to do anything.

TWELVE

At Millgarth, Walsh and Jackson were poring over a map of the city centre and trying to make plans for Thursday. 'You know,' Harper said as he watched them, 'we're working on the assumption they won't do anything before then.'

The superintendent's head shot up, eyes filled with panic.

'God, you're right, sir. We . . .'

'I know. But the way this gang operates, I wouldn't put it past them. Some misdirection; make us look one way while they do something utterly different.'

'I'll tell the constables to stay alert,' Jackson said, and hurried off.

'They have today and tomorrow,' Harper said. 'And I wouldn't trust them to be straightforward on Thursday. We need to be prepared for a trick or two.'

'There's only so much we can do, sir.'

'Let's make sure we're ready.' He thought. 'More than that, able to adapt. They're going to keep us on the hop.'

He'd stirred them, he thought as the car passed Woodhouse Moor, then into Hyde Park. Made them think differently. Would it help? Who knew?

Charlotte Radcliffe lived on Shire Oak Road, detached houses all set back from the street in Headingley. Everything calm and quiet and ordered. She had the first floor of a Victorian mansion, everything exactly as he remembered from his last visit.

Dressed in black, but her mourning frock was fashionable cotton that followed her figure and ended halfway down her calves. A necklace of jet beads and a jet cameo.

'I'm sorry about your friend,' Harper said.

She bowed her head, then raised it again. The sorrow on her face managed to reach her eyes. 'Thank you. Ben was . . .' She searched for the words. 'Lovely. Gentle.'

'It must be a huge shock, coming right after your brother.'

'He and Charles . . . they were best friends. They met at prep school and after that they were inseparable.' She blinked. 'Do his parents know? Oh God, his sister.'

'We've informed them,' Harper told her. 'It sounds as if you were close to him.'

'We went out together,' she replied. 'Not all the time, nothing too serious, but quite often. I suppose we were close. Certainly for a while.'

'Was there anyone who disliked him?'

He saw her expression change. The grief vanished, and wariness took its place. Interesting.

'Disliked him? How do you mean?'

'Arguments. A rivalry, perhaps.'

Anger began to flare at the back of her eyes, but she hurriedly forced it down, back in control once again. He'd hit a nerve.

'No. Nothing like that. Everyone loved Ben. He was a sweetheart of a chap. Why?'

'We're not sure, but we think someone might have run his car off the road and caused the accident that killed him.'

She hadn't known that. She became very still, hardly daring to breathe.

'I'm sorry,' he said into the silence.

'No, no.' The woman began to regain herself. 'It was just . . . I can't imagine anyone doing that to him. Do you mean it was on purpose?'

'We don't know,' Harper told her. 'We're not even absolutely certain that's what happened.'

'I see.' She opened a box, took out a cigarette and lit it. He saw the slight tremor in her hand. Genuinely upset, or was Charlotte Radcliffe worried about something?

'Do you think it could be connected to your brother's death?'

'I don't know, Chief Constable.' A drawn-out sigh. 'I can't imagine how. Or why. This is the first I've heard about it. I have no idea what to think. It's like everything collapsed. I've been racking my brain, trying to understand why Charles would kill himself. There must have been something he couldn't talk about to anyone, even to me. I definitely can't believe someone would kill him. I just can't. And now this with Ben . . .'

'Were they lovers?' Homosexuality was illegal, but everyone knew it happened.

'No. I'm certain of that.' She gave a knowing smile. 'Believe me, they both had appetites for women.'

'The other factor is Alderman Thompson's letters and the black-mail attempt. I'm sure you remember he was given a beating.'

'Yes. How is he?' The question arrived as an afterthought. She'd long since moved beyond Ernest Thompson.

'Greatly improved. But I'm convinced the letters are at the heart of all this. Your brother and Mr Rogers could have been the pair who assaulted him.'

She shook her head. 'They'd never do that.'

'Someone did, and it was connected to the letters.' As they stared at each other, Harper tried to read her expression, but the mask held firm. 'Do you know where they are?'

'No, I don't.' She tried to sound honest, but he didn't believe a scrap of it. 'I told you. I told those men of yours. Someone must have taken them from here.'

'It could have been Mr Rogers and your brother.'

She hesitated. 'They'd have no reason.' A tiny hesitation. 'But maybe it was.'

The calculation was there. Shifting all the blame and respon-sibility to two dead men and carrying none of the guilt herself.

'Have you searched their rooms?' she asked.

'Your brother's. Mr Rogers's place is today.'

'Then I don't know what else to tell you, Chief Constable.' A tiny hint of a smirk flickered across her lips, sliding away almost before it appeared. She knew the police wouldn't find anything. 'I gave you the names of our crowd, and I told you a number of people could have taken them.'

There it was: she was challenging him. He was completely certain now; the letters were here. Hidden away in a drawer or tucked at the back of a cupboard. Under a loose floorboard. He had to prove it. Find enough evidence for a search warrant and take her by surprise.

Meanwhile, two men were dead. If it had really begun as a bit of fun, something to break the tedium, it had lost the punch-line. But Charlotte Radcliffe would never admit anything until she was faced with no other choice. Possibly not even then.

Harper stood and put out his hand. She shook it, skin dry and cool.

'I'm sorry I can't do more to help you.'

'We'll find whoever's responsible,' he said. 'Don't you worry about that. Doesn't matter who it is.'

He left her with the threat hanging in the air.

'Town hall,' he told Bingham as the car tyres sang over the gravel drive.

'Alderman Thompson has been asking for you,' Miss Sharp said. 'He's rung twice this morning.'

'I'll go and see him in a minute.' He inclined his head towards the door of his office. 'Are Ash and Sissons in there?'

'Just Mr Ash.' She placed a hand on a pile of papers. 'I have a few things that need your signature. You're still the chief constable until the end of the month. You can't swan away from everything.'

A quick nod. 'No, you're right.' It was easier to give in than start a discussion.

'I'll bring you a cup of tea.' Grudging, but it was still something.

Ash was sitting, pen poised, notebook open.

'Any discoveries?' Harper asked.

'We went through Rogers's rooms. No letters.'

'I won't say I'm surprised.' After all, they were still somewhere in Charlotte Radcliffe's flat. They'd never gone anywhere. 'Anything incriminating?'

'Not really. A little cocaine in a vial, and some cannabis.'

Interesting. Under the new law, cocaine would become illegal in a few months. For now, though, there was nothing wrong with possessing either drug.

'Plenty of money?' he asked.

'That whole crowd,' Ash replied. 'Far too much of it and not enough to do.'

An entire world had shattered and was struggling to rebuild itself, while people like this played around and acted as if nothing bad had ever happened, that nothing could touch them. The complete opposite of the Model T gang. Yet every bit as ruthless and deadly.

He told Ash about his visit to Miss Radcliffe. 'What are you going to do next?'

'I thought I'd talk to a few people, sir. A couple of people who supply drugs.'

It might bring some information; more likely nothing. It was an admission that they were casting around in the dark.

'What about Sissons?'

'He's out talking to one of his contacts.'

Very cryptic, but they all guarded their sources.

Alone, he ploughed through the papers. Miss Sharp was as good as her word, tea and one biscuit; he was back in her good graces.

Alderman Ernest Thompson looked a little stronger today, more like his old self. The familiar bluster was starting to return as the wounds disappeared. A pity; Harper preferred him when he showed a more humble side. All he wanted was news, and there was little to give him.

'Just make damned sure you keep me up to date,' he said as Harper left his office.

He glanced out of the window of the Kardomah. Up in the sky a balloon was slowly moving, carried by the wind. It took him back to the year before, the big RAF show in Roundhay Park. They'd built hangars, displayed planes that had fought in France, so many other things. He'd been there as chief constable, taken up in the balloon that was the big attraction. Terrifying to be up so high, but thrilling, too. Able to look down and see Leeds all spread out. His city.

Mary had been there too, but she'd had to pay a princely ten bob to go up for a few minutes, then another shilling to shoot a rifle. He'd expected her to be gushing when she arrived home, full of everything she'd seen. Instead she'd been worryingly quiet. He wondered now if the bullet and the recoil had somehow planted the very first seed of change, and the Great Silence brought it along. Maybe she didn't even know the answer herself; it could have simply been time.

She was wearing a different dress today, cotton again, soft spring colours. She must have thrown the old, stiff corset away.

'Buying a whole new wardrobe?'

'It's hardly that,' Mary told him with a smile. 'Only three of them. I haven't broken the bank. Besides,' she added with a grin, 'just one or two would seem very strange, wouldn't it?'

Each day he spotted a few more women dressing in the new style. It was catching on. He glanced around the café. The place was busy, women taking a break from shopping, men eating dinner before rushing back to work. No need to order; it was the same thing every time they met for lunch.

'My mam was feeling a little better this morning. Julia told me what yesterday was like.' She put her chin in her hands and stared at him. 'Are you sure you'll be able to take care of her? You and Julia. She's growing worse, you know that, Da.'

Yes, he did know. He'd gone through all the possibilities, time and time again.

'I'll do my best,' he told her. 'Always.'

Millgarth was quiet when he entered. All the beat constables out on patrol, the detectives' room almost empty, only a plain clothes sergeant searching through papers. The superintendent was busy in his office. Through the window, Harper could hear the bellow of an instructor putting new recruits through their paces in the yard. Even with his bad hearing, it all rang loud and clear, taking him back to his first days on the force, when he was so young and callow. So eager.

Harper shook that memory from his mind.

'Well?' he asked Walsh. Each day, the man looked more ground down. He did an excellent job of running A division, but this case was eating away at him. The dark circles under his eyes kept growing larger and his skin had turned coarse.

'Still nothing concrete.'

These men were leading them a merry dance. 'Are we prepared for Thursday?'

'As much as we can be, sir. We'll have constables close to the jewellery shops. They should be able to get there in seconds.'

'As long as they're ready. Remember, the gang haven't said *when* something will happen on Thursday. Or even what it's going to be. If our constables have been standing around for hours, will they be quick enough off the mark?'

He believed in the Leeds force. They were his; he was proud of them. But he was under no illusions. Coppers were human and far from perfect.

Walsh gave a wry smile. 'We'll have to hope so, sir. I know they've all had enough of being played for a bunch of idiots by this mob.'

'It's still only Tuesday. I said it yesterday: they have time to pull a few tricks yet. That's what worries me.'

They went over the plan again. He listened, trying to poke holes in it as the superintendent ran through everything. It seemed simple, straightforward. In theory, little should go wrong. But that was always a long distance from reality. Harper offered a pair of suggestions to make things move more smoothly.

By the time he glanced up at the clock, it was almost five. Outside, the day had faded, no more marching feet.

'Now we wait and see.'

Harper stood outside the door of his house, key in hand as Bingham drove off down Hawthorn Street. He hesitated, not sure what he'd find inside.

Julia was chattering merrily away. Annabelle turned her head as he entered. The words came slowly, aching out of her.

'Hello, Tom.'

He felt the rush of gratitude. Almost as if everything was normal. Until the next time.

THIRTEEN

Patches of blue sky as the clouds skittered past. But there was a touch of warmth in the breeze again, another teasing hint of spring. Just a few more weeks now, Harper thought . . .

'Where first, sir?' Bingham asked as he turned the car on to Harrogate Road and headed towards the city centre.

'Town hall,' he said. If anything important had happened overnight, his telephone would have been ringing. He could take care of business early and have the rest of the day for the Model T boys.

Harper glanced as they passed Alderman Thompson's house. The upstairs curtains were still closed. Was he enjoying a peaceful sleep, or was guilt weighing heavily on him? But if it hadn't been him, Charlotte Radcliffe would have found another fool. Perhaps one who didn't have any clout in the city.

Miss Sharp seemed surprised to see him so early.

'We're usually an afterthought,' she sniffed. 'Or is everything quiet at Millgarth?'

'I don't know.' He smiled at her. 'You're my first port of call today.'

'The important post is on your desk. I suppose you'd like a cup of tea.'

'I could murder one.' He gave a short laugh. 'Probably not the best thing for a chief constable to say.'

Harper worked steadily for an hour, reading and signing, knowing he'd remember none of it by this afternoon. Putting on his raincoat, he turned back and looked at the room. Would he miss this place? Very much, he decided, at least in some strange way.

'Will you be back later?' Miss Sharp asked.

'I don't know.'

Downstairs, he stopped to see Dickinson, the deputy chief.

'Wishing you'd never accepted the job yet, Albert?'

'It's not that bad,' he replied with a grin and a shrug. 'I've always had a knack for reports and forms. They're not that taxing.'

'No,' he agreed, 'just boring. Don't worry, you'll find your days full once you take over the whole job.'

'How are things coming along with that gang?'

'They've promised they're going to do something special tomorrow. Daring us to catch them.'

Dickinson raised his eyebrows. 'Crooks issuing challenges to the police? We need to stamp all over that.'

'They're too clever, that's the problem. They're keeping us foxed.'

'I haven't seen anything about us catching the ones who assaulted the alderman.'

'That's taken a strange turn,' Harper said, and the man stared with interest. 'I'll have to tell you about it when it's done.'

If it was ever done, he thought as he stepped out into spring sunshine. That whole thing was a murky pit, each character worse than the last, with the woman at the heart of it all. He'd trust Ash and Sissons to take care of it. Harper knew he wasn't going to be able to trap her; she was too sly for that.

By the time he reached Millgarth, he had a thin sheen of sweat under his hatband. With luck, they were going to enjoy a long, warm summer. God knew they deserved it after everything that had happened in the last few years. War, influenza, and now businesses were closing, too many out of work, and hardly any of those homes needed for the returning heroes had even been started yet.

No more than a few minutes' walk, but he passed three men begging. One was missing a leg, selling boxes of matches from a tray. Another had an empty sleeve pinned against his jacket. The third held a sign that said: *Will work at any job. Wife and three children to support. I fought every day of the war.*

How many more like them in Leeds? he wondered. In the country? The government had let them all down. What might happen if things didn't change?

It wasn't a question he wanted to consider. Besides, he thought, as he pushed open the door of the police station, he had more immediate things on his mind.

'Anything new?'

Jackson shook his head as he stubbed out a Black Cat and lit another. 'Not a peep. We're just marking time. I tell you, sir, I'm wound so tight I feel ready to explode.'

'It's the anticipation,' Harper said, and the man nodded.

'The same as when we were ready to go over the top and waiting for the whistle.' He grimaced at the memory. 'Do you really think they'll try to steal a march and do something today?'

'I don't know,' was all he could offer after a moment's thought. 'I certainly wouldn't put it past them. That's why we need to be prepared.'

The morning dragged by. Harper read through all the witness interviews again, hoping some clue might jump out at him. But he didn't find anything to spark his suspicions.

*   *   *

The café at the market for his dinner, staring down from the balcony. Cheese on toast, simple, not too filling, just right for a day that kept growing warmer. Carrying his coat, he wandered around, over to Kirkgate and into the tall coolness of the parish church.

The only person around was a verger, polishing the brass of a plaque. It was the first time he'd been here for anything but a funeral or memorial and the quietness unnerved him. Harper heard his footsteps resound upwards as he wandered. After a few minutes he left, striding along Somerset Street, back to Millgarth.

'They did it again,' the desk sergeant told him. 'The super and the inspector are down there.'

Caught them wrong-footed. It didn't matter that he'd been right. 'Where? Anybody hurt?'

'Albion Street, just above the Headrow. I haven't heard anything about anyone wounded or more, sir.'

That was one small relief, Harper thought as he hurried through the streets. By the time he arrived he was breathing hard and pouring with sweat under the April sun. Jackson was in charge, talking to people and giving the orders. Walsh stood apart and studied the scene.

'The usual performance?' Harper asked.

'To the last note,' Walsh replied. 'It's down pat. Pull up, run in. Shot into the wall, grab the jewellery, out and drive off. Away in seconds.'

'Did they get much?'

The superintendent nodded towards the shop. 'We'll find out soon. We have witnesses, but there's nothing can tell us that we haven't already heard.' He sighed. 'Looks like you were right about the misdirection, sir.'

Harper shrugged. 'I can't say it gives me any pleasure.'

They began the walk back to Millgarth.

'Do you think they'll still do something tomorrow, sir?'

He'd wondered about that as he dashed through the streets. Had it been a lie to keep them off balance?

'Yes, I do,' he answered eventually. 'I think this was another taunt. They probably always intended to do it. Something's going to happen. I've no idea what, but I bet they'll try to rub our noses in it again.'

'We know their names, we know the number plate on their car,' Walsh smacked a fist into his palm. Pure frustration. 'The only thing we don't have is the three of them in bloody custody.'

'Maybe tomorrow,' Harper said, and wished he could believe it.

A report from Ricks: the shoplifters and pickpockets were on the streets of Manchester.

He snapped awake in the darkness. The hands of the clock glowed green: a little after five. Quietly, Harper washed and dressed and let himself out of the house. Chapel Allerton was silent, no lights in the houses as he began the walk towards town.

This was the day. This was the challenge the gang had promised. They'd do something. He felt it. He *knew* it. What, though? Where?

Walsh and Jackson were already at Millgarth, the atmosphere so tense he could probably have sold it by the slice. At least they both looked like they'd slept, Harper thought. He needed them fresh and sharp.

'There's nothing going to happen yet,' he said. 'Come with me.'

The café in the market was raking in money from the traders. Harper ordered cooked breakfasts and large mugs of sweet tea for each of them. Something to keep bellies full; when things began to explode they'd have no time to eat.

'Any ideas, sir?' Jackson asked.

'No more than you,' he answered with a smile and glanced at Walsh. 'Any little birds giving you hints?'

The superintendent shook his head. 'Nothing.'

As soon as they finished, they marched back to the station. Then tension caught them; no time for idle talk. The station sergeant shook his head; everything was quiet.

The men on the day beat were already out on the streets, the only sounds the murmurs of the night patrol before they went home. All so familiar, but with his hearing, it was nothing more than a background of noise.

Harper poked through a sheaf of papers, looking at the words but unable to remember a single one of them. He looked at the clock: two minutes since the last check.

* * *

A little after nine, the station sergeant burst in.

'Fire on York Road, sir, about three-quarters of a mile past Harehills Lane. The brigade are out there, but someone's taking shots at them.'

Harper was already on his feet, reaching for his hat. 'Pistols for the three of us.' His voice was calm, in control, while jolts of electricity surged through his body. His pulse was hammering in his neck. 'Do you have a good shot among the men?'

'Hopkinson, sir,' Jackson replied. 'He had sniper training during the war.'

'He's with us. Issue him a rifle. I want a squad out there now and a car for us as soon as it can get here.'

'Very good, sir,' the sergeant said as he hurried off.

'Is this it?' Walsh asked.

'I'm sure of it.' His mouth was dry. A swig of cold tea for his throat. 'It's not like anything else they've done, but . . .' It would make the perfect diversion. Draw the coppers out there and they'd have a free run at the city centre.

Harper stopped for a moment at the desk, 'I want those in town to stay exactly where they are. Tell them to hold their positions and be prepared.'

Just in case.

The driver parked two streets away from York Road. Safe, out of the way. Smoke was rising from an empty building as the firemen gathered behind the engine for cover.

'Anybody hit?' Harper asked. These were his men, too; the brigade was part of the police force.

'We're all fine, sir,' the fire inspector answered. He was a hard-looking man with a grizzled face. 'But we daren't go close enough to put out that blaze in case they try again.'

His report was brisk and clear. They'd responded to the alarm and just started to roll out their hoses when the shots came.

'They came from that wooded area on the other side of York Road, sir. Poke your head round the corner and you'll see it. We ducked back.' He sounded apologetic. 'No choice.'

'It was the only thing you could do,' Harper agreed.

'One of the lads went to ring your lot, sir. We were pinned down. They fired twice more—'

'How many shots in total?' Walsh asked.

'Five. I'm positive of that. I heard enough bullets in France.'

'Did any come close?'

The reply was slow. 'When someone's shooting, you just try to duck out of the way. But now you mention it, I don't believe they did.'

'Are you certain of that?' Jackson pressed him.

The fire inspector looked thoughtful. 'You know, I'd say they were shooting high, sir. Trying *not* to hit us, if that makes any sense at all.'

'It does,' Harper said. Perfect sense.

The gang was behind this. No doubt in his mind. They'd kept their promise for Thursday. By now they'd be about their usual business. Robbing. He had to hope the constables in the city centre were alert.

'What do you want to do, sir?' Walsh asked.

'We're agreed on who's responsible?'

'Definitely, sir,' Jackson said. He was grinning, eager for action.

'They'll have long since gone, but we still need to clean out the area,' Harper continued. 'Let's do it properly. Send three men around to sweep through from the back. I want Hopkinson to be one of them. Make sure they keep their eyes peeled. We'll be going straight across, and I don't want our own men firing at us.'

Five minutes for everyone to be in position. Quick, covert glances across the road, but the small, wooded patch seemed empty.

The gang had done a good job when they picked this place. Excellent cover. Setting fire to an empty building, so nobody would end up hurt. Clever.

He checked his watch, then took out the Webley he'd collected at Millgarth.

'Ready?' he asked. Walsh and Jackson gave their grim nods. A deep breath. 'Let's go.'

Two constables waved traffic to a standstill. Harper knew the shooters had gone. He was completely certain of it. Yet that tiny grain of doubt rubbed in his mind. What if he was wrong and a bullet was waiting for him?

Harper strode out into the road, keeping his hand tight around the butt of the gun. His eyes were fixed on the woods, watching for the slightest movement, any glint of metal.

He tried to swallow. Impossible. He was terrified, trying to keep his expression steady and stop his legs from shaking.

Keep moving. Even, steady strides. A chief constable couldn't show fear in front of his men. You never asked them to do something you wouldn't do yourself. The sweat ran down his back. Never falter, never hesitate. Particularly if all you wanted was to walk away.

He reached the far pavement and kept going. His palm was damp and slick. Eight, nine, ten paces and Harper had soft dirt under his feet. A second to glance around. More shadows, the trees coming into leaf high above his head. This would be the gang's last chance to fire.

There was only silence.

Walsh and Jackson stood either side of him, pistols in their hands.

'They've gone.' His voice was cracked, dry and dusty. He exhaled, filled with relief and fear of what was ahead. 'Let's go and see what havoc they've caused in town. The men can handle the details here, and the brigade can put out that bloody fire.' Harper shook his head. 'One hell of a diversion.'

'A couple of times there, I thought I was going to have a heart attack.' Walsh laughed. Easy to joke about it now the tension had passed. Harper pushed down the safety catch on the Webley and slid it into his pocket. Jubilation coursed through him. They'd survived. There was never much chance of danger, but that single germ of fear had been powerful.

Christ. All done here. Now to tally up the real damage. This mob had it all worked out. Were they too good for the police? He felt the chill that came with the thought. He wouldn't let himself believe that.

FOURTEEN

The car pulled up outside Millgarth. Walsh dashed inside while Harper and Jackson waited on the back seat.

How bad was it going to be? Harper closed his eyes and hoped.

When the superintendent came back out, it was impossible to read his expression.

'No need for us to rush off. It didn't turn out the way they expected.'

A constable was waiting in the detectives' room. Young, very nervous, mouth twitching and eyes darting around. Probably too young to have served during the war, a suggestion of a moustache on his upper lip. Harper smiled; he'd done exactly the same when he started on the force, trying to make himself look older. The officer had his helmet tucked under his arm, snapping to attention as the chief constable entered.

'Tell these men what you told me,' Walsh ordered.

'Yes, sir.' Now he stared straight ahead, the way he'd been taught. 'I'm PC Woodford, 6782, sir. I was keeping watch on Briggate, close to those two jewellery shops by the corner of Commercial Street.'

Harper listened intently. Jackson gazed at the floor, picturing it all in his head.

'At three minutes past nine, a Model T Ford pulled up on Briggate outside one of the shops. Two men ran from the car. They were both wearing caps and had gauze masks covering the bottom half of their faces. Another man remained in the car with the engine running.'

Woodford paused.

'Go on,' Walsh prompted him.

'I began to run towards them.'

Harper interrupted. 'How far away were you?'

'Probably two hundred yards, sir. Our orders were not to be too close.'

More distance; they'd agreed on that. A few more seconds to reach the crime, but harder for the gang to spot as they approached.

'Go on,' he said.

'I heard a shot from the shop and began to speed up. By the time I was close enough for them to know I was there, the robbers were already outside. One of them opened the passenger door of the car and jumped in. The other tried the back door, but it wouldn't open. He saw me coming and started to dash around to the driver's side. As he ran out into the road, he went straight into the path of a lorry.' He recited every fact in the same monotone coppers were trained to use, as if he was giving evidence in court, but he couldn't hide the horror in his expression. Poor lad, Harper thought. He'd probably never seen anything like that before. Christ Almighty, he hadn't expected it himself.

'I see.' Harper shuddered. He could almost feel the lorry's impact. Jackson was shocked, mouth open, eyes wide. Walsh was shaking his head. 'How bad is he?'

'I don't know, sir. He was taken to the infirmary. He looked like death.'

'What about the other two?' Jackson asked.

'As soon as they realized what had happened, they drove off, sir.'

'What?' Harper asked in disbelief. 'Before they even knew if their friend was hurt?'

'Yes, sir,' the constable replied. 'But believe me, sir, from the bang, it couldn't have been good.'

So much for comradeship, he thought. Callous bastards. Leaving one of their own to die or be arrested. In the end it came down to looking out for number one. Not much honour there, only survival.

'Very good, Woodford,' Harper said. 'Write it up and make sure Inspector Jackson receives a copy.'

'Yes, sir. Thank you.' He beamed at the praise, then marched out.

Harper glanced at Jackson. 'Ring the hospital. We need to know which one of them it is.' He paused. 'Sorry. You know your job better than I do.'

Someone placed a mug of tea by his hand and he drank, suddenly aware of how thirsty he was. The inspector had the telephone receiver by his ear, waiting for someone at the infirmary. All around him, people were busy, bustling. He could only stand and watch. The whole thing seemed impossible to believe. The fire, shooting at the brigade, that walk across the road feeling completely exposed. Then for it all to come crashing down on one of the gang. Hit by a vehicle. It seemed so ordinary. All of it in under an hour.

Another swallow of tea and Harper marched out to the front desk. 'Where's the lorry driver who ran over the robber?' he asked.

'Down in the interview room, sir.'

'Do we have all his particulars?'

The sergeant nodded. 'When he was brought in, sir.'

The man was slumped in his seat, elbows on his knees, face cradled in his hands. He didn't stir as Harper sat across from him.

'Mr . . .'

'Harris.' Very slowly he raised his head. About thirty, his hair cut close, a pale, jagged scar across his skull. 'Is he alive?'

'As far as I know.' That was the truth, little as it seemed.

'There was nothing I could do. He dashed out from behind the car. One second there was nobody, then he was right in front of me. Never even looked to see if anything was coming.'

Harper wrote it all in his notebook. The man's statement, to be typed later.

'Once you spotted him, what did you do?'

'I stamped down on the brake so hard I thought the pedal would go through the floor.' His eyes implored. 'What else? I tried to steer away from him, but there was a car coming the other way. A man with his wife. I could see two little kiddies in the back.'

'Did the man you hit see you?'

Harris shook his head. 'I don't think so. He was trying the door handle. Yelling something, by the look on his face.'

Harper handed over the rest of the tea and the driver took a grateful swig.

'You hit him and stopped. What did you do after that?'

Harris stared, reliving the scene. He was dazed, still in shock. 'I wanted to make sure he was alive. Before I could reach him, the car he'd been trying to get into took off. There was a copper blowing his whistle. Plenty of people. A woman who said she was a nurse . . . the only thing I could do was stare at him on the ground.' He cocked his head and blinked. 'I remember I kept saying sorry over and over again.' When he looked up again, the driver seemed helpless. 'It was the only thing I could think of.'

Before Harper could say more, the door opened. Walsh.

'Sir.'

'Mr Harris, you're free to leave. We might need to talk to you again, but we won't be bringing any charges.'

A nod. 'I hope . . . I hope he's all right.'

'The robber's alive. The doctors say he's going to survive, although he'll never be the same.'

Harper's mind slipped to the lorry driver. He'd never be the same either, and no fault of his own.

'Who's with him at the hospital?'

Walsh gave one of his dark, knowing smiles. 'Clough. Inspector Jackson's sergeant.' He paused long enough for a heartbeat. 'He's prised out the gang's address. I've put together a squad, they're already on their way. The car's waiting for us.'

Harper was suddenly aware of the Webley in his pocket, its weight dragging his jacket down. He'd completely forgotten he was carrying it.

'Where are we going?' he asked as they settled and the car moved off.

'Not far from Temple Newsam,' Jackson said.

He knew the grand old house with its huge, rolling grounds. For centuries the home of rich, titled families. People who moved in a much higher orbit than a chief constable.

'Right.' Time to put everything in order. 'Now tell me which of the killers we have in hospital.'

'David Templeton,' Walsh answered. 'Both legs broken, pelvis shattered.'

'I managed a word with the surgeon,' Jackson continued. 'Templeton's going to be lucky if he ever walks again.'

Harper thought about the fear the gang had caused, and the dead man who did his duty and tried to stop them. 'Don't ask me to feel sorry for him. Mind you,' he added after a moment's thought, 'he might be very bitter once he realizes what the rest of his life will be like and the way his pals took off. Let's see if we can use that. See if he's willing to turn King's evidence.'

'By then we should have the last two in their cells, sir.'

'Let's hope you're right.'

Something had gone wrong on this last robbery, or they wouldn't have netted Templeton. But this gang never moved without an escape plan. They'd probably already scarpered, off to their next bolt hole.

He'd been lost in his thoughts, and came back to earth as the car parked behind a dark van. The back doors were open, six uniformed constables clambering out.

Harper stared down a rocky dirt drive. In the distance, perhaps two hundred yards, he could see the roof of a house. It stood in a small hollow.

'Is there a way they can get out at the back?'

'Not a clue, sir.'

Jesus. They were going in blind. It might be better if the pair had already run. These two weren't going to surrender meekly. Finding the place empty would be safer than a gun battle where some of his men were bound to be hurt.

Jackson was hurriedly sketching out a plan to the bobbies. They spread out, crouched down as they moved across the open ground.

'You see the house sits in a dip,' the inspector said as he returned. 'The men will wait on the lip of that, ready.'

'What about us?' Harper asked.

The inspector grinned. 'We're arriving in style, sir. Driving right up to the front door. They won't be expecting that.'

Maybe not, but he wouldn't put it past them to have a contingency for it, too.

The driver put his foot down on the accelerator and let out the clutch. He felt a rush, the tingle in his fingertips. They were close to action. The car rocketed down the drive, bumping and jolting, sending up a thick plume of dust. A leap in the air as it crested the hill, skidding as it landed heavily but never losing speed.

Harper glanced at the others. They both had pistols in their hands, bodies braced, faces set. Ready. He held his breath and drew his gun as the car slewed to a halt outside the front door.

It was a small stone farmhouse, with a pair of dilapidated outbuildings. Plain, ordinary, woodwork in need of a lick of paint. Hidden away, isolated. He didn't think there were any like this still left so close to town. They'd seemed to be everywhere when he was young. Different times; these days the city sprawled. The thoughts flickered through his mind in a fraction of a second. He looked again. Nothing to mark it as a killers' hideaway.

Jackson had his foot raised, kicking at the lock of the front door. Walsh had vanished around the back of the building. Harper kept his gaze on the windows, watching for any movement. The Webley was in his hand, safety catch off, finger resting on the trigger. Small, shallow breaths. His body was taut, every muscle aching.

The door crashed back and banged against the wall. That was the signal for the uniformed men to start running, following Jackson into the farmhouse.

Harper stayed outside. Their quarry had gone. He could feel it. The surge that had pushed through him began to ebb. He slid the revolver back in his jacket.

There was already a crowd inside, no need for him to add to it. Instead, he walked around the farmyard, glancing into the outbuildings. One had been a barn, he thought. A long-ago smell of cows seemed to hang in the air. A perfect place to keep a car out of sight.

He squinted. Something that could be tyre tracks. Harper squatted, feeling the creak in his knees, and rubbed his fingertips across the dirt floor. A trace of something slick and viscous. He brought it closer to his face. Oil.

Out in the light, some of the constables were making their way back to the van. Walsh and Jackson were standing in the kitchen. Plates had been washed and dried and sat on the draining board where the gang had left them before they set out that morning.

'They can't be more than an hour ahead of us,' Jackson said. 'Grabbed what they could from the bedrooms, by the look of it. Left a fair bit behind for us to go through.'

'An hour or a day, it doesn't matter. They're still in front,' Harper pointed out. 'And we don't have a bloody clue where they've gone.'

Walsh sat at the table, head in his hands, quietly saying, 'Bastards, bastards,' over and over.

The scent of them lingered. Sweat, soap, cooking. This was the closest the police had come. But not near enough. They were still frustratingly beyond reach. Cigarette butts in the ashtray. Ashes from a fire in the hearth of the main room. They'd made a home of sorts here. How long had they stayed? That should be simple to discover, all they needed was to find the owner.

But where had they gone? That was the real question. Did they have a place they could run to?

After the constables left, Harper climbed the stairs, peering in the rooms. Beds neatly made. The army discipline had stayed with the men. The clothes that remained were carefully folded. Shoes polished to a high, gleaming shine.

Very different from most criminals he'd ever encountered. They were planners. Did they have one for losing another man, or were they running now, desperate and struggling to stay free?

They did, he decided. They were too organized for anything else.

FIFTEEN

Harper knew exactly what he ought to be doing: he should be in his office at the town hall, taking care of correspondence that needed a chief constable's full attention. The afternoon was slipping away. Soon enough, Miss Sharp would cover her typewriter and go home.

Instead, he was in a car with Superintendent Walsh, pulling up in front of the infirmary. He wanted a look at David Templeton. He needed to hear his voice.

The man had a room to himself, a constable on duty outside who stood to attention as he saw two senior officers approaching.

They'd spoken to the doctor and the nursing sister. Templeton was in pain, he drifted in and out of consciousness. If he ever walked again, it would never be more than an awkward stumble with a pair of sticks.

When they entered Templeton looked as if it was taking every ounce of control to contain what his body was doing to him. So far the painkillers hadn't been properly effective, the doctor said, shaking his head. He'd seen it before, caring for the wounded in the aid stations just behind the lines.

'From the look on your faces, you didn't catch them.' Templeton spat out the words, eyes taunting.

He was scrawny, a creature of sinew and bone, not much muscle on a thin frame. He gritted his teeth and closed his eyes for a second as pain pulsed through his body, opening his mouth to breathe as it passed.

'Why have you been doing these robberies?' Walsh asked.

'The army. They made us this way.' A grimace of a smile through the pain. 'It's the first time we've felt alive since the war.'

'Where will the others go?'

'The lance-jack always took care of that. Corporal Hobson knows what he's doing.'

'Did he tell the rest of you?' Harper asked. 'Or did you just follow his orders?'

The man's face hardened. He pushed his lips together as another wave of agony washed through him. 'Good soldiers follow orders. Was you never in the army?'

'A lifetime in the police,' Harper replied as he stared at the man. 'It's not so different.'

Walsh glanced at the chief. He wanted to take over. Harper stepped back into the shadows near the door. He'd had his glimpse. Templeton was so ordinary. No hero, no ogre; he passed dozens just like him on the street every day.

'Why don't you tell me what happened to Trevor Curtis?' Walsh asked. 'One of you executed your own comrade. Were you the one who pulled the trigger?'

Harper slipped out into the brightly lit corridor with its harsh smell of carbolic, then out into the late afternoon. Not dark yet, but the light was starting to dim. It was only a short stroll along Great George Street to the town hall, but as he climbed the steps, it felt like moving from one world to another.

Miss Sharp was ready to leave, making her final inspection to be certain she hadn't forgotten anything. She raised her eyebrows as she saw him.

'I'd given up on you for the day.'

'My wife used to say that all the time.' He grinned, but she was having none of it.

'Everything's in your office. It'll keep you occupied for another hour. Just put it all on my desk as you go out and I'll take care of it in the morning. Alderman Thompson rang twice. I told him you were out and I had no idea if you'd be back. I heard what happened. Nobody hurt?'

Any of the police, she meant. 'No, but one of the robbers is in a bad way.'

She gave a brief nod. 'I'll be off, then. Am I likely to see you tomorrow?'

'I'm sure of it. The bad penny always comes rolling back.'

He began working through the pile of papers, but his mind kept straying to Templeton. The gang had abandoned him, it came down to that. He'd been hit by the lorry and they'd used the confusion to escape. It would be something for Walsh and Jackson to explore with him.

A long report from Ricks about the shoplifters in Manchester. They'd had coppers at the station, questioning all the women coming off the London trains and arresting any who couldn't give good accounts of themselves and where they were going. It was heavy-handed, the sergeant noted, probably illegal, but it was working. Arrest, then shipping the women back home was working. A few managed to slip through, but it was enough to keep them contained. A sharp contrast to Liverpool, where the police had been taken by surprise and the women had run riot in the shops. Ricks thought Leeds needed to duplicate the Manchester plan, but stay ready to make changes.

It all made sense. This was why he was glad someone from the Intelligence section was in charge.

An hour almost to the minute, and he picked up the piece of paper at the bottom of the pile. A note in Ash's copperplate writing: *We'd like to see you on Friday morning.* He and Sissons must have found something. He'd need to wait for tomorrow to discover what.

Harper had barely started down the stairs when a bellowing

voice called his name. He look around to see Thompson beck-
oning. He sighed and turned.

The jowls sagged on the alderman's heavy face. He looked
careworn, still bulky and with the low flames of a fire inside.
But it hadn't quite become a roaring blaze again yet. He was
still smaller than he'd once seemed; maybe he'd never fill a place
the way he once had.

'I hope you have news for me,' he said once the door to his
office closed behind him.

'Today's been full of other things,' Harper told him. 'You
might have heard.'

'I did.' He waved it away as if it was nothing. 'I need this
business resolved.'

'Still heard nothing more?'

Thompson shook his head. 'That bit seems to have come to
an end, thank God.' He looked around and lowered his voice.
'But I need those letters back. Look at me, I'm hardly sleeping.
My wife's noticed I'm not eating much.'

'Soon,' he promised. It was his job to take care of things like
this. But sometimes it felt so, so hard.

'You'd better be right.'

Annabelle seemed to be with them as they sat and ate. Still silent,
but her eyes flickered towards whoever was speaking. She seemed
to be listening as Mary told them tales from work. While Harper
and his daughter washed and dried the pots, Julia tried to coax
his wife into completing a jigsaw of the Houses of Parliament.

In bed, he held Annabelle close. When they met, she'd had a
little bulk to her. Now there wasn't much left, skin hanging over
bones. Her body was disappearing, ounce by ounce.

'Tom.' Her voice took him by surprise. So soft that he wondered
if he was imagining it. But it was there. Husky, tentative and
small, feeling its way in the darkness.

'I'm here.'

'I'm frightened.' She paused for so long that he wondered if
she'd drifted to sleep. Then the words came, as if she'd been
saving them all up and needed to speak them while she still
could. 'I looked in the mirror this morning and I saw a strange
old woman I didn't recognize. Yesterday I realized I was having

a conversation with my mother.' The pain rose up in her voice. 'She's been dead for donkey's years, Tom.' Annabelle dug her fingers into his arm, hanging on to him. He didn't say anything, waiting. 'I feel lost. I know it's this . . . senility. I know it right now, but I'm not sure if I will tomorrow. I'm not even sure how I know it. Half the time I can't even tell who I am.' He felt her head shift towards him. 'Do you see?'

She was beseeching him for help, although she knew there was nothing he could do. If he could lift it all from her, put it on himself instead, he wouldn't hesitate. Which was worse: to know what was happening and be unable to stop it, or to wander through it like an innocent?

Stupid question, Harper told himself. There was no good choice.

'I do,' he told her softly as he stroked her hair; it was coarse under his fingers. 'You know I'll always do everything I can for you. From the end of the month you'll have me under your feet all the time.'

She was silent for a moment. He felt her body tense, then relax. 'You're going to retire. I remember now.'

'I'm ready for it. We'll be able to do things.'

'Will we?' So much in two words. Bitterness, sorrow. Hope.

'We will,' he said. Tom Harper, he thought, you're a rare man for promises today.

SIXTEEN

'Do you know the Leylands?' Harper asked Bingham as the driver pulled away from the kerb in the morning. The man chuckled. 'Spent my first six months on the beat down there. Picked up a decent smattering of Yiddish when I worked it, too.'

It would have been astonishing if he hadn't. The Leylands was where Jewish immigrants from across Europe came when they arrived in Leeds, Yiddish their common language.

'Let's go down there before the town hall.'

Maybe it was the conversation with Annabelle, but in his

dreams, his mother had visited. A short woman with a kindly face but determined eyes. Even when he was sixteen, working five and a half days a week rolling barrels at Brunswick's Brewery, she'd encouraged him never to lose sight of becoming a copper. It had been his ambition since he was a young boy, following Constable Hardwick as he patrolled the streets. Sometimes the copper would give him a clip around the ear, other times a sweet; it depended on his mood. Nellie Harper had died young, not long after her son was promoted into plain clothes. But she'd returned in the middle of the night to stand in front of him, wearing her old, faded apron, a shawl around her shoulders, that gentle smile turning up the corners of her mouth. She reached out to him and Harper extended his hand until their fingers almost touched. Then, in a blink, she was gone, only the darkness left.

'Park on Noble Street.'

He climbed out, ignoring the boys who ran towards the novelty of a car. Even now, they'd see very few in a place like this.

It was smaller than he recalled, but that was always the way. Growing up played its trick on reality. Shabbier, too. He remembered the first influx of Jewish families, running from the Russian pogroms and not sure they'd ever find safety. Harper glanced around. Down on the corner, colourful advertisements in English and Yiddish were pasted to the gable ends of houses.

Hands in his overcoat pockets, he strolled along to number twenty-seven. The windows were clean, the step donkey-stoned. But it seemed impossibly tiny. His father had been a large man; how had he ever been able to fit through that front door?

No familiar faces, of course. The last of those would be long gone, dead or moved elsewhere. It probably wouldn't be many years before all this was torn down as unfit for human habitation. Then only ghosts would stroll around here, the ones who didn't need to see the flagstones and cobbles and bricks. It could become their home for eternity.

'You wanted to see me.'

Ash and Sissons sat in the chairs on the other side of the desk.

'We believe we've found the driver who hit Ben Rogers's car and sent him off the road,' Ash said.

To his death.

'Believe?' Harper asked, taken aback by the word. 'Aren't you certain?'

A pause as Miss Sharp bustled in with a tray of teapot, cups, and a plate of biscuits.

'We're certain we've discovered the vehicle that did it.' Sissons explained. 'It was parked on the road outside the owner's house. He came out one morning and saw the damage to the coachwork. Thought someone had hit the car as they passed and never stopped. He was furious, but . . .'

'He didn't report it?' Harper asked.

'He did,' Sissons continued. 'Told the man on the beat and went down to the station to fill out the form. That's how we found him. A copy came through the Intelligence section and one of my men brought it to my attention. But he had no reason to imagine it might have been involved in the crash.'

'The car is back like new now.' Ash picked up the story, his voice full of disappointment. 'We talked to the place that did the work. All the old panels have already gone for scrap, unfortunately.'

'Takes away the proof. Who was driving it? Does the owner know?'

'No, sir. He had an alibi for the night it happened. We checked. But . . .'

Harper waited. 'Go on. But what?'

'There's a man: Timothy Gordon. Another of the crowd that seems to revolve around Charlotte Radcliffe. He was already on our list. We'd talked to him before, but he didn't seem a likely suspect.'

This was incestuous, Harper thought, with Miss Radcliffe at its heart. 'What about him?'

'He lives just a few doors from the man who owns the car, sir. Quite close to you in Chapel Allerton, in fact. Evidently it's common knowledge on the street that the owner leaves his car unlocked because he keeps losing his key, and he keeps a spare one under the mat.'

He exhaled slowly. 'So Gordon might have known and could have done it. That's fine. It's certainly a coincidence. Do we have anything to show he was in the vehicle?' He looked from Ash to Sissons. 'Fingerprints? Anything at all?'

'We've taken fingerprints, sir,' Sissons replied calmly, 'and we asked Mr Gordon if he was willing to be printed. He agreed, but we couldn't find a trace of him in there. Of course, he could have been wearing gloves.'

'And *why* would he do it? Is there any kind of motive for him to kill Ben Rogers? I assume they all know each other. Does he have an alibi for the night Rogers died?'

'He claims he was at home, on his own.' Ash shrugged. Impossible to prove either way. 'We've questioned everyone on the street, nobody saw him in the car. For motive . . . anything we come up with is guesswork, sir,' Ash said. 'We know Gordon and Miss Radcliffe have been involved—'

'Christ, is there anyone in that crowd she hasn't had?' Harper rubbed his temples, feeling the start of a headache.

'It doesn't seem like it, and she has them all under her spell. You were there when we gave her the news about her brother.' Harper remembered the shock and sorrow on her face that quickly fell away as she began to scheme. 'My belief is that she thinks Rogers killed her brother and persuaded this man Gordon to run him off the road. Or indicated that she'd like someone to do it.' Ash looked up, helpless. 'Honestly, it's all guesswork. No proof and I don't see how we can find any.'

'Meanwhile, Timothy Gordon denies everything.'

'Told us to show our evidence or he'd have his lawyer on us.' A long sigh. 'The thing is, sir, he's right.'

'Then we'd better come up with some proof.'

Ash turned his hands, palms up. 'I said, sir: we can't, not without some sort of break. We've looked at it from every direction.'

'We're not giving up,' Sissons told him. 'We're agreed that Miss Radcliffe is behind it all. The problem is, she's untouchable at the moment. We don't have anything on her, and she's grieving her brother's possible suicide and his best friend's death.' He poured a world of disgust into his words.

'We have the beating of a city alderman.' Harper counted it all off on his fingers. 'We have two people dead in very suspicious circumstances. Behind it all we have blackmail. None of the people involved are professional criminals. We're trained police. Between us we have over a century of experience. We must be able to take them apart.' He turned to Ash. 'Those two former policemen you're using, are they effective?'

'Yes, sir. They've provided us with much of the information.'

'Would one or two more help?'

He shook his head. 'Not if you want to keep all this quiet. The more people, the louder an investigation becomes. It's the way of the world.'

Ash was right: the last thing they needed was a reporter coming around. It was a story with plenty of meat: an older councillor having an affair with a younger woman, blackmailed by the wealthy children of privilege. Thompson had been a fool but he didn't deserve that.

'How do we prise these people apart?' Harper asked. 'Make them turn on each other.'

'They're all close,' Sissons answered in his careful, studied voice. 'The families are friends; they went to the same schools. All the men have been with Miss Radcliffe at one time or another. They're as much a gang as those killers in the Model T.'

'And both of them are losing members,' Harper said. 'We need a lever. I'm damned if I'm going to let people like that beat us.' He pressed his lips together as he thought. 'They must have chars, someone who comes in and does for them. Cooks. Let's find them and talk to them. People like that always see more than anyone imagines. Let's go in by the tradesman's entrance and surprise them.'

As they left, Miss Sharp slipped by them. With a flourish, she placed a small pile of papers in front of him.

'Before you have chance to do your vanishing act,' she told him. He felt like a boy sitting under the teacher's glare, even when she'd returned to her own office. Half an hour later, everything complete, he placed them on her desk.

'Can I go now?'

She snorted. 'Am I likely to see you again today?'

'I don't know.'

She stared at him, but it was an honest answer. It depended on what happened.

The air was warmer and the breeze blowing against his face felt pleasant as he walked over to Millgarth. He was doing this so often he was probably wearing a rut in the pavement. Someone in a gauze mask and cap walked towards him, and for a split second he tensed, thinking it was one of the gang. But the man walked right past without a glance. Nothing more than a sensible citizen.

'Anything more from Templeton?'

'He's had two operations, so he's barely been conscious,' Walsh said. 'My best interrogator is over at the infirmary, waiting for him to come round properly.'

'Catch him while he's groggy and we might drag more truth out of him,' Harper ordered. 'What about the farmhouse?'

'You saw it for yourself, sir – they cleared out in a hurry. Took papers, a few clothes, the jewellery they'd stolen. Jackson spent most of yesterday there.' He shrugged. 'Nothing to indicate where they'd gone.'

'Can they carry on, just two of them?' He'd been thinking about it as he marched along the street, weighing the possibilities.

'It's feasible,' Walsh replied. 'One stays in the car, the other runs into the shop. People know who they are now, they have a reputation, so everyone will already be scared. The way I see it, sir, they don't have any choice. If they stop, everyone's going to believe we've beaten them. Can you see them accepting that?'

'No,' Harper agreed. 'Not really.' Too much was at stake for them to withdraw quietly. Pride, honour: things that were the death of young men. 'Then how do we put an end to it? They'll be growing desperate, and that's going to make them even more dangerous.'

'All we can do for now is keep our eyes peeled, sir. Hope we can spot their car by a house.'

Harper snorted. 'We might as well try the power of prayer.'

'If I thought it'd work against this pair, I'd be on my knees right now.' Walsh sounded exhausted. No surprise. This gang had been outfoxing them for too long.

'I'll sit down again with the files on the pair that are still standing. Maybe there's something in there that can give us a clue.'

'You're welcome, sir,' the superintendent told him doubtfully, 'but we've been through them time and again.'

Yet what else could he do? He had nothing to offer out on the streets these days. He was the chief constable, a glorified clerk who spent his days with papers. Probably the best he could give would be going through folders and reports.

He began with John Booth, the man who'd been raised Baptist and seen his religion shatter in the trenches. Booth had grown up in Armley with five brothers and sisters, all adults now. Five and a half feet, dark hair, brown eyes. Barely skimming eight stone in weight and pigeon-chested, according to the doctor who examined him. No venereal diseases during the war; not too surprising, since he'd been raised in a church.

Slightly below average intelligence, according to a test. Not much initiative, unlikely to rise above private. Good reports from his commanding officers. Obeyed orders well, worked with the others in his squad. One of nature's followers.

Finally, the interview with his parents after he'd been identified as a member of the gang. Sorrow, disappointment. He'd returned from France a changed man; someone they couldn't understand. He didn't want to go to church, said he didn't believe in God any more.

Booth had gone back to his old labouring job, but only lasted a few weeks before he moved on. Other work, never causing problems, but not happy, not settling. Only his war comrades seemed to matter to him, his mother said. He spent his evenings with them and finally left his home to share a house with them. He didn't give his parents the address.

His father blamed everything on the war. Before it, he'd been a good, steady lad. He cared about his family, and God. The young man had returned corrupted, the father said: that exact word. Tainted in his mind and his soul and his heart.

Harper set the folder aside. In his friends, Booth had found something to replace the certainty of the church. Something tangible; the men who kept each other alive. Lance Corporal Will Hobson was their preacher, and the others were his flock. He led and they followed meekly behind.

Harper sighed and glanced at the clock on the wall. He'd spent most of the morning learning about John Booth. He understood more about the man, but none of it would help the police find him. He lifted the telephone receiver.

'I know it's not our usual day, but do you fancy some dinner?

My treat.' He listened for a moment. 'I was thinking we could go to Youngman's for a change. Outside your office in a quarter of an hour?'

Hints of blue sky when the clouds parted. Harper stood on the corner of Albion Place and Briggate, watching people as they passed. Not just the faces, but the way they walked and held themselves. It had been drilled into him by Superintendent Kendall, back when he was a young detective. You could learn a lot from it, the man had said, and he was right. But Kendall was a quarter of a century in the ground now. Hard to believe.

'You're miles away,' Mary said as she slipped her arm through his.

'Years, more like.' He smiled at her. His daughter was always a picture in his eyes. 'Ready for fish and chips?'

They talked about Annabelle, Mary's business, her trip to France in the summer. She was wearing another of her new style of frocks. A complete convert, but how could anyone go back to the restrictive old fashions after such a drastic change? He'd very quickly grown used to seeing her like this. The colours were brighter, the shape was flattering. The dresses made her look like a woman in her twenties, not someone who wore her clothes as a penance.

'Are you any closer to catching those men?' she asked. 'The ones in the Model T. I read that one of them is in hospital.'

'He's going to be there for a long time. Only two of them left now.'

'Will you catch them?'

'Yes,' Harper answered. Unless they suddenly vanished, there was no doubt of that. 'The big question is how long it might take us.'

Her eyes widened in understanding. 'Ah, it's like that.'

'Exactly like that.'

During the war, Mary had been a member of the Voluntary Patrol, women police constables of a sort, but with very few powers. She'd seen how things worked. Now Leeds had one proper woman constable, an official, paid position. But she still couldn't arrest anyone; the Watch Committee had created the job as a sop to the times, nothing more.

Mary had an impish grin on her face. 'You can tame that back garden after you retire. Have you taken a look out there in the last few days?' He shook his head. 'The grass is already starting to grow back where you dug.'

'I'll work on it on Sunday,' he said, wondering if he'd have chance. Harper finished his food, pushed the plate away and patted his belly. 'It'll do me good.'

Dinner with Mary had been exactly the tonic he needed. A spot of brightness to raise his spirits in the middle of a bleak day. Back at Millgarth, Harper opened Will Hobson's file and began to leaf through the sheets. Twenty-four, a bright young man. One of life's leaders, his sergeant had written on an evaluation. The kind of man who inspired, who people followed without question, had been an officer's assessment.

He was certainly the leader of the gang, the same way he'd been in charge of his squad as a lance-corporal. He had their loyalty in peace as much as war. Or perhaps they couldn't settle now the fighting was done, so they kept it going.

He'd been working at the sewage plant when war was declared. Joined up the day it all began. Showed plenty of initiative, quickly promoted to lance-corporal. Mentioned in despatches at the Somme. Could have become a full corporal or even a sergeant but showed no interest in further promotion. He seemed content with his section, a captain noted. He developed a close bond with his small group of men.

Interesting, Harper thought. Hobson had enough ambition to acquire a little power, but no more than that. A section kept everything personal. Did that tell him much about the man? Anything he could use?

He sat, drumming his fingers on the small stack of paper. No, nothing that would be helpful.

After he was discharged from the army, Hobson had returned to the sewage plant. Six more months and he applied to become a foreman; he was being trained for the post when he suddenly left the job.

He was quiet, well-behaved at home, his parents said. Each time they tried to ask him about the war, he gently deflected them. Most evenings he'd be out with the members of his old section. Never brought them home, his parents had no idea who they were. He said nothing about them. Never withdrawn or sullen, simply quiet and polite.

They'd been astonished when Will told them he was moving. Work had been shocked when he suddenly threw over the job. No inkling it might happen. Hobson had dropped no hints, hadn't been in touch with his family or anyone from the sewage plant since he'd gone.

Will Hobson's brother had died in the fighting and left him the only valuable thing he owned, a Model T Ford. His parents hadn't wanted to believe when a detective came and said their son might be using it to commit crimes.

That was the end of the file. It wasn't so much, really. Still, he felt as if he had a clearer picture of Hobson. The man wasn't going to surrender. He'd never walk away. Hobson would keep fighting until the end; this was all he had. Leading men like this probably felt like the only worthwhile thing he'd done in his life. But how violent was he willing to be?

SEVENTEEN

He was tired, he expected to sleep well, but it had been fitful. No telephone calls, simply too much time lying awake, going through the cases in his mind and frustrated by them both. They were making progress, but at the speed of a tortoise. It wasn't enough. Finally, a little before five by the hands on the clock, Harper gave up on trying to rest.

The air was definitely warmer. Walking down Harrogate Road he saw others, men on their way to work for the final half-day of the week.

From a distance, the city looked black. Generation after generation of factory soot had coated the bricks and stones and stolen all the colour from the place. Now the industries were closing down, fewer chimneys feeding their smoke into the air. Too late; the damage had been done. Brush against a building and you came away with a dark stain on your clothes. It was the mark of Leeds.

He passed through Sheepscar. The Victoria was locked up tight, curtains closed upstairs where the landlord slept. Strange; Harper felt no tug drawing him back there.

Millgarth was filled with noise, the day shift preparing for work. But the detectives' room was quiet, still too early for them to arrive.

The telephone began to ring in Walsh's office. Without thinking, he lifted the receiver.

'Chief Constable Harper.'

A heartbeat of silence, then a woman's voice, close to frantic: 'Thank God. I was looking for anyone who could give you a message.'

She was speaking so rapidly that his hearing tumbled all the words into one.

'Who is this?' he asked.

'Nancy. Nancy Ash.'

Harper felt cold panic creep across his skin. He gripped the receiver more tightly. 'What is it? What's happened?'

'It's Fred. He's had a heart attack. I'm at the hospital.'

The world seemed to stop. Ash . . . Christ.

'How is he?'

Her voice wavered on the line. 'The doctors say it was mild. I keep asking them but they won't tell me if he'll be fine, and they won't let me see him—'

'I'll be there as soon as I can.'

The streets were quiet as he hurried along. Faster than a walk, not quite a run. Imagining the worst. Ash had come back from his shooting three years ago. Not the man he was, but still active and vital. He'd been relishing this case. And now . . .

An image of Billy Reed came into his head. The man had been his sergeant when Harper was a detective inspector. Years ago now. They'd had a falling out and Reed had asked for a transfer. He'd ended up an inspector himself, and after he began running the force in Whitby, they'd enjoyed a reconciliation of sorts. Then Billy had simply keeled over one day as he was walking. Dead before he even hit the pavement. So young. At least Ash was still alive.

Not even ten minutes and he was at the infirmary, sitting and holding her hands in his. She was a small, round woman, looking helpless as she perched on the bench in the waiting room, tears winding through the powder on her face.

'Would you talk to them, please?' she asked. 'They're all giving me the runaround.'

'Of course.' It was the least he could do.

The doctor was young, full of his own knowledge and an air of superiority because he could heal the sick. Harper listened for a minute, then began to speak. Fast, sharp words, ripping the physician into shreds. It wasn't something he liked to do, but he needed the information, the truth, and to make sure Nancy Ash was treated with respect, not pushed aside because she was a woman.

He brought her a cup of tea, sweet-talked from the canteen.

'They say they can never promise completely in these cases, but I have the sense they think he'll recover,' Harper told her. Her body sagged with relief and she began to cry. Harper passed her his handkerchief. 'He was very lucky. He's going to need to rest for a while.'

She nodded. 'I'll make sure he does, don't you worry about that.'

'No pushing himself. Only small walks, and definitely no more working for me on the side.' He smiled; she didn't return it, but how could she? Her mind was brimming over with fear and worries and loneliness.

'You should go home,' Harper told her. 'You won't be able to see him for hours.'

'I'll stay here.' She placed her handbag on her lap and stared straight ahead, an immovable object.

'If there's anything I can do, someone will be in my office at the town hall.' He took out his notebook and wrote down the telephone number, then added the line at home.

'I need to send some flowers to the hospital,' he told Miss Sharp. 'To Frederick Ash. The message something like get back on your feet soon.'

'Our Ash?' Her head shot up.

'He's had a heart attack. I've just come from there.'

'How . . .?' she asked.

'You know what doctors are like – they'll never properly commit themselves one way or another. But they seem hopeful and the nurses believe he'll pull through.'

Sissons had just arrived, still hanging up his raincoat as Harper told him. His face tightened. Without thinking, he placed a hand over his heart.

'How much work has Ash been doing on this case? An honest answer.'

'Quite a bit, sir,' the superintendent replied. He glanced around his department. 'I have to run all this, too.'

'Could one of the others do that for a while?' He needed Sissons to handle the blackmail and deaths. With Ash out of action, he was the only one with intimate knowledge of the case.

'If it's not for long. You have Ricks working on those shop-lifters. That's taking up a lot of his time.'

'Then we'd better make sure we wrap this Thompson case up quickly.' The humour fell flat. 'Do you have anyone you can trust to work on this?'

'Ash had those two retired policemen, sir, but they reported directly to him. I've only met them once. Anyone coming to it fresh would be starting from nothing and it's complex.'

That was one way of putting it, Harper thought. Twisted was better. A sudden realization came.

'I know the case. Some of it, anyway.'

Sissons gave him an encouraging smile. 'You do, and you've interviewed Miss Radcliffe.'

Crossed swords, more like. 'I've been working with Walsh on the Model T gang, but there's not much I can contribute there. Tell me truthfully: do you think I can do anything to help on this? Ash had all his old contacts. I don't. Mine all disappeared long ago.'

Sissons considered his answer. 'You have the rank to deal with these people, sir. And the circle of suspects keeps decreasing. Not many left now. We're down to Timothy Gordon – he's the one we're sure ran Rogers off the road – and two more men. Plus Miss Radcliffe, of course.'

'Of course. The spider in the centre of the web. How much of what you've done is written down?'

'Just the bare bones, sir.' Sissons's eyes widened. 'You said—'

'I know.' That was his order, everything verbal, no trace for people to find. Now it was going to come back to haunt him. But what he needed to do was obvious.

'I want everything you have in my office in five minutes, then tell me how I can help.'

'Are you back here to work now?' Miss Sharp asked as Sissons delivered a pile of papers.

'For the moment.'

She rolled her eyes. 'You're like a yo-yo. I suppose you want a cup of tea.'

He winked at her. 'And a biscuit, if there are any going.'

He skimmed through the papers in the file, then ordered them differently and went over them all again, reading more slowly. It was like studying a sketch, a quick drawing with the details left out. But those had been his own orders; too late to carp about it now.

Sissons reappeared a little before half past ten. 'Been able to make much sense of it all, sir?'

Harper rested his palms on the papers. 'What there is.'

'We kept most things in our heads. But we talked about them.'

For the next hour he led the chief constable through everything they'd done. The people they'd interviewed, the answers they'd received, whether they believed them. He'd heard some of it in their summaries; now he made notes as Sissons fleshed it all out.

'That's what we have, sir,' Sissons told him as he finished. The man had a towering memory; that was what he needed for intelligence work.

'Thank you.' He rubbed the back of his hand across his jaw. 'I have a much clearer picture now.' Not a pretty one, either. A group of people with far too much time and money and no responsibilities. 'What do you suggest I do?'

'You could start by going to talk to Timothy Gordon again. He denies he ran Rogers off the road, and what we have is tenuous at best.'

'But?' With so little, there had to be some good reason to go back to him.

'Mr Ash believed that he might crack under some pressure. He wanted to give Gordon a few days to believe he was free, then come down hard on him.'

'That's fine. I'll go and see him. The other two you mentioned, Daniel Anderson and Robert Wilton. I don't think I've heard about them.'

'They're all part of the same set. Anderson works as a stock-broker on the exchange, and Wilton has a position at a bank.'

He snorted. 'Not a clerk, I take it.'

Sissons chuckled. 'Hardly. But at least the pair of them earn their crust, even if they don't need it.'

'Family money there too?'

'Bags of it, sir. The same school as the others, that's how all the men met.'

'And all enchanted by Charlotte Radcliffe?'

'Every one of them. Apparently she's had involvements with them all at one time or another.'

'Right,' Harper said. 'You've given me somewhere to start.'

'You'd mentioned talking to the chars and cooks these people have, sir,' Sissons reminded him. That was right; he had. 'Those former officers Ash uses are doing that.'

'Very good.'

The car pulled up on the Headrow.

'Where to, sir?' Bingham asked.

He started with an address, then changed his mind. 'The infirmary.'

Nancy Ash was still sitting on the same chair, looking as lost as when he'd left her, hours before.

Harper found the ward sister. He'd known her for years, from the time she was starting out as a nurse probationer. Sister Carter had become a briskly efficient woman who frightened her nurses. But she was good at her job. My patients don't die, she told him once. They're too scared of me for that.

'Barring something very bad, Mr Ash is going to be fine,' she said through her gauze mask. She'd made him put one on, too. Still, he heard the note of caution in her voice and lifted his eyebrows. 'You should know better than to expect guarantees in a hospital, Mr Harper,' Sister Carter told him. 'At the moment

everything looks well. A few days' rest and observation in here
and he'll be fine to go home. But after one heart attack there's
always an increased risk of a second. That could prove fatal.'
She stared into his face. 'Mr Ash is the right age for it.'

A year younger than him. 'I understand.'

'Is he one of yours, Chief Constable?'

'Yes.' And always would be.

A nod. 'I'll make sure he's well looked after. Why don't
you persuade his wife to go home? She can see him at visiting
hours this evening. He ought to be awake and ready for her
by then.'

Nancy Ash was quiet in the car, sitting and wringing a handkerchief through her hands.

'Try to sleep,' he said.

'I won't be able to. I'll be worried every minute.'

'He's in the very best hands. I promise you that.'

Harper could see her reluctance. Even as she turned the key
in the lock of her house, he expected the woman to turn around
and march to the tram stop. Finally the door closed behind her.

'Mr Gordon.'

His rooms were elegantly furnished, the entire floor of a
house at the top of Allerton Hill in Chapel Allerton, barely
more than three minutes' walk from Harper's own, but far more
luxurious.

They sat close to a tall window that overlooked the garden.
The grass was a striking green rectangle, closely mowed, daffodils
and tulips bringing colour to the beds that surrounded it.

'I trust this won't take too long, Chief Constable.' He checked
his wristwatch. 'I'm meeting some people for cocktails before
dinner.'

'It's just after three,' Harper said pleasantly. 'We have plenty
of time.'

Timothy Gordon was just short of six feet tall with a young
man's litheness. The kind of assured handsomeness that seemed
to come with money. But there was something else underneath
that. A prickle of fear, Harper thought. It was there in the way
he couldn't quite settle in his chair, nervously shifting around.

'You knew Mr Rogers, I believe,' Harper said.

'I did. There was a whole group of us at school together,' Gordon replied. 'But I'm sure you're aware of that.'

'I am. And you're all friends with Charlotte Radcliffe.'

'Yes.' He took a cigarette from a silver case and tapped it on the chair arm before lighting it.

'Your set is shrinking, Mr Gordon. First there was Charles Radcliffe's suicide, then Mr Rogers dying so soon afterwards.'

'I know.' Gordon didn't look at him, but stared out of the window towards the garden.

'Was there a falling out among you?'

The man moved again, as if he was uncomfortable. 'Not really. No, nothing like that.'

Almost a glimpse of the truth. *Not really* . . . what did that mean?

'There's you left, Mr Wilton and Mr Anderson.'

'And Charlotte.'

Harper dipped his head. 'And Miss Radcliffe, of course. Tell me, what do you think is happening with these deaths?'

'I don't know.' He flicked ash into the ashtray. 'I wish I did.'

'No? You must have thought about it.'

'Yes, of course.' The words hurried out of his mouth. 'But I don't have any answers.'

'A pity, Mr Gordon.' He stayed silent for a moment. 'You know, it's curious that the car which ran your friend off the road was taken from right around here.'

He turned his head to face Harper. 'What are you trying to say?'

'Nothing.' He raised his hands, the innocent. No expression on his face. 'Merely that it's curious. Did you know the car was left unlocked with the key under the mat?'

'Your men asked me all this. I'm sure you know the answer.'

'I do. But I'm asking again.' Harper gave a brief, dark smile. 'I want to look at your face as you tell me.'

'There's nothing to say, really.'

'No?'

'No,' Gordon insisted, but he might as well have scribbled the lie across his face. As Harper stared, he began to blush, the colour rising from the collar of his shirt.

'Are you sure about that?'

'I just told—'

'I don't believe you, Mr Gordon.'

'But—'

Harper's smile remained, but his voice became iron. 'Let me tell you something. If I arrest you, you'll be interviewed by people who have years of experience in taking suspects apart to discover the truth. They drag it out of hardened criminals. I don't imagine they'll have too much of a problem with you.' He let the threat hang in the air. 'If you're thinking of making a run for it, you won't even reach the door. I might look old and slow, but I have plenty of practice in stopping criminals. Now, what's it going to be?'

'I wasn't involved in Ben's death.' His gaze remained through the window and he blew a plume of smoke before angrily stubbing out the cigarette. 'That's God's honest truth.'

'Let's say I accept that.' He was watching Gordon's eyes. 'You weren't involved.'

'That's what I said.'

'You mean you weren't directly involved.'

A small gap, but long enough for the truth to come crashing down. 'I said I wasn't involved.'

'But you know who was.' He slapped his palm down on the wood of the chair arm. 'Don't try to split hairs. You know who took that car. You know who ran Ben Rogers off the road. I thought Ben was your friend.'

'He was. So was Charles Radcliffe.'

'Were they?' His disgust curled at the edge of the question. 'Then why are you protecting the man who killed him? Or is that the way you do things in your set? Loyalty doesn't stretch to honesty?'

'I don't bloody know who did it.' He shouted it out, then seemed to shrink into himself, astonished by his outburst.

'But you have your suspicions.' A nod as a reply. 'Who, Mr Gordon?'

The other two names on their list; it had to be one of them. But he wanted Tim Gordon to confirm it.

'I told Dan Anderson and Bobby Wilton about the car. We'd been out, and passed it when we came home one night. It's a bit of a joke around here.'

'I see.' It all made sense so far. 'Why would either of them want to hurt Ben? You were all friends, weren't you?'

'Yes, yes, of course we were. Are. Have been for years.' His eyes were glistening, on the verge of tears.

'Then why?'

'I don't know. I don't. Something was going on, they'd be talking, but none of them would ever tell me what they were doing.'

'Did you ask?'

'Of course I did.' The question seemed to surprise him. 'They said I was imagining things.'

It hadn't taken long to scrape away the lies. Harper believed him now. Easy to see how things stood in the group. Gordon was the one who was tolerated. Always there, for as long as they could remember, but never quite one of them. Wanting to belong, but never quite managing it. Try as he might, he couldn't imagine Timothy Gordon behind the wheel of a stolen car and forcing his friend off the road. He didn't have the steel for that. He tried for the bravado and insouciance of the people he called friends, but the man was a terrified rabbit.

Harper stood. Gordon was still sitting, looking out of the window.

'I'm going to give you a word of advice. Don't tell anyone about our conversation. Absolutely *nobody*, you understand? If you do, I'll find out and I'll make sure you pay for it.'

Gordon turned pale. 'I won't. I swear.' He'd talk. Let him stew for a day or two and he'd start, although he wouldn't want to admit he'd betrayed the others, taken the first step to moving away from them. There might not be any of them left soon; they'd all be dead or in prison.

'Did you have evenings with Charlotte?'

'Yes. Twice.' His face lit up at the thought, and Harper felt sorry for the man.

'Town hall,' he told Bingham, then changed his mind. 'No, Millgarth first.'

'If you're looking for the superintendent, sir, he dashed out an hour ago,' the station sergeant said. 'Inspector Jackson was with him.'

Harper felt his jaw muscles tighten. His pulse was beating faster. 'What was it? A lead? A tip?'

'I don't know, sir, sorry. But they were out of here like their lives depended on it.'

EIGHTEEN

Anderson was a stockbroker, Wilton a banker. God forbid either of them should be at work on a Saturday.

'Not a chance, sir,' Sissons told him with a chuckle.

'Tell me a bit more about them,' Harper said.

'Wilton's father is a senior man at the bank. Go back a few generations and one of his ancestors is among the founders.'

A lucrative family trade. But for some, that was how their lives went; they walked through it all on a thick carpet.

'The job is a sinecure?'

'Sinecure, birthright.' Sissons shrugged. 'Wilton's passion is horses. He has three or four. Hunts, rides point-to-points. When I was digging around, I found out he's taking part in one tomorrow in Collingham.'

'He was at school with the other young men?'

'All of them. That and the way they've always danced around Miss Radcliffe seem to be what bind them.'

'What do you make of her?' Harper was curious.

'She has something, I suppose,' he admitted grudgingly. 'She has all those young men under her spell.'

'We'd better not forget Alderman Thompson.'

A small laugh. 'And old men, too. I don't quite see her charm, sir.'

'For the right man, perhaps.'

The superintendent nodded. 'It must be there.'

Not much of an answer, but maybe a man either fell under that spell or didn't. 'What about Anderson?'

Sissons took his time before answering. 'He's the odd one out, sir. Fought in the last few months of the war. All the others, their families used connections to keep their sons at home. Anderson's father insisted that Daniel did his duty.'

'Did he see action?'

'Amiens.'

Everybody knew the name. The Hundred Days Offensive. It had led to the Armistice and the end of the fighting.

'I see.'

'The way I understand it, he's been a drinker since he came back. Still part of the same crowd, but he seems to spend much of his time soused.'

He'd seen too many drunks to ask how the man functioned. Plenty managed to keep it at a level at which they could work, except when they went on a toot.

'Does being a stockbroker keep him busy?'

'Probably not, sir. But he makes money.'

'I'm sure there's a fair bit in the family, too.'

'The Andersons are very well off. Daniel has a place in Shadwell. His parents bought it for him.'

Well away from town, about as close to the country as it was possible to be while still within touching distance of Leeds.

'Any interests?'

'None that I've discovered. He goes out with the others.'

'And with Miss Radcliffe?'

'A few times after he came home. He was a bit of a hero among them for a while.'

'A short while?'

Sissons smiled. 'Very brief.'

'You and Ash interviewed them both. Could either of them have forced Rogers off the road? Or pushed Charles Radcliffe in the path of an express train?'

'We didn't talk for long, but I'd say it's possible, sir,' he replied after a minute.

A cautious answer, Harper thought as he walked along Great George Street to the infirmary. The spring warmth still hung in the air. The people he passed were smiling, cheerful.

Inside the hospital, though, all that disappeared. He tied on his mask and saw the grave, serious eyes, everybody earnest. Sister Carter glanced up as he entered the ward. Her stern expression faded.

'It's not visiting hours yet, Chief Constable.'

'I was hoping you might make an exception.' He was hoping for charm. It had worked when he was a younger man. Now, though?

'Go on, then,' she said. 'It's the last bed on the left. Five minutes only, though.'

'Any more word from the doctors?'

'He's improving. Barring problems, we'll send him home on Monday.'

Ash looked shaken. The bedclothes were pulled up around his neck and he stared at the ceiling. The table was piled high with flowers and fruit.

'You should have just told me if you needed some time off,' Harper said as he sat.

The man tried to smile, but it was a weak effort. 'Well, you're always such a slave-driver, sir.'

'You gave us a scare. Your wife rang to tell me what had happened. She'll be in later. I think she'd be camped outside if she had her way.'

An attempt at a smile. 'Nancy's a good woman.'

'You're going home on Monday. She'll look after you.'

A small chuckle. 'That's what I'm afraid of, sir.' His face grew serious. 'I'm sorry to let you down on the case.'

'Don't apologize. I'm taking over. I've already been to talk to Timothy Gordon. Anderson and Wilton soon. What did you make of them?'

It took Ash's mind off being in the hospital. He was thinking instead of gazing. Sister Carter drifted past and coughed, pointed to the watch pinned to her apron.

'Hints,' Harper said. 'I'd better not outstay my welcome. You'll be home before you know it.'

'Can't come soon enough.'

'One last thing. I'd suggested you talk to the cooks and chars these young people use. Did you ever have chance?'

'Those two former coppers I know are doing it. They'll have a report.'

That was good enough; it was in hand. 'I'll stop by and see you next week. Just do what your Nancy says.'

'I don't imagine she'll give me much choice, sir.'

It was strange to see the man in bed and helpless. In all the years on the force he'd been active, always there, knowing every little thing. Even his wounding and retirement hadn't really dimmed his energy. This, though: it had been a rough blow.

His car was waiting on the Headrow. 'Millgarth again,' he said. The final call for the week. Then he wanted a quiet Sunday.

'I hope you have something,' Harper said as he walked into Walsh's office. 'I could do with some good news.'

The superintendent let out a long sigh and glanced at Inspector Jackson. The inspector's left hand was bandaged, the side of his face scraped and bloody. His clothes were torn, covered in dirt and grit.

'We came very close, sir. Very damn close.' His voice was thick and slurred, eyes a little glazed. He swayed as he stood. Harper raised an eyebrow. 'The doctor gave me some medicine, sir. I broke a couple of fingers.'

'You need to go home. Get some rest. Ask someone to give you a lift.' He waited until the inspector hobbled away. Harper turned back to Walsh. 'How bad is he really?'

'He's in pain. That's why the doctor gave him something. Right now he's mostly woozy, sir. He'll feel it when that wears off. Apart from the fingers it's mostly superficial. Thank God.'

'How did it happen?'

'We had a tip, sir. Someone said they knew where the gang's Model T was being kept. A garage out in Woodlesford. A woman said she'd seen two men putting it away the night before, locking the door and walking off.'

'That sounds worth investigating.'

'The garage was unlocked when we arrived. No car there.' He shook his head in dismay. 'Of course.'

'What did you do?'

'Jackson was sure they'd be coming back, so he stayed close enough to keep watch.'

'I take it he was right.'

Walsh snorted. 'I'd barely reached the end of the street, just turned the corner, when I saw the Model T. Two men inside, heading towards the garage. I was driving our car, and I tried to turn it around and go back. You know what a beast it is.'

He did. An old vehicle from before the war; you had to fight the gearbox.

'You missed what happened?'

'I heard the thump as the car hit him.' He was silent for a moment, listening to it happening again in his mind. 'The blessing is that they'd slowed for the garage. Jackson ran into the road, trying to stop them. From what he told me afterwards, it was the side of the car that banged him. He caught hold of the door handle and they dragged him along for about fifty yards. As soon as they started to speed up, he had to let go.'

'Where were you?'

'I was coming up behind them, sir. I could see it all by then. When Jackson fell, I could have gone after them or taken care of my officer.'

'You made the right choice,' Harper assured him. 'One of ours has priority.'

'Yes, sir.'

'You scared them. Any kind of panic is good.'

'I don't imagine they'll go back to the place, but I have someone watching it.'

No, they were too canny to return. The questions flooded through his mind. Would they have somewhere else lined up? Possibly. Were they growing tired of running? They'd lost half their number. They had to be feeling the strain by now, and today must have made them realize that the end was close. They wouldn't surrender, not a chance of that. Could they vanish, move to another city? No. They were both born and raised here. This and the trenches were what they knew.

Still, how could he talk? Trips to the coast, a couple of times to London. He hadn't exactly seen the world himself.

'What about Templeton? Have you been able to squeeze anything more from him?'

'Honestly, sir, I don't think there was ever much in him.' He sighed. 'He's going to have the next few months full, thinking about his operations.'

The telephone rang. For a second, they both froze. Then Walsh reached out a wary hand and answered.

'For you, sir.' He handed over the receiver, relief showing in his eyes.

'Harper.'

'It's Ricks, sir. Superintendent Sissons suggested I try to reach you there.'

'Anything new to report on these women?'

'Manchester's tactics seem to be working. The force there is containing them. I've been keeping in touch with the man in charge there. He says it's been an invasion, but he's sure it's stopping. Still a few stragglers in the city, but they're gradually arresting those.'

'Going to be us next?'

'That's the intelligence coming out of London. We need to be prepared, sir.'

'Yes.' More demands on his men. He'd need to see where he could spare some. 'What kind of numbers will you need?'

'You're not going to like this, sir. Probably eight to meet every London train for a few days, and wagons to haul them away.'

Inwardly, he groaned. But it was his fault. He hadn't given this the attention it needed. 'And apart from that?'

'Not many.' He hesitated. 'These are women. It means our woman police constable is going to be busy.'

He hadn't considered that. She wouldn't be able to cope with it all. He'd need to swear in a few female Specials. Something for Monday.

'I'll take care of it.'

He felt the weight as he sat in the car. Everything was pressing down on him. The gang in the Model T, Charlotte Radcliffe and the young men in thrall to her, the dead they'd left in their wake. The frustration of trying to catch them and prove their guilt. Now the shoplifters who would be descending on the city. To top it all off, Ash's heart attack and the fear that he would die.

Then there was the constant thread that ran through every day of his life: Annabelle's illness. Tugging at him, pulling him, shaping his life for seven years since the first diagnosis.

He leaned back, feeling the movement as they passed through Sheepscar. Sometimes he wished he could sleep the clock around; perhaps he'd feel rested when he woke and his problems would have vanished.

It cost nothing to dream, as long as you never forgot the reality.

Bingham's voice sliced through his thoughts. 'Home, sir.'

'Thank you.'

'Anything tonight? Will you need me?'

Harper shook his head. 'A quiet night. Go and enjoy yourself and I'll see you on Monday.'

He turned the key in the lock. The sound of voices from the kitchen. He cocked his head, trying to pick them out. Julia, then Mary . . . and finally Annabelle's slow rasp. He let out a sigh. A good day. Things could change in a heartbeat, but at least the evening would begin well.

Another jigsaw, this one a beach scene. Annabelle looked at the picture on the box.

'Do you remember when we used to go to Whitby, Tom?'

'Of course. Once we walked along the beach all the way to Sandsend.'

'Yes.' Her face lit up with a broad smile. 'We had an ice cream, then we walked back again. We stayed in a lovely hotel, and saw . . . was her name Eliza?'

'Elizabeth,' he said. 'Billy Reed's wife.'

'That's right. I liked her.' She frowned. 'I can't remember why we lost touch.'

'It was after Billy died. We just drifted apart.'

'Yes.' Her face cleared as the memory returned. 'He had a heart attack. Just like Ash.'

Her mind was agile today. Everything working, clicking into place. 'Ash should be going home on Monday,' he told her.

'Is there anything we can do, Tom?'

He gave her a gentle smile. This was how she used to be. Caring, ready to help however she could. 'His wife will take care of everything.'

'We should go to Whitby.' Annabelle's words were a croak. 'This summer. One day when it's sunny.'

'I could drive, Mam,' Mary said.

'How can I refuse?' he asked, winking at his daughter. By summer, his wife would have forgotten all this. Even if she remembered it, he doubted she'd be well enough for the trip. Hours in the car over roads that would rattle anyone's bones. Still, it cost nothing to dream . . .

Her mood was steady all evening. Twice she went silent for

a few minutes and Harper was wary. Both times she returned to the conversation with a smile. While Mary and Julia prepared Annabelle for bed he made his nightly rounds, checking the doors and the windows. Exactly the type of thing he did when he was on the beat, he thought with a chuckle, testing every doorknob and inspecting each window.

Back in those days, all he wanted was to become a detective, to work in his own clothes. What would that young man in uniform make of who he'd become? They lived in different worlds. He held no real nostalgia for the past, but things had definitely been simpler then.

All too often now, he felt as if time had managed to slip past him to leave him flailing in its wake. He'd lost his sharpness. But he wanted these cases cleared before he retired. It was a matter of pride.

'You've been quiet tonight,' Annabelle said as they lay in bed. He had his arm around her shoulders, her body pressed against him.

'Work,' he told her. 'Retirement coming up.'

'I know we can't go to the seaside, Tom.' She pushed her face against his neck. 'I'm sorry.'

'For what?'

'Being like this. What I do to you.'

He rolled to face her.

'Don't. You have no reason to apologize. You didn't want all this. I love you, no matter what. In sickness or in health, remember? I promised.'

'But . . .' He waited, but the words she wanted stayed unspoken.

'You're my wife. I love you. Mary loves you.'

He felt her tears trickling over his fingers and pulled her close again.

'Sometimes I'm so scared.'

'I'm here. Soon enough I'll be here all the time.' He smiled, even if she couldn't see it in the darkness. 'You'll wish you had some peace.'

Annabelle was silent for a moment, then she giggled softly. The first time he'd heard that in far too long. The shadow in her soul had passed. For now, at least.

'Give over, Tom,' she said. Her lips found his and they kissed. How had he ever been lucky enough to find her?

NINETEEN

Monday morning. Harper walked into Millgarth. Inspector Jackson had reported for work. Battered, bruised, with cuts to his face and hands. He had that glint in his eye; he craved revenge. Determined to catch the rest of the gang.

'Are you sure you're ready to be back?'

The man stared him in the eye. 'Yes, sir.'

He probably wasn't, Harper thought. But sending him home for another day's rest would dent Jackson's pride. He'd been that way himself. Right now his own body hurt from a Sunday spent digging in the garden. Muscles he'd forgotten he possessed ached. But nothing like trying to stop a motor car.

'Fine. Now find them.'

'How's Mr Ash, sir?' Walsh asked. They'd served together for several years, both part of Harper's squad when he ran Millgarth.

'I telephoned the infirmary first thing. If the doctor approved when he made his rounds, he should be on his way home by now.'

'There'll be plenty on the force glad to hear that.'

Very true. Ash knew everyone; his network extended far beyond the police, across the city. Everybody liked him. The offers of help would pour in.

The bank was a solid building on Park Row, two minutes' walk from the town hall. The financial institutions stood there, banks, insurance companies, all gathered together in a small area. An elaborate stone carving rose high above the high door. It was probably meant to show prosperity, or something similar, he supposed. Solidity and reliability.

A mention of his rank saw him ushered straight upstairs to Robert Wilton's office. A polished brass nameplate on the door, thick carpets everywhere to absorb all the footsteps. As hushed and reverent as an undertaker's parlour. More expensive, though. Good paintings on the walls, heavy leather club chairs and a large desk. Windows that looked down on the street.

'Chief Constable,' Wilton said. He came around, ready to shake hands. 'I'm not sure what you think I can do for you.'

He had that moneyed sleekness, a well-cut suit, the precise haircut that probably cost far too much. The sense that nothing had ever touched him, and never would. A bruise stood out high on his cheek.

'A souvenir from your point-to-point?'

Wilton rubbed it and winced. 'How did you know about that?'

'I'm in charge of the police. It's my job.'

They sat on either side of the huge desk, as if it was a continent that divided them. Wilton rang through for his secretary to bring them coffee.

Once they were all settled, the man repeated his question: 'So, what do you want?'

'I'm sure you know. Charles Radcliffe, Ben Rogers.' He paused. 'Do you need me to say more?'

'I've lost two of my best friends. We've—'

'—known each other forever. I've heard that line a few times. And you've all been with Charlotte Radcliffe. I imagine you're all still in love with her.'

Wilton looked amused at the idea. 'Maybe we are. After all, she was the first for us.'

'First?' Harper asked.

A small, soft laugh. 'What do you think I mean, Chief Constable?'

Interesting. A fact to store away.

'How well do you know Timothy Gordon, Mr Wilton?'

A moment of panic crossed his face. His eyes flickered towards the door, hoping that some saviour might walk in.

'As well as I know all the others.' He took a cigarette from the case on the desk and his thumb snapped against the lighter. 'Why?'

'Then you might well be aware that a neighbour of his had his car stolen and damaged.'

'No.' Wilton's voice was bland. 'Bad luck for him, but isn't that too trivial to have someone of your rank asking questions?'

'Ordinarily, yes. But we're sure the car was used to force your friend Ben off the road. The crash caused his death.'

His body stiffened. 'I'm very aware of what happened to Ben. I was one of his pallbearers.'

'What you probably won't have heard is that we've taken finger-prints from the car, and there are a couple we can't identify.'

Gordon had kept his word; he hadn't spoken to the others. Wilton did a good job of not letting his expression fall. But Harper could almost see the man's mind racing over everything: he was sure he'd worn gloves, but was there a moment when he might have touched something in the car without them?

'What are you suggesting?' The smoothness was sucked away for a moment and Harper had a quick glimpse of a lost little boy. Better.

'Nothing,' he replied with a smile. 'We're trying to eliminate all the possibilities. I'm sure you'll be happy to let us take your prints, Mr Wilton. It can help bring some justice to your friend. I'm certain you want that.'

'Of course. But . . . I need to check with my solicitor first.'

'Naturally.' Harper placed the cup and saucer on the desk and stood, bringing out a card from his pocket. 'We'll be in touch and arrange a time for you to come in. It doesn't take long. I appreciate you're a busy man.' A nod of the head. 'Good day.'

As simple as that. A huge bluff. It would be interesting to see what Robert Wilton did next.

The Leeds Stock Exchange was in an imposing building at the corner of Albion Place and Albion Street. He'd been inside a couple of times before, always surprised at the quiet and decorum as men conducted their business.

Daniel Anderson had a drinker's face. Bloated and fleshy, with a red crackling of tiny veins across his nose. The same age as the other men in this case, but he looked a generation older.

His office was little more than a cubbyhole upstairs, the desk thick with paper, with barely enough space for two chairs, the kind of room where the walls seemed to press in as soon as the door was closed.

'You fought in the war, I understand.'

'Yes.' Anderson lit a cigarette, taking quick, short drags. 'I was a lieutenant. Joined in '18, trained up just in time for Amiens. Started as a subaltern, then promoted to full lieutenant in a month. Only two of our intake were still alive by then.'

'It must have been awful.'

He bowed his head, looking down at the floor. 'I was barely out of school. My only experience of life had been the officers' training camp.' He stared at Harper. 'What do you think?'

'What you went through, it must have set you apart from your friends.'

'We're chums, I still see them often.' He frowned. 'There's a distance between us. There has to be. They can't understand what it was like.'

'Nor can I,' Harper said. 'My daughter's fiancé vanished at the Somme.'

Anderson nodded. 'Some of my men fought there. Said it was worse than Amiens.' A raw grimace. 'Hard to believe.'

'You were involved with Charlotte Radcliffe?'

'For a week after I returned from the front. It was a bit of fun.' A sour smile. 'Her gift to a hero, perhaps.'

'And since?'

He shook his head. 'I'm not the best company, Chief Constable.' A bemused smile. 'You might have heard that I like a drink.'

'I have.' No point in lying.

'It's how I cope. With all this, with life. With everything that happened. It means I can sleep.'

'Were you close to Ben Rogers?'

'Once,' he said after a long hesitation. 'A long time ago. But I was close to them all back then.'

'Do you resent them?' Harper asked. 'After all, they all managed to stay at home. Safe in Leeds.'

'When I came back, I did. They seemed like children. Now?' He shrugged. 'I don't really think about it.'

'How did you feel when you learned that Charles Radcliffe and Ben Rogers had died?'

He was silent again, finishing the cigarette and stubbing it out in a metal ashtray. 'Surprised. Charles had everything, no worries in the world. I can't imagine why he'd take his own life. And Ben . . . he could be reckless in that car, but it shocked me.'

'Did it touch you?'

'I suppose it did. I'd seen so many die, but this was different.' He glanced up at the ceiling, then back. 'These happened *here*. The war's over, we're supposed to be safe. I helped carry both coffins.'

Time to surprise him, Harper thought.

'What if I said that both those deaths were murder?'

'What?' He craned forward, his expression suddenly intent. 'But . . .'

He wasn't lying, not try to cover up anything. He genuinely didn't know. It had jolted him.

'We're not certain, but it appears that way.' A small hesitation. 'What do you know about blackmail, Mr Anderson?'

'Me?' He seemed astonished by the question. 'Nothing. Why would I?'

The words had the clear sound of truth. Anderson was a drunk, trying to fumble his way through the world, but he wasn't a killer. He hadn't been part of the blackmail; probably the others decided he wasn't reliable, and they might have been right.

'Alderman Thompson would like to see you,' Miss Sharp said. 'So would Mr Dickinson, when you have chance. And Superintendent Walsh rang. He said to tell you that they're still searching. All the papers to be signed are waiting on your desk.'

He laughed. 'Is there anything else?'

She sniffed. 'Do you want a cup of tea or not?'

'As soon as I've talked to the alderman.'

'Any more word on Mr Ash?'

'All being well, he's at home even as we speak.'

Thompson had a face like thunder, the storm about to break.

'You don't have the letters yet.'

'No, I don't. But I have two bodies, both of them probably murdered, and one of my investigators just left the hospital after a heart attack.'

'Who?'

'Ash. He's going to be fine. We hope so, anyway.'

'I'm sorry, I didn't know.' At least he had the decency to apologize. 'Who's replacing him?'

'Turns out you're getting your first wish. I've taken over. I've just come from talking to two people.'

'Good. No more excuses, then.'

'Excuses?' Harper could feel temper beginning to stir.

'Always some reason for not having it done, and it's grown out of hand.'

'Let me remind you of something, Alderman. You were the one who began all this. I don't know what you were thinking when you started something with Miss Radcliffe. But everything that's happened since is because of that. You asked me to clean up your mess, to sweep it all under the carpet and make sure it stays there. Now you tell me I'm not doing it fast enough to please you. You need to make up your mind.'

He stood and stalked out of the office, leaving the door open. He'd probably been stupid to let rip like that, but by God, it felt good. What did he have to lose? Thompson didn't have a hold over him any longer; he'd be retired before you could say Jack Robinson. Harper smiled to himself as he walked along the corridor, suddenly rid of all the frustrations that had been plaguing him.

'I appreciate you taking the weight of the paperwork from me.'

Deputy Chief Constable Albert Dickinson shrugged. 'It's like I told you, sir, I enjoy it. Some people are made for that sort of thing. I must be one of them.'

'Ready to move into this office next month?' Harper asked. 'It's not long now.'

'I'll have big shoes to fill. That's what everyone tells me, anyway.'

Harper laughed. 'Don't believe a word.' He paused while Miss Sharp appeared with tea and biscuits.

'I'm just a place marker until they appoint someone new.'

True enough; at least he understood that. 'You'll be fine.'

'I wondered if there's anything else bubbling up that might be important.'

'There is.' He explained about the shoplifting gang. 'Apart from that, it's just the two outstanding cases. Everything else is minor.'

'Any progress on those two, sir?'

A quiet snort. 'Just what you'll have heard. Not enough.'

'That one with Thompson seems to have taken some bizarre turns. Do you really think one of the men who beat him committed suicide?'

'We don't know,' Harper answered. 'It's possible.'

'The scuttlebutt is that there's another death involved.'

He sighed; secrets were hard to keep in the force. It was a miracle they'd managed to keep Thompson's blackmail quiet.

'It's possible.' At least the rumours about Rogers being forced off the road hadn't spread. Thank heaven for small mercies. 'There's so much we don't know. I'm not sure we'll ever untangle it fully.'

But he hoped to God that they would.

He walked and thought. Almost mid-April and warm enough to be outside without an overcoat. Close to the Cork and Bottle he passed a man begging, an empty socket where his left eye had once been, burns on the skin all around. Another victim of the war. They'd be around for years to come, the reminders of it all. He put sixpence in the man's tray. It wouldn't change things, but it might make today easier for him.

Every week, fewer and fewer bothered with gauze masks. Deaths from the Spanish flu were still falling. With luck, the epidemic seemed to be almost over. One day they might discover exactly how many it had killed. Only the Model T gang still liked the masks, he thought wryly.

He cut down Lands Lane to Commercial Street and through towards Briggate. The streets were busy; he had to squeeze between people and keep a wary eye out for traffic along the road.

Daniel Anderson. He was a shell of a man, really, someone who managed to function from day to day. Everything inside had been blasted away at Amiens. God only knew how much killing he'd seen there. But Harper was convinced he hadn't been involved in the murders of Charles Radcliffe or Ben Rogers. The man didn't have that in him, and the others wouldn't trust him enough.

Robert Wilton? Guilty of pushing Rogers off the road. Harper knew it, he felt it in his water. The man was terrified. But the police still didn't have a scrap of evidence. Bluffing a confession out of him would be the only way.

Was he also the mystery man who'd pushed Charles Radcliffe in front of the express train? Maybe that one really was suicide; the statements on a second man were so thin they were hardly there. He wondered if they'd ever really discover the truth.

Then there was Charlotte Radcliffe, the spider who waited for victims at the centre of the web. It all began with her, and the power she seemed to exercise over men. But after two deaths, it was careening out of control.

In court she'd beguile all the men. Judge, jury, lawyers. He was sure of that. But if she ended up in the dock, everything about Thompson would spill out . . .

Without even thinking, his feet had led him down to Millgarth. Old habits.

'Nothing more, sir,' Walsh told him. 'We're scouring the area where we found them—'

'They'll have moved somewhere different.'

A nod. 'We still have to check, sir. With this pair, you can never tell.'

'They'll strike again. If you want my guess, they'll be out there tomorrow. They need to prove something to us. Where's Jackson?'

'I sent him home. He wants the gang, but he needs another day of rest. He took quite a battering when he tried to stop that car.'

'Let's have him fighting fit.' He paused for a moment, weighing a thought in his head. 'Tell me, how tightly stretched are you between this case and running the division?'

Walsh pressed his lips together, worry in his eyes. 'About ready to snap, sir. Why?'

'There's something I need from you. You were always my best interrogator.'

'Thank you, sir. I think . . .'

He'd wait to ring Wilton. Let him begin to feel secure and start to smile again. Then an invitation to Millgarth for fingerprinting later in the week. A statement while he was there, just the things he'd said in his office. Purely a formality, sir, nothing out of the ordinary. Enough time for his fear to build and leave him on edge. Then Walsh could start work on him. Put him in one of the interview rooms, where the scent of terror seeped out of the plaster.

He'd need to give the superintendent all the background, bring him into the secret. But he knew he could trust the man.

Things were beginning to move. Slowly, creakily, but by the end of the week he'd have plenty more. Still no idea what he could do about Charlotte Radcliffe, though. That needed more thought. Maybe Wilton would give him a direction.

'Sergeant Ricks,' he said as he poked his head around the door of the intelligence section. 'Anything new to report on these women?'

'Same as it was, sir. I'll let you know when there's a change.'

'I've arranged for these men to be available.' He handed over a list. 'I talked to our policewoman. She'll come up with the names of ten women who served on the voluntary patrols to act as special constables for this.'

Ricks beamed with pleasure. His first command, and it was going to be a big one. 'Thank you, sir.'

Ten o'clock the next morning, his car pulled up outside Ash's house. Harper knocked on the door. No flowers, no fruit, no arms weighed down with magazines. Just himself, in an overcoat today, the weather chillier again, more the way April should be.

'Is he up?'

'Of course he is,' Nancy Ash said. 'I'm not going to have him lazing around in bed all day. He's in the parlour. Go through.'

TWENTY

Harper stood outside the house, talking to the two men who'd been visiting Ash. They had the look of retired coppers: substantial, solid. When they moved, they had the rocking gait that came from years spent walking the beat.

'Your timing's very good, sir,' Ash had said when Harper

entered the parlour. He introduced the men. 'This is the pair who've been helping on the case.'

Sitting in an easy chair, with a rug tucked around him, face pale and jowls hanging, the man looked every inch an invalid. But there was a light in his eyes, and an impish delight in his smile.

'How are you?'

'The hospital gave me very good care, but there's nothing like your own bed for a proper rest.'

A quarter of an hour, then Nancy was shooing them out into the tiny front garden: Harper, along with Richard Thornton and Joe Franklin, both a year or two off the force and glad of something to fill their time. They squeezed into the car and back to the town hall, gazing around with a mix of suspicion and pleasure as he led them into his office. Their first time with a chief constable.

They'd done work on the case, digging up background on Rogers and Charles Radcliffe. A little more on the other men in the set.

'Did you talk to the cleaners and the cooks?'

Most of Thornton's hair had gone, the scalp shiny as he ran a hand over it and glanced across at Franklin. They were both bulky men who looked as if they'd added weight since they stopped pounding along the streets.

'We did, sir. Plenty of gossip. If it's true, they're not a pleasant bunch. But we didn't come up with anything of use to us here.'

It had been worth a shot. 'I have another job for you. See what you can find out about Robert Wilton in the next two days.'

'Very good, sir,' Thornton answered. 'We'd already put together a few things for Freddie before he took poorly. We can let you have that and see what else there is.'

Simply arranged. If Ash thought they were good, that was enough for him. But he had no memory of either man in uniform. Getting old, he thought, getting old. Back in the office, he lifted the phone.

'Do you have a few spare minutes for your da to buy you a very late dinner?'

Maybe she'd given away all the old frocks. Today it was a cotton dress, a dark rose colour, reaching to the middle of her calf. A short fox fur jacket and a small hat. A woman of the moment, moving confidently through life.

Their usual meal, the same chat as every time. About Annabelle's health, Mary's business. His plans after retirement. So close now, but still so far away, waiting on the other side of Charlotte Radcliffe, the Model T gang and the shoplifters.

'You look tired, Da.' He heard the concern in her voice. 'Are you all right?'

'Fine.' Harper found a smile for her. 'Nothing to worry about.' He shrugged and sighed. 'Just the old story: cases.'

'You can walk away from them at the end of the month, you know.'

'I know.' He tapped his head. 'Well, I know it here.' Another tap over his heart. 'This hasn't received the message yet.'

'You won't change, will you?'

'No,' he agreed. 'It's probably too late for that.'

He felt her eyes peering into him. 'Tell me something: what will you do if they aren't solved by the end of the month?'

He didn't know. He'd never considered the possibility. Everything would be tied up, because . . . because it had to be. A neat ending to a long career. It couldn't be any other way.

'I don't know,' he admitted.

'You can't stay on.'

'No.' He chuckled. 'Poor Albert Dickinson would be chucking me out of his office.'

She placed a hand over his. 'Maybe you ought to think about it, Da. Life doesn't always do what we want.'

An image of Annabelle came into his mind. 'Believe me, I know that.'

The child being mother to the man, he thought wryly. Had he really reached that age?

It hadn't been the distraction he'd hoped, Harper thought, as he escorted Mary to her office then strolled back down to Millgarth. Still, maybe it had been the one he needed, hearing a few truths spoken out loud.

Walsh sat at his desk, head in his hands.

'Again?' Harper said.

A nod. 'The bastards.' He looked up, a man pushed to the verge of tears.

'Where this time?'

'Less than two minutes from here. Just up on Harewood Street, that little place that buys old gold.' Not just proving something to the police, this was stamping their faces in it.

'Same way?'

'To the last detail. Gone before anyone can react. I've got to tell you, sir, I'm at the end of my tether with this.'

'I've felt that way on cases before. Something will happen.'

Walsh sounded beyond hope. 'When?'

Not as chilly in the morning, as if the weather couldn't decide what it was going to do. Harper opened the door and stepped outside to wait for the car. He felt something hard under his shoe and looked down. Another brown paper bag. No need to look; he knew exactly what was inside. He picked it up, weighed it in his hand and stuck it in the pocket of his jacket. They were giving two fingers to Leeds City Police.

'Where are we starting today, sir?' Bingham asked.

'Millgarth.'

The scrapes and cuts on Jackson's face and hand were scabbing over. His two broken fingers were splinted and taped together. In a fortnight they'd be a memory, a pain to bother him when the weather turned damp.

Harper brought out the bag and tossed it on the desk.

'Where was it?' Walsh pushed his fingers through his hair.

'Waiting on my doorstep.' Definitely rubbing their faces in it. 'That's the second time. Let's find them. I've had enough.'

In his office, the papers he needed to read and sign were waiting on his desk. If it wasn't something requiring attention before the end of the month, he wondered, why bother? But he did his duty for the first part of the morning, then sat back and considered when to see Charlotte Radcliffe again.

After Walsh had questioned Robert Wilton, he decided. The superintendent would drag the man's answers and guilt out of him. After that he'd be ready to face her again. Retrieve Thompson's love letters and hand them back to him. But whatever debt the alderman felt wouldn't extend beyond Harper's retirement.

The bag on the doorstep right as the day began had soured his mood. A few arrests would improve it, but he wasn't about to hold his breath.

Harper picked up and waited as the operator connected him to Wilton's bank.

'This is Chief Constable Harper.'

The title always brought results. A few seconds and he was speaking to the man.

'I know you answered my questions when we talked, Mr Wilton. You were very generous with your time.' That was the bait. 'Did you talk to your lawyer about giving us fingerprints? Good. For the records, we'll need an official statement, too, just what you told me when we met. It keeps everything formal and means we have it on paper. Could you come to Millgarth police station on Saturday morning to give one?'

'I'm supposed to be riding on Saturday,' Wilton said.

'This won't take long.'

A long pause. 'If we do it early.'

'As early as you please.'

'How about eight o'clock?'

'Excellent. Thank you.' Now the trap was set.

A call to Walsh. 'That favour I mentioned. There's a man called Wilton coming in on Saturday morning. He's due at eight. I questioned him, and he believes he's coming in to give his fingerprints and make a statement. He lied to me and I want you to tear him apart.'

'Yes, sir, but—'

'Don't worry. I'll see you have all the background and the notes from my talk with him.'

'You haven't said what this relates to, sir.'

'No,' Harper agreed. 'At the moment, it's part of something that doesn't officially exist.'

'Sir?' He sounded completely confused.

'I'll buy you dinner and explain everything. It'll do you good to take a break from the office. And I'm sorry about earlier. I know you're all doing everything you can.'

'This pair are going to be the death of me.'

'Not before I retire, they're not. I don't want to have to appoint someone to run A division.'

At least it made Walsh laugh. Harper took a pad, dipped his nib in the inkwell, and began to write.

They met at the café in the market. Up the iron steps to the balcony where they could gaze down on the stalls. Walsh was sitting at the table, looking relieved to be away from the station.

'Here,' Harper said, and brought a thick sealed envelope from his jacket. 'This is everything I can remember of the questioning. The man's name is Robert Wilton. He's some high muckety-muck in the bank his father runs.'

'I see.' Walsh tucked the envelope away. 'What's he supposed to have done, sir?'

'Stolen a car and helped to kill someone.'

The man didn't flinch or jump in shock. He'd been a copper too long for that, Harper thought. Just nodded and said again, 'I see.'

'There are wheels within wheels going on here. Whatever you think you know, there's more to it.' That brought a look of bafflement. Harper produced another envelope. 'This is all the background. Read this one first and you'll understand.'

Walsh handled it like it might explode. 'And if there's anything that doesn't make sense, sir?'

'You ask me.' He hesitated, then emphasized the words. 'But only me. Understood?'

A frown. 'Of course.'

'Don't worry, there's a logic of sorts. But you can't talk about it with any of your men. Not even Jackson. Sissons is the only other person on the force who knows everything. He's been working on it.'

'Was Mr Ash involved?'

Harper smiled. 'I've taken over what he was doing. That's why I'm not breathing down your neck on the Model T gang.'

Reminded of his failure, the corners of Walsh's mouth turned down. 'Nothing new on that, sir.'

'We've chopped away at them. Have you questioned the one in hospital again?'

'Templeton? A couple of times, sir.' He chuckled. 'He's not

likely to run off. As soon as he's well enough, we'll have him
in court. Then the hospital wing at Armley gaol.'

'How much has he given you?'

'Very little. I don't think he was ever privy to a lot. Hobson
told the others what they needed and nothing more. He arranged
everything and kept it to himself.'

'Were they happy with that?' If it was him, he'd be asking
questions, needing information and answers.

'He's their lance-corporal. He kept them alive when they were
all on the line. They trust him.'

He thought of Trevor Curtis, the executed man. 'And he's
responsible for their deaths.'

'According to Templeton, they all agreed on that. Curtis had
broken the rule, he'd put them in danger.'

They kept their own, brutal laws. Hobson had to be a hard,
unyielding man. Maybe that was what they needed to stay alive
in wartime France. But this was England, and the country was
supposed to have ended its fighting.

An hour, Harper decided as he hung up his raincoat. That should
be long enough for Walsh to read both documents and wonder just
what the hell he'd agreed to do. He was presuming on the man's
loyalty. Not to the force, but to him. It was a great deal to ask.

When the phone rang, he took out his pocket watch. Fifty-three
minutes. Close.

'Sir, you—' Walsh began.

'I am. I'm very serious.'

'We're covering up crimes.'

'I know exactly what we're doing. Officially, we're investigating the beating Alderman Thompson received. As I wrote, the
motive is unknown. One of the suspects apparently took his own
life. We have no idea why. The other drove off a road. His car
might have been hit by another. You're interviewing the man we
believe stole and drove that other car.'

'What if he admits it?'

'I'm sure he will. We'll need to come up with some charge.'

'You know that none of this comes within a mile of the truth,
sir.'

'I do. And you understand why.'

'We're protecting the alderman's reputation.'

'That's right.'

'I'll do it, sir but I want to ask a question first.'

He knew what he was about to hear. 'Go ahead.'

'Is Alderman Thompson really worth it, sir?'

Harper sat, exhaled slowly, then said, 'I'll give you an honest answer. I don't know.'

He lowered the receiver. Well? He asked himself. Was the man worth what they were doing?

'Two men to see you.' Miss Sharp had closed the door as she entered, speaking in a low voice by his good ear. 'They wouldn't give their names, but they're both getting on a bit. They look like they might have been policemen.'

'Show them in, please.' Ash's retired friends, bringing information. 'Tea if you can.'

The pair had worked quickly and effectively. A day and a half and they'd turned up plenty of information on Robert Wilton to fill out the little that Sissons had provided. Harper scribbled notes as they talked, stopping sometimes to ask questions, then crossing out and changing phrases.

By the time they finished, his notes were scratchy and messy. He'd make a tidy copy and pass it to Walsh before Saturday's interrogation. With all this, the superintendent would know Wilton better than he knew himself.

'I'm impressed,' he said when they were done. In a short time, they'd put more together than he could ever have managed. 'You should have been detectives.'

Thornton glanced at Franklin and the pair of them shared a grin. 'No offence, sir, but we was never that interested. Happy on our beats, talking to people. Funny how many you end up knowing across the years.'

'I remember,' Harper said. 'I had those old courts that were torn down to build the arcades. A long time ago now.' He studied the pair. Earnest, honest faces, although that didn't mean a thing. 'Tell me, would you be interested in more work?'

Thornton hesitated before answering. 'I thought you were retiring very soon, sir.'

He laughed. 'I am, but the man in charge of our intelligence section might be able to throw something your way.' He stood. 'Come with me.'

Sissons looked unnerved by three people squeezing into his little domain. Polite as ever, he stood awkwardly as Harper introduced the two men.

'They're friends of Mr Ash,' he explained. 'They've done some work on our case.' No names, definitely not in the town hall where the walls might have ears. 'I've just heard some of their results, and they're good. I thought I'd introduce you to them. For the future.' He nodded. 'Gentlemen, I'll leave you to it, and thank you. That's excellent work.'

Alone in his office, Harper copied out the notes and sealed them in an envelope, then tore the old sheets into tiny shreds.

Almost ten o'clock. Annabelle was already in bed. He was sitting in the parlour, reading through the *Evening Post* as the phone began to ring. His body ached as he pushed himself upright and strode into the hall. Growing old. Older, anyway.

'Inspector Jackson, sir.' He sounded out of breath.

'Our gang again?' What? It was too late for a robbery.

'We have a dead copper, sir. Shot.'

'What? Who?'

'I'm in a telephone box in Beeston, sir, and I don't have any more change. Despatch has the address.'

The street stood at the top of a hill, looking down over Elland Road football ground. The neighbours were standing on their doorsteps as constables grimly moved from house to house, asking questions. The body had been taken away for the post-mortem. Jackson was directing everything, capable, handling it all well. Harper had just arrived, and was talking to Chambers, the local division superintendent, when another car pulled up and Walsh stepped out.

'What was the constable's name?'

'Endicott,' Chambers replied. 'Simon Endicott. Joined up last year, as soon as he turned eighteen.'

Maybe it had been his dream, becoming a copper as soon as he was old enough, Harper thought, just the way he'd been himself.

'Poor lad.' Walsh shook his head.

A funeral with full honours. But someone of that age should have had years to look ahead. Certainly now the war was done.

'Looks like it was this gang of yours,' Chambers said.

'How did it happen?' Harper broke away from his thoughts.

'We're just guessing. Seems like the gang had just moved in here, no more than three days ago. People heard the shots—'

'Shots?' He leaped on the word. 'More than one?'

'Three of them, sir. Nobody's claimed they saw the killing. But two men driving off in a car with dirty number plates right after the shots . . . it has to be them, doesn't it?'

'It does,' Walsh agreed. 'Why, though? Why now? Do we have any idea?'

'Not really. We can piece things together, but we'll never know for sure. Endicott's body was on the doorstep. Plenty of blood, so he was shot there. He must have spotted something to rouse his suspicions and went to the house to ask questions. The bastards shot him where he stood. He probably never even had chance to speak. Grabbed what they could and ran.'

'Did anyone here know them? Harper asked. 'Had anyone talked to them?'

'We're trying to establish that, sir.'

Walsh had gone, talking to Jackson and gazing at the scene.

'Tell me about Endicott,' Harper said.

'As pleasant a lad as you could hope to meet,' Chambers replied. He was close to tears. 'I know we always say that, but it's true, sir. His family live down the street from my brother. Eager, learning fast. He'd have made a good copper . . .'

'If he'd had the time.'

Chambers nodded.

Christ Almighty, what a waste. So bloody young. Like the soldiers who died on the battlefields.

'These two are really going to be desperate now, sir.'

'They already were,' he said. 'That's why they did this.'

Harper walked up and down the road. A long row of terraced houses with small front gardens, two steps up to the front door. So many streets in Leeds looked exactly the same. The killing was the only remarkable thing about this place. Lights were burning in most of the houses. Knots of people gathered, talking.

There was nothing more he could do here. Nothing to see. Suddenly he felt weary all the way to his bones.

'Take me home,' he told the driver.

TWENTY-ONE

'What do we have?' Harper asked.

He stood in the detectives' room at Millgarth, at a little after seven in the morning. Walsh and Jackson were both unshaven, suits creased, the bags heavy and shadowed under their eyes.

'We're still guessing as to exactly what happened,' Jackson answered. 'One neighbour had talked to Will Hobson. They'd only been there since the start of the week. The house was furnished when they rented it. The two of them arrived with a suitcase each. Probably left with what they were wearing and that's all.'

'And now they've killed a policeman. Nothing they can do will make up for that.'

'Might make it easier to find them, sir,' Walsh said. 'People will let us know.'

'Maybe,' he agreed. 'But they're going to hang. They probably always were, but there's no doubt about it now.' He waited the length of a heartbeat. 'Make sure every officer knows to take care. Don't approach these men alone. One copper or a dozen, it's not going to make any difference to them now.'

'If I were them, I'd leave Leeds.' Jackson's voice spilled into the silence.

'Maybe they have. Be sure you send an alert to all forces.'

Walsh nodded and scribbled in his notebook. 'It'll go out this morning.'

They were doing everything possible, he thought, men already pushed as far as they could go. Now they had more reason than ever to keep going, with one of their own on a cold table in the morgue.

Before he left, Harper slipped into the superintendent's office.

'I know you have this on your plate, but you haven't forgotten the other thing I need, have you?'

'No, sir.' He sighed. 'It's just—'

'You're the best I have at asking questions. I know you don't like what we're doing. I don't blame you; I can't say I relish it, either. But this is how things are.' He brought out an envelope, the evidence from Ash's retired coppers. They'd had long lives, he thought. More than Endicott managed. 'This will tell you more about him. I don't think he'll give you much trouble.'

'We're stretched to breaking point here, sir.'

Harper calculated how many officers he could spare. He'd already agreed to let Ricks have some, but that was before a copper was murdered. That took precedence over everything else. 'I can give you eight men now. More very soon. Three more detectives.'

He'd be stripping every division to do it, but this was vital.

Relief flooded across Walsh's voice. 'You're a lifesaver.'

'No, I'm not.' Not when one of his officers had died. He shook his head sadly. 'I wish I could be.'

'I heard,' Miss Sharp said. 'Poor boy.'

'I know. I know.'

In his office, Harper settled in the chair. After he'd reached home last night, he'd slept. No troubled dreams; now that ease of rest left him full of guilt.

Papers waiting on his desk. Work as usual while the world turned upside down. A policeman murdered. He read and signed and wondered when he'd become so inured to death that it no longer disturbed his nights. Had it happened to soldiers during the war, when the number killed each day was beyond comprehension? During the flu, perhaps. Definitely a sign that it was time to retire.

He picked up the telephone receiver. A series of calls to make.

Sissons perched awkwardly on the seat at the Kardomah. He'd eaten the toasted cheese right down to the last crumbs and now he was sipping his coffee and gazing around as if he was trying to memorize every face in the restaurant.

'How do we trap Charlotte Radcliffe?' Harper asked. This was the reason he'd brought him here, away from the town hall and curious ears.

'The only way I can see it happening is from someone else's testimony, sir. You said that Walsh is going to talk to Wilton.'

'On Saturday.'

A nod, and his Adam's apple bobbed up and down. 'Is he guilty of running Rogers off the road?'

Harper thought back to sitting in Wilton's office at the bank. 'I'm certain of that. What I'm not sure about is whether he'll implicate the woman.'

'Maybe she didn't do anything directly, sir.'

He narrowed his eyes. 'What do you mean?'

'Do you know those mechanical toys, sir? You wind them up then put them on the floor and they start to walk.'

'Yes.'

'Maybe it's like that; all she did was wind up these men and point them in the right direction. We know they're under her spell, they have been since they were very young. Start them on the blackmail and let it take its course from there.'

'It's an interesting idea,' he allowed. 'But doesn't she strike you as the type who craves control?'

Sissons smiled. 'There's control in causing chaos, too.'

Harper rubbed his chin. This was hard to understand, never mind believe. 'Even if it causes the death of her brother and another of their friends?'

'For that to matter, you need to assume she cares about these men.'

'She must. Surely . . .' The idea shocked him. 'Her own brother . . .'

He grimaced. 'I know. I don't have any evidence. It's just an idea, sir. But it makes a certain amount of sense.'

He examined the idea as he walked down to Millgarth, looking at it from every direction. In forty years on the force, he'd faced all sorts on the job. Killers and people who ended up dead. But it was hard to believe that Charlotte Radcliffe would be so indifferent to these people. Even her own brother. He'd need to think much more about that.

*   *   *

Men were busy in the detectives' room. All the new faces he'd drafted in to help. Someone had pinned a photograph of PC Endicott to the wall. Harper studied it as people moved all around him. He stood tall and proud in his uniform, so young and earnest and hopeful. The way all of them had once been, many years ago. Now he'd never share the joys of those who remained.

It was good to keep the picture where everyone could see it. It reminded them what could happen and why they were doing this.

'A constable marched in and put it up,' Walsh said. 'I could hardly tell him to take it down, could I, sir?'

'Maybe it'll be a good spur.' The air was thick with smoke from pipes and cigarettes. 'Have all the extra men I arranged reported?'

'Already busy chasing leads.'

When this case was done, the superintendent would need a break. A little time away from here. Each day he seemed a little smaller, ground down by the frustration and disappointment.

Harper glanced around the room. Experienced men with hard, determined faces, and the constant reminder of why they were doing this.

The desk sergeant brought in the *Evening Post* and handed it to Walsh.

POLICE KILLERS STILL ON LOOSE, the headline read, and underneath, in slightly smaller type, WE ALL NEED TO HELP WITH JUSTICE.

'Think it'll make much of a difference, sir?' he asked in a weary voice.

The story took up most of the front page. He'd spoken to the editor himself; they'd worked up the coverage between them. Something similar for the *Yorkshire Post* in the morning. There would be stories in the national dailies, too.

Full descriptions of Booth and Hobson and the car. Everything he'd asked the editor to include.

'The tips should start to flood in very soon. Let's investigate every single one. You never know . . .'

'Yes, sir.'

'But make sure they're careful. Emphasize it.' He nodded

towards Endicott's photograph. 'We can't risk another of those.
Telephone me if you have anything solid.'

Definitely spring. He reached the crest of the Headrow, the hill
falling away in front of him, down towards the town hall. The
tower rose high, the clock large enough to read the time from a
quarter of a mile away. By its sheer size, the building dominated
the city.

A man walked towards him, wearing a cap and gauze mask.
The gang had used a clever disguise, no doubt about that. But
life was trying to find some new kind of normal after the war
and the influenza. What would it be like? The trench and barbed
wire had shorn Leeds of a generation of young men. Every family
carried some pain. The trick would be to look forward and fashion
a life on top of it.

'Your wife's nurse rang,' Miss Sharp said as soon as he entered
the office. Her voice was clear and grave. 'Can you go home as
soon as possible?'

'How long ago?' His stomach lurched. Fear crawled all over
his skin.

'About ten minutes. I'd just missed you at Millgarth. I'll ring
for your car.'

The drive seemed to take forever, even with Bingham going
as fast as he dared. He'd telephoned Mary and her Model T
was parked outside the house when his car pulled up.

'I hope it's nothing, sir.'

'Thank you.' But Julia would only ring him at work if it was
serious.

He could hardly breathe as he unlocked the door. Voices from
the parlour. But when he opened the door, he blinked in disbelief.
The mantelpiece had been swept clean, ornaments, the clock,
shattered in pieces on the floor.

Annabelle sat in her chair, eyes open but looking at nothing,
lips pinched together, completely divorced from the world. Julia
and Mary hovered by her and the doctor was closing his bag.
He stared at Harper and nodded.

'She's drained herself. I've given her something. She'll sleep.'
He wore his morning coat and striped trousers, along with the

old-fashioned wing collar and tie, as if they gave him authority. 'I'll let myself out.'

'Thank you for coming,' Harper said. He picked out the sound of the front door closing and turned to Julia. 'What happened?'

The nurse had a cut on her face, another along the back of her left hand. For the first time since she'd come to work for them, she looked shaken.

'She had a good morning. She didn't speak, but we played Ludo and she was doing well. She was alert. Just . . . empty, somehow.' Her eyes were moist. 'After dinner she normally has forty winks. But she didn't want to sleep today.' A small hesitation. 'She stared, but she seemed fine. About an hour ago, I went to make us both a cup of tea.' Julia took a deep breath.

'Go on,' he said.

'When I came back, everything felt different. I know it doesn't make sense, but the atmosphere had changed. I'm not sure I can explain it. It felt . . . darker, somehow.'

'Was Annabelle any different?'

'Her voice was sharper. She snapped at me. She does that sometimes when she's bad, but this, it was . . . I don't know. Something was going to happen. She started to push herself out of the chair. I thought she needed the toilet. I helped her stand up.' She hugged herself. 'When I did, she began to hit me. Scratch me. She pushed me away. I fell down.'

Harper glanced at his wife. She seemed small, frail. Weak. But he knew full well that when things turned, anyone could become strong and violent. A force outside of themselves took over.

He nodded towards the damage. 'That's when she did that?'

'Before I could stop her,' Julia answered. 'I'm sorry.'

'It doesn't matter.' They were just things; they could be replaced. 'I'm more concerned about you.'

'I'm fine, honestly,' she said, although she was pale. 'I didn't think she could move so fast. I couldn't believe it. I had to hold her and help her back to the chair. She'd have destroyed half the room otherwise.'

'You did very well,' Harper told her.

'Whatever the doctor gave me mam is starting to work,' Mary said. 'She's looking woozy. We'd better get her to bed.'

Julia began to move. Harper placed a hand on her arm.

'Thank you. Once she was sitting . . .?'

'Everything fizzled out of her. Just went away. I rang the doctor and then you.' Another wary smile and she moved to work with Mary.

It felt as if they'd arrived at some kind of turning point, he thought as he started to clear all the broken pieces from the floor. Fragments of china and glass, a porcelain dog they'd bought somewhere, now missing its head and tail. Harper set letters and papers aside on a stool.

He'd read about things like this. Now it had happened here. A milestone, not one he ever wanted to see. As he worked, he thought about the question Mary had asked: how long would he and Julia be able to cope?

As long as humanly possible. It was the only answer he could imagine.

Harper smiled to himself. At least it had pushed Charlotte Radcliffe and the Model T gang from his mind for a while.

'Are you sure you're all right?' he asked Julia.

'I'll put something on the cuts.'

'I'm sorry she . . .'

The nurse gave a sorrowful shake of her head. 'We both know it wasn't really her. It's . . . whatever this is.'

This disease that was robbing Annabelle of her mind and her life.

'Yes. Thank you. Truly.'

She was sleeping. Harper sat on the edge of the bed, studying her face and stroking the back of her hand. He looked and he saw the love, the beauty of all the years; that was simply the way of things. The rush and joy of their wedding day. The way he felt when he walked in and saw Annabelle in bed, holding a baby so small that the fragility scared him.

The memories would remain. She'd have them too, but they were tucked away in pockets that were gradually being sewn up. All her past was being stolen from her. And he couldn't stop the theft.

How much longer?

TWENTY-TWO

He felt exhausted as he washed and dressed and break-fasted. Harper had slept, but last night had gnawed at his heart. Things with Annabelle were only going to grow more difficult. Nothing could stop it.

She'd looked so peaceful when he eased out of bed, a tiny smile on her face as she slept. Very likely she'd never recall a thing. The violence was an aberration; that was what he told himself as he hurried out of the door and into the car that was waiting for him on Hawthorn Road.

'Town hall or Millgarth, sir?' Bingham asked as he drove towards town. For two pennies he'd have said to turn around, take him home and leave him there. His wife needed him more than anyone. But another fortnight, that was all. Two more weeks of duty, and the desire to close the final cases.

'Let's start at Millgarth.'

The murder team was busy, the room packed as Jackson stood under the photograph of PC Endicott and addressed the detect-ives. Harper stood at the back of the room, next to Walsh, and strained his poor ears to listen.

'Essentially, we're no further along,' he said when the inspector finished.

'No, we're making progress, sir.' Walsh gave a cautious smile. 'Slow, but it's there. Constables are physically checking every garage. We're going to find that car—'

'Sooner or later. We need sooner. Have you seen the morning paper?'

He'd stopped at the newsagent's on Harrogate Road and bought the *Yorkshire Post* and two of the national dailies. The shooting was still front-page news; the murder of a policemen on duty would always draw attention.

'No, sir.' He didn't need to say he'd been too busy.

Harper put them on the desk. 'They're all wondering why

we haven't arrested anyone yet. Questioning how good we are.'
He hesitated. 'One suggested bringing in Scotland Yard.'

'Sir, I—'

Harper held up his hand. 'I know you're doing everything
you can. If you need more men, I'll find them. I'm sure I'll
have reporters coming round today. I'll tell them that the responsibility for the force in this city is mine. I'm the chief constable.
And that I know you're all doing all that it's possible to do.
Endicott was one of us.'

The relief on the man's face was obvious. 'Thank you, sir.'

'No need. But let's catch these bastards sharpish. When's
Endicott's funeral?'

'I heard from the family yesterday. Monday at one.'

Harper sat in his own office, Sissons across from him.

'Is there anything you can do to help Walsh and Jackson find
these killers?'

'Not really, sir.' The superintendent frowned. 'Things are
moving faster than the flow of information that reaches us.'

'Anything, anything at all that might help, pass it on. Even if
it's a couple of days out of date. It's all vital.'

'We have been, sir. By messenger or telephone.'

'Very good.' He needed all the departments working together
on this. 'And there's the other thing.' A dark smile. 'The killings
and the blackmail that doesn't really exist.'

'You have everything we've been able to find, sir.'

'Right now, it looks as if it all hinges on Walsh breaking Robert
Wilton when he questions him tomorrow.'

'He'll do that, sir. You've met Wilton.'

'Yes.' Harper shook his head. 'My bet is that he'll crack him
in under an hour.'

'I'd go ninety minutes.'

Too ghoulish for a proper wager, though.

The ring of the telephone took him by surprise.

It was Saturday morning, eight o'clock. Harper was pacing in
his office, drinking tea. It would be more than an hour before
he'd hear from Walsh, but he already felt the anticipation bubbling
inside. Wilton would admit to driving Rogers off the road, he

was sure of that. But what else? Would he give up Charlotte Radcliffe?

'Chief Constable Harper.'

'Walsh, sir. That man hasn't shown up yet.'

Just after the hour. He chewed his bottom lip for a moment.

'Give him five more minutes.'

'Very good, sir. After that?'

'Ring his local police station, get them to send someone to his house. I'd like a man to check his office, too.'

He might be late. He had every reason to be scared. Would he have had the courage to run?

Five more minutes and he grabbed the receiver as soon as the bell sounded.

'No sign yet, sir. I've dispatched constables.'

More waiting. Minutes passed as if they were moving through treacle. He wanted to do something, anything, but he was stuck here until he had news.

It came just before half past.

'His door was unlocked, sir,' Walsh said. 'The constable went in. Found him in the bathtub. The water was stone cold. Wilton had tried to slash his wrist with a straight razor. It looks like it happened last night. He did a poor job, though. Lost blood, but he's still alive. The ambulance is taking him to the infirmary.'

Harper replaced the receiver and sat down. He could scarcely believe it. Christ Almighty. Trying to kill himself. It was one thing he hadn't expected. He'd caused this, made someone try to commit suicide. Was it really worth it?

'Could you ring for my car, please?' he asked Miss Sharp.

'Well,' Ash said. He was sitting with his fingers in his lap, face bleak at the news. A fire blazed in the grate; the parlour felt oppressively warm. But he still wore a heavy cardigan over his waistcoat, a jacket on top of that. 'Well.'

'What do you think?'

'Apart from the fact that he's guilty, sir?'

A thin smile. 'Yes.'

'I'd say he's a very troubled young man.'

The heart attack had left Ash looking older. All the humour

had gone from his eyes. He seemed deflated, fragile and wary
of the world.

'I'll go and see him.'

'Push him, sir?'

'You never know,' Harper said. 'He might have something he
wants to get off his chest. Any suggestions?'

He looked up with a face full of sorrow. 'I'd say be gentle,
sir.'

But he didn't have an opportunity to see Wilton.

'No, Chief Constable,' the doctor said. 'He's lost blood. He's
resting and I want to let him stay that way.'

'It's important.'

'He's in no fit state to be badgered by the police.'

'Tell me something. He slashed his wrist. Why didn't he
die?'

The doctor shook his head. 'It's not as simple as you think to
commit suicide that way.' He held out his right arm to demon-
strate. 'People believe that all you need to do is cut across the
wrist.' He made a slicing motion with his left hand. 'It's not
effective. Most people who try that survive. You need to cut
along, from elbow down to the wrist' – another demonstration
– 'and even then, you have to cut deep to be certain. Best part
of an inch. That's harder than you think.'

'I see,' Harper said. A shudder rippled through his body.

'I gave him something to make him sleep. You can talk to him
this afternoon.'

Suicide, he thought as he walked back to the town hall, hands
in his pockets, wrists pressed tight against the fabric.

A little after noon, he snatched the phone from the cradle, thinking
it might be news of Wilton. He'd already heard Miss Sharp pack
up and wished her a good weekend.

'Da?' It was Mary's small voice. She wanted something. 'I'm
glad you're still there.'

'No rest for the wicked.'

'What are you doing for your dinner?'

Harper needed to escape the four walls of his office. To see
something that didn't involve death.

'How about spending it with you?' he said.

'Half an hour?'

The weather had caught up with her clothes. Sunny, proper spring, just perfect for the cotton frock in soft pastel colours and the small pale blue hat on her hair.

They settled at their regular table in the Kardomah.

'Me mam,' she said after the waitress brought their food. 'What happened . . .'

'What do you suggest?'

Her eyes were moist. Mary tugged an embroidered handker-chief from her sleeve and dabbed them dry.

'I don't know, Da. That's it, I just don't know.'

'It's never happened before. We can—'

'Do what? Hope it never happens again?'

'That's more or less the size of things, isn't it?' Harper asked.

'It doesn't seem like enough. She hurt Julia. She could have hurt herself.'

'I know. Believe me, I know.' She'd had a dangerous strength. 'We need to make the parlour safer. Remove things she might be able to use. Just in case.'

'In case there's a next time,' Mary said. Her voice was bleak.

'Yes.'

'I know it's not deliberate. It scares me.'

'It terrifies me,' he admitted. 'It seems like . . .' he moved the salt cellar around on the table as he tried to find the words, '. . . something's changed.' He lifted his face to look at her. 'Like we're moving more towards the end.'

'Maybe I should cancel my trip. Len's mum would understand.'

Harper shook his head. 'You go. I'll be at home.'

'But if she died when I wasn't there . . . I'd never be able to forgive myself.'

'There's no telling when any of us might go. But unless things change quite drastically, your mother will be with us this summer.' A wan smile. 'I hope so, anyway.'

There was nothing to decide, he thought as he walked back along the Headrow. She simply wanted to release her fears. They weren't very different from all the things inside his own heart.

But none of it was in his control. All he could do was to be there. For Mary, and for Annabelle.

He kept going, along Great George Street to the infirmary. Afternoon, the doctor had said. The town hall clock struck two as he climbed the steps.

Wilton's bed sat at the far end of the ward. His face was pale. His arms rested on top of the blanket, his left wrist heavily bandaged. As he approached, Harper felt a burst of guilt. The man wouldn't have tried this if it hadn't been for him. It passed almost as soon as it arrived. Really, Wilton had brought this on himself.

He managed a ghost of a smile and Harper sat on the visitor's chair.

'I wondered whether you'd come.'

'Who else has visited?'

'My mother. Tim Gordon, Danny Anderson. Five minutes each. Word spreads quickly.'

'Not Charlotte Radcliffe?'

A small, tight shake of the head was his answer.

'I'm not going to ask you why.'

'Really?' He sounded surprised. 'Everyone else has.'

'No need. All you did was make perfectly clear what I already knew.' He gazed around. About half the beds were full. Nurses moved from patient to patient, handing out pills and watching until they'd been swallowed. 'Anything else would be lies, wouldn't it?'

As he'd walked along the corridor, Harper had decided not to pussyfoot around the topic. It would be pointless when they both knew the answers. At least he might discover some small pieces of the truth.

'If I say yes, you can arrest me,' Wilton replied. His voice was flat.

'I'm not going to arrest anyone for the death of Ben Rogers.'

That was enough to make him turn his head and stare. 'I don't believe you.'

Harper shrugged. 'It's true. There were no fingerprints. That was a lie.'

'Then I'm free?'

'No, Mr Wilton. You're definitely not free. You're going to be haunted by what you've done for the rest of your life.' He leaned closer and lowered his voice. 'I want to ask you this: who put the idea in your head? Who made you do it?'

The man stared up at the pale paint on the ceiling for a full minute.

'Ben killed Charles,' Wilton said finally. 'Pushed him in front of that train. They'd beaten up that alderman—'

'Thompson.'

'—and Charles suddenly felt guilty. It was all meant to be a game, you see. Some fun to make an old man sweat. But it got out of hand.'

Taken on a life of its own, far beyond their grip. 'Go on.'

'Charles went to London for a few days. To do a bit of soul-searching. Ben thought Charles would confess and they'd end up in jail. He suggested meeting at Garforth station—'

The words tailed off into silence. Both men were dead and the truth of that had died with them.

'Did Rogers tell any of you what he'd done?'

'No. He didn't have to. We all knew.'

'Including Miss Radcliffe?' He was building up to the heart of it now.

'I suppose so.'

'She never said?'

'No.'

'Nothing at all or nothing specific?'

'I'm not going to answer that.'

His words were enough of a response. 'What else did she say?'

'She'd lost her brother. It had just been the two of them. You know their parents are dead?'

'Yes.'

'She'd always been the strong one. Maybe she liked him relying on her. I don't know.'

'When did she work out what had really happened to him?'

A shake of the head. 'I have no idea. She never told me if she did.'

'You were a pallbearer at his funeral. Mr Rogers's, too.'

'Yes.'

'You'll feel their weight on your shoulder for as long as you live.'

Wilton raised his left arm to show the bandage. 'That's one

of the reasons I did this.' He turned his head towards Harper. 'Now you tell *me* something: how do you live with something when you realize you just can't live with it any longer?'

'I can't answer that for you. I'm a policeman, not a doctor or a priest.'

'I know exactly what you are, Chief Constable. I've answered all the questions I'm going to answer.'

'I wish you well, Mr Wilton. Eventually, I hope you find some kind of happiness.'

TWENTY-THREE

W ilton had been his great hope. But he could never take the man to court. There had never been a chance of that. What he said might as well have happened in the confessional. None of it would bring a conviction.

Maybe the weight would rest too heavy on him and Wilton would try to commit suicide again. Nothing Harper could do about that; it was a choice for the man's conscience.

Wilton hadn't given him Charlotte Radcliffe. He'd stayed loyal to . . . who? A woman who existed more in his imagination than reality. An ideal. A girl whose body he'd known a few times. She remained untouchable, pulling the strings, controlling the lives and deaths of all those men.

She was guilty. He knew it, Wilton knew it. But what could the police prove against her? Absolutely nothing. She insisted the letters that began the blackmail had been stolen. She'd kept her distance from Thompson's beating, from the two deaths. Everything at arm's length. Charlotte Radcliffe manipulated her admirers like they were chessmen. She was clever. She was ruthless.

How the hell could he catch her?

Sitting in his office, he telephoned Millgarth. One more day of frustration. No sign of the two remaining members of the Model T gang.

'It's as if they have the power to vanish,' Walsh said. His voice was so tight it might explode; he was at the end of his tether.

'You said that once before. Why don't you go home? Let Jackson handle things.'

'I can't, sir.'

'Yes, you can. When did you last spend some time with your wife?'

'I . . .' he began, but he couldn't answer. Harper knew it all too well. He'd been the same when he was a superintendent. Cases dug their claws into you.

'Go and see her.' He turned and glanced out of the window. 'It's still afternoon. The sun's shining. Take her for a walk. Rest. It'll give you a different perspective. But no coming back to the office until tomorrow.'

'Yes, sir.' He sounded crestfallen, as if the order meant he'd somehow failed. 'How's the man I was supposed to . . .?'

'Wilton. Alive and very unhappy. Still keeping faith with the woman. I don't know how she does it. A spell or something.'

'You don't believe that, sir.'

Harper chuckled. 'Sometimes I wonder. Go home. Things will look brighter.'

'I hope you're right, sir.'

'That's why I have this job. It means I'm always right.'

The woman plagued his mind on the drive home. Had she snared him, too?

'She's been this way since the middle of the morning,' Julia said. Harper stood in the doorway of the parlour and watched Annabelle gently rocking to and fro. Just a couple of inches each way, thin fingers gripping the arm of the chair.

'Has she said anything?'

'Not a word.' The scratch stood out, red and vivid on the nurse's cheek. 'Ignored her dinner. I'm not even sure she knew I was there.'

He pulled up a stool and sat by his wife. She kept moving, staring straight ahead, unaware of his presence.

'Can you hear me?' he asked softly. Nothing, nothing at all. He stroked her arm for a minute, two. No reaction.

'I don't know where she is,' Julia said when he moved away.

'Somewhere. Nowhere.' She wasn't hurting anyone. Not even herself. 'Let's leave her for now. I'll make a cup of tea and sit with her.'

The rocking was a slow, constant motion, some need inside her. Then, quite suddenly, she stopped. There was no other change. She still didn't seem to hear when he spoke to her. She didn't respond to his touch. Then, as quickly as she'd stopped, she began again.

She was still doing it when Mary came home.

'Come on, Mam, we'll get you ready for bed.'

By the time he wrapped his arms around Annabelle in bed, she'd stopped moving. But she hadn't returned from wherever all this had taken her.

Harper stepped outside into Sunday morning. Still early, the soft pale light of dawn and redness in the high clouds off to the east. A shepherds' warning? It looked set to be another warm day. Harper breathed in the air. Clear up here, so much cleaner than Sheepscar.

At the very corner of his vision he caught a slight movement.

A fraction of a second. He stepped back inside the house and slammed the door just as the shot rang out. The sound pierced his hearing as it hit the stone work and the ricochet whined away. Harper turned the key in the lock. Jesus Christ.

His hand was shaking as he dialled Millgarth. He hadn't imagined the gun or the bullet. They'd been real. His heart was racing. As soon as Inspector Jackson came on the line, the words flooded out.

'Hobson and Booth have been out by my home. Parked down the street. When I stepped outside, they took a shot at me.'

'A shot? Are you all right, sir?' Jackson's voice was calm, soothing.

'Yes, yes. It hit the front of the house.'

'I'll be there in a few minutes. Please stay inside, sir. Don't go looking through the window in case they're still around. I'll get someone from the Chapel Allerton station to check the street.'

Speaking to him like he was a civilian. He'd been shot at before, even close to where he'd lived. But this was . . . different. It was terrifying and he couldn't explain it.

'Da?' Mary was standing beside him. He hadn't noticed her. 'You look like you've seen a ghost. Come on.'

She took him by the sleeve and led him through to the kitchen. He followed, an obedient child.

'That was a bullet, wasn't it?' No fear in her voice; nothing more than a simple question. But he saw the fury starting to build behind her eyes.

'Yes.' As the kettle boiled and she made the tea, he sat at the table and told her. Before she could pour from the pot, a firm knock on the door. A copper's knock. Harper started to rise, but she gently pushed him down again.

He could make out the sound of voices, but his hearing wasn't good enough to pick out words. Harper turned as she entered the room.

'The constables have looked all around the area, Da. No Model T with dirty numberplates. We're safe.'

No, he thought. The last members of the gang had just proved they weren't safe. They never would be until Booth and Hobson were arrested.

'It's me they're after.'

'I daresay they are. But do you think you're the only one here?' She tried to keep her voice low, a hiss, but it rose as the fear and anger tumbled out. Her eyes flamed. 'There's me mam. Me. Julia. Or do you think a bullet would swerve around us if we got in the way?'

Her voice weakened. Harper took a breath. 'You know what I mean.'

'I know what just happened.' She stormed out of the room. A few seconds later he heard the front door close, then the sound of her car.

He stood on the doorstep with Jackson, talking him through what had taken place. The inspector still looked the worse for wear, scrapes on his face, hand bandaged.

'I don't know that I really thought at all,' Harper said. 'Maybe I spotted the car; it was the only one down there. But even that didn't really register until I caught a glimpse of some movement. Then it must have clicked into place. I dashed back inside.'

'They were parked about twenty-five yards away?' the inspector asked.

'Yes.' The shock was fading, and a cold, solid anger was taking its place.

'If they still just have Webleys, it's impossible to be accurate at that range.'

Harper tried to think. 'I don't remember anything like a rifle barrel, but . . .'

Jackson smiled. 'You were too busy getting out of the line of fire.'

Harper nodded his agreement. 'More or less. A copper should be able to tell you more, I know. Pity we're always some of the worst witnesses.'

'It's not as if there's any doubt about who it was. I just don't know what else we can do, sir.'

'What if I'd come outside with my daughter? She made sure she pointed it out to me: this isn't just me, it's my family.'

'We could put a constable outside the house.'

'You know full well what I'm going to say to that. I've barely got ten days before I retire.'

'Your choice, of course, sir.'

'Just give me a leaving present and put these bastards in the cells before I go.'

Jackson sighed. 'Believe me . . .'

'I know.'

'I'm glad nobody was hurt, sir.'

A slow exhalation. 'So am I, Inspector. So am I. These people seem to think they can violate my home life to make their point. We *have* to stamp on them.'

Annabelle hadn't heard any of it. Thank God for that, at least. He didn't know how he could have coped with her fear on top of everything else. His had finally passed. The fury remained, along with a sense of impotence. There was nothing he could do to find the gang. There was little he could do to bring down Charlotte Radcliffe. He was stuck. His time as chief was going to end in a pair of failures. Maybe he'd have more luck with the gang of shoplifters.

Annabelle spoke a little during the morning. No more than five words, with long, long silences, but it was something. Yesterday was another country, left behind and forgotten. Only the present and the distant past seemed to exist for her.

In the warmth of the afternoon, they put her in the wheelchair.

Harper went outside, alone. A precaution. In his head he knew they wouldn't return, but his heart refused to be convinced.

Feeling a flutter in his chest, constantly glancing around, he pushed her to the park. He had to do this, to try and force some normality back into things. A broad-brimmed hat kept her face shaded. Annabelle began to smile as she heard the band playing tunes she'd known most of her life.

The familiarity, the pleasure of the music. For an hour she seemed happy, raising a hand to conduct, trying to hum along in her gravel voice as she sat in the warm sun. Eventually she seemed to be flagging, looking up gratefully as he took the handles and guided her back towards home.

Time in the park with her had cleansed his mind. He could still see the car, sense the shot, but it was starting to drift away from him. His chest didn't feel as tight. Annabelle gave him that, even if she could no longer know it. She'd never understand how much he needed her.

Mary had returned while they were gone. She gave him a tentative smile. Thank God for that, at least.

An hour of digging. Harper attacked the ground, trying to work off his anger and frustration with the cases. He knew he was out of condition for this, puffing and panting as he worked while Mary sat inside with her mother, pointing everything out.

She didn't seem to notice. The joy had gone from Annabelle's face again. She was showing empty eyes to the world.

By late afternoon the ground was all dug, clods chopped, everything raked and ready for the plants. Maybe he wouldn't catch all the crooks, but this would be one promise he could keep.

TWENTY-FOUR

Sergeant Ricks was waiting for him on Monday morning, suit brushed, hair neatly combed. Harper was formally dressed in his uniform.

'The information is that we can expect the women on

Wednesday,' he said. 'They had such a difficult time in Manchester that the men organizing it feel we might make an easier target.' He grinned. 'They're going to be in for a shock.'

'Are you prepared?'

'I am, sir.' He produced a folder from under his arm. 'This is the plan I've made. Now we know when they're coming, I've taken the liberty of arranging a meeting with the heads of the department stores for eleven this morning, as well as the man who heads up the Association of Briggate Shopkeepers.'

Harper stared in astonishment. 'I had no idea there was such a thing.'

'You'd be amazed. I'd like you to be there, sir. It would lend the proper weight to everything.

'Miss Sharp,' Harper called. 'Do I have anything this morning?'

'No,' she answered. 'I never know if you'll be here. Nothing until Constable Endicott's funeral this afternoon.'

He cocked his head. 'That's your answer,' he told Ricks. 'Where is it?'

The young man looked down, abashed. 'I was hoping we could hold it in here, sir.'

Harper laughed. 'You'll go far. Here it will be.'

It was strange to see them all gathered together. Men all around his age who controlled so much of the retail trade in Leeds. Apart from the Briggate man, there were the general managers of Schofield's, the Pygmalion, Mathias Robinson, Marks and Spencer and Marshal and Snelgrove. Important men. He'd met most of them before, at charity galas and business luncheons.

But this was different. He sat and let Ricks handle everything. The man was prepared, he'd come armed with suggestions on a typewritten sheet.

'We'll have a female special constable in each store to take care of the women you arrest. I suggest you set aside an empty, locking room to hold those you stop. Please make sure your floor walkers are alert.' A small pause to be certain he had their attention. 'This isn't going to be a single day. At best, it'll last for the rest of the week, and that's if we're lucky. The faster and harder we clamp down on them, the sooner it will be over.'

The men had questions, but they seemed satisfied. By the time he shook their hands as they left, Harper felt everything was in hand.

'You've done a thorough job,' he told Ricks.

The sergeant gave a nervous smile. 'Words are fine, sir. It's what happens once the women arrive that counts.'

True. Now all they could do was wait. One more item for the list.

'We've got something.' Walsh sounded jubilant on the other end of the line.

'Arrests?' There would be some poetic justice on the day they buried the copper the gang had killed.

'No, sir.' The vigour went out of his voice. 'One of them wrote to his mother.'

It only took a second to work out who. 'Booth?'

'Yes. Asked them to forgive him. The war had made him this way, all sorts of twaddle like that.'

Was it rubbish? There could be more than a bit of truth in that sentence. The fighting had changed so many of those who survived. But that wasn't something for the police.

'Anything to indicate where we can find him?'

'The postmark is Harehills, sir. Jackson's already organized men to go round all the shops there with everything we have on the pair.'

'Good.' It was a start. But with these two, it could just as easily be a false trail.

The funeral for Constable Simon Endicott was solemn. Harper said a brief talk, looking at the parents who knew nothing could bring their son back.

Very few officers had been killed on duty, thank God. It was easy to recall all their names. He listened to the eulogies, sat and stood, sang the hymns and added his amens to the prayers. But none of it would bring the man back.

A few words with the family, condolences and sympathy, then striding over to Millgarth with renewed determination.

'Do we have anything yet?'

'Harehills is a big area, sir,' Walsh replied. 'If I thought it would make a difference, I'd be out there asking questions with the rest of them.'

'It's a bloody murder investigation. I've just had to promise Mr and Mrs Endicott we'll arrest someone very soon. I don't want to be a liar. Not when they're going home to grieve all over again.'

'Most of the men are on it. I've kept a few looking at other leads, just in case. We know how slippery they are.'

At least the superintendent believed in the pair's slyness.

'Do we have a copy of the letter?'

'The Booths gave it to us. I said we'd return it.'

Harper read. It was made up of short, stumbling sentences, but everything was genuine and heartfelt. The words of a man who didn't know how to express himself, but was trying.

More than that, he thought, it was a farewell letter. He didn't expect to live to see his parents again. Not like Endicott, who'd believed he'd go home at the end of his shift until Booth or Hobson murdered him.

'Sounds like he's made his decision.'

'That's how it struck me, too, sir.' Walsh pushed his lips together. 'When we know where they are, we need to go in armed. It's either that or risk losing more men.'

They'd gone with weapons to York Road and the farmhouse the gang had run to afterwards. Now the reasons seemed stronger than ever.

'I'll sign the chits right now. And your sharpshooter . . .'

'Hopkinson.'

'Keep him ready and make sure there's a rifle for him. I'm not going to another funeral because of this pair.'

'Very good, sir.'

'Once we know where they are, I want to be a part of it.'

He'd seen it develop. He needed to be there when it ended.

In his office, Harper brooded. The day was nearly done and it felt as if he'd achieved nothing beyond saying farewell to a young man. Weary, he picked up the telephone.

'Superintendent Walsh.'

'Any results yet?'

'Nothing definite, sir.' His voice was wary. 'We have come up with two possibilities. Shopkeepers think they recognized one or other of the men. An assistant at the Co-op on Harehills Lane was quite sure.'

'Do you have an address?'

'No, sir. The possibilities are in different parts of the area, too.'

'When was the most recent?'

'Yesterday, sir. That's the day after Booth sent the letter to his parents.'

Maybe it wasn't a ruse; they might still be there. The man could have written and sent it without telling Corporal Hobson. His little gesture of atonement. Of penance.

Perhaps they really were close. But he'd thought that often enough before, and the gang had slipped away.

'Be careful,' he told Walsh. 'If they really are round there, we don't want to risk warning them. They probably have another bolt hole waiting.'

'They must be running out of those by now.' The superintendent spoke slowly, as if he'd been thinking things through. 'I just wondered about that letter. Maybe this is where they've decided to make their stand. They can't go on much longer. They never sold any of the jewellery they stole. They have to be broke by now.'

Stony. A time to end the story. 'Maybe so, but let's take them by surprise if we can. There are too many people living in Harehills for us to just roll in. If they start shooting, it won't be just coppers who get hurt. Civilians, too. I'm not going to take that risk.'

'I agree, sir.'

'Keep your marksman on standby.'

'He is, sir.'

A final telephone call, up to Carlton Barracks.

'Colonel? It's Chief Constable Harper. I have a favour to ask, if you'd be so good.'

Finished, he slowly stood. His knees ached and the serge of the dress uniform was scratchy against his legs. Time to go home.

'She's been silent all day,' Julia told him. She kept her voice low, as if conversation might disturb Annabelle. 'She swallows when I put food in her mouth, but everything is reflex.'

He sat and read the paper to her for a while, but there was no
reaction. He stared out of the window at the patch of earth he'd
dug. Come the weekend, he'd buy some plants and put them in
the ground. Some colour Annabelle could see during the summer,
plus a rose bush for under the window. Exactly the way she
wanted.

'We've narrowed it down to a few streets, sir,' Walsh said.
Tuesday morning and he stood in the superintendent's office at
Millgarth. 'The Bellbrookes, off Harehills Lane and Compton
Road.'
    'How many houses?'
    'Seventy, sir. All through terraces.'
    Coming closer. He could feel hope starting to bubble up inside
him.
    'I don't suppose there's a Model T with muddy number plates
outside any of them?'
    Walsh snorted. 'We should be so lucky. But five different
shopkeepers have said the sketches of Hobson and Booth look
a lot like some customers who've just moved into the area.'
    'That's good enough. They don't know exactly where,
though?'
    'No, sir.'
    'What about the men on the beat? They're supposed to know
exactly who lives where.'
    'People come and go all the time round there. It's impossible
to keep track.'
    'Every street has its busybody. The constable will know them.
Make sure they ask. No house-to-house enquiries, though. I'm
not risking any of my men.'
    'Very good, sir.'
    'I want some results by the end of the day so we can make
proper plans.'
    'I'll have Jackson up there working with them.'
    'No,' Harper said. 'Not him. Booth and Hobson have seen
him, they'll know his face. You go up and take charge.'
    'Yes, sir.' A smile that looked like relief. Probably happy to
do something more than sit in an office. 'Glad to.'
    'As soon as you know exactly where they are, tell me. This

time they won't have chance to slip away. We'll have plenty of men to watch the house.'

He wore a grim smile as he walked along the Headrow. A shilling into the cup of a one-armed man begging on the corner of Albion Street.

'Alderman Thompson rang,' Miss Sharp said as soon as he walked into the office, 'and Sergeant Ricks would like to see you.'

'Tell Ricks I'll see him in five minutes. Could we have some tea, please?'

Thompson was surly, as if he was doing Harper a favour by answering his phone.

'You'd better have some good news for me.'

'Everything is where it was the last time we talked, Alderman.' He waited for the explosion. Instead, there was only a sense of exhaustion.

'How much longer do you have on the job?'

'A few days yet.'

'Will you find those letters?'

'Yes.' Harper didn't know where the confidence came from. There was no cause for it. Nothing had altered. Maybe he'd started believing in luck.

'I hope to God you're right.'

Ricks's shave was so close that his skin shone pink, hair neatly greased down with lotion. Why not? His big moment was almost here.

'Is everything in place, Sergeant?' Harper sipped some tea, watching the man's face.

'As much as it can be, sir. We're going to find a few variables, of course, and some will evade the net. If the floor walkers in the department stores do their job, we should be able to catch most of the rest.'

'Most.' That was the important word.

Ricks reddened. 'I can't guarantee we'll catch every single one of them, sir. But enough to stop them doing any real damage.'

'Let's hope you're right.'

'I believe I am, sir.'

The certainty of the young, Harper thought after the man had left. Had he ever been that way? Stupid question; of course he had.

Charlotte Radcliffe. Harper stood, hands in his pockets, staring down at Great George Street. He saw people move but didn't really notice them. Just figures scuttling along.

He needed to unnerve the woman. He'd seen her mask slip a couple of times, just for a second. He had to discover a way to burrow under that, to shatter those defences.

Harper turned away, picked up the telephone and rang the infirmary. Robert Wilton had been discharged. He looked through the file and found the man's number at home.

The voice that answered was shaky, weary as it recited the number.

'This is Chief Constable Harper. I wanted to ask how you were.'

He could hear the drawing in of breath. 'Do you want the polite answer or the honest one?'

'Honest,' he said. 'Always.'

'Then I'm sorry I failed, but glad I did. Does that make sense?'

'More or less. Now, though, you need to find a way to live with your guilt.'

'I could do something about it,' Wilton said.

'You could,' Harper agreed. 'But I don't believe that helps at all.' He hesitated. 'Tell me, how do you feel about Miss Radcliffe?'

'She . . . I suppose we all loved her.'

'Loved or love?' Harper asked.

'Both, perhaps. She's a year older than the rest of us and she . . .'

'Was your introduction to women?'

'You could put it like that, yes. It creates a bond of sorts. I'm not sure that ever completely goes away.'

'Were you all eager to please her?'

'Fell over ourselves when we were younger. The smallest thing and we were scrambling. Why?'

'I was wondering if that's still true.'

'It may be,' Wilton said after a long pause. 'I had some time to think in hospital. I know I wasn't there long, but you'd be amazed how inaction can set your mind to work.'

'I'm sure.' It sounded as if Wilton wanted to unburden himself, that he'd realized the weight he'd carried, and felt ready to shed it.

'Even Charles, her own brother, he was in thrall to her, you know. She and he . . . I know it sounds awful, but it was true. She broke taboos, she didn't care.'

Harper could believe that. The woman had learned to rein herself in a little but the sense of it remained. She wanted her fun, her experiences, and damn everyone else.

'Does that disgust you?' Wilton asked.

'I'm not here to judge her. Not today, at least. Did you know about the blackmail with Alderman Thompson?'

'She and Charles cooked it up with Ben Rogers. They thought it would be something different. Before you ask, I have no evidence, just hints and winks. I can't testify to it in court.'

'I wouldn't ask you. How did you become part of it?'

'After she realized it was falling apart. Charlotte never expected the police to become involved. Once they were, Charles panicked. I think that's why he went to London, then . . . I think she maybe persuaded Ben to kill Charles to save them both. Maybe she promised him— I don't know. So much of this is me guessing.'

But it made an awful kind of sense. 'Tell me about what you did.'

'She hinted she wanted revenge for Charles. I suppose I was happy to be her white knight. I'd never found anyone else to match her.'

'I see.'

'Do you?' he asked. 'I wish I did. Perhaps I should do the same as Danny and drink my way through everything.'

'There are doctors who can help you, Mr Wilton.'

'Are there? Who knows? Still, maybe there's something I can do.' He put down the receiver.

A strange conversation. It confirmed what he already thought, but it disturbed him, too. Would Wilton try to kill himself again? There was no way to tell, and he couldn't have a man constantly watching him.

Harper sighed. It was time to see Charlotte Radcliffe again.

TWENTY-FIVE

All the leaves on the trees were out, casting gentle shade over the drive of the house, sunlight dappling through the branches. Very peaceful; hard to believe he was only a mile and a half from the city centre.

Harper rang the bell marked Radcliffe and waited on the deep porch. No answer. Again, but nothing. He'd come without warning; that always meant taking a chance.

As Bingham drove away, he glanced back at the large house. He'd be back here very soon.

'Millgarth,' he said, and hoped for progress.

'We're being careful, sir,' Jackson told him. 'Narrowed it down to four possibilities.'

'Four? I'd hoped for better by now.'

The inspector reddened, embarrassed. 'The constable who covers the area isn't up to snuff, sir.'

'What's his name? I'll replace him.'

'Edmondson, sir. But that's not going to do us any good right now. I have Sergeant Clough and a pair of detective constables up there asking questions. Very cautiously.'

'Are we certain that Booth and Hobson are still there? We might be putting in all this effort for nothing.'

'No, sir.' Jackson gave him a plain answer. 'We can't be sure. We're still looking around, but this is the best lead we have. It's the *only* one we have, so we're pushing it.'

'As soon as we establish exactly where they are, we're going to take time to put together a plan. I'm not going to risk any civilians for this pair, and I don't want any of our coppers hurt.'

'That's the risk we take,' Jackson said. 'We all know it.'

Harper nodded. 'It is. But let's make it as small as possible. Yesterday I went to the funeral of a policeman they killed. I don't want to go to another.'

'Of course, sir. None of us do.'

'Then let's be very careful. Here's what we can do . . .'

Not even five minutes' walk to Briggate, then across the road to Albion Place. He'd barely reached the stairs when he heard footsteps coming down.

'Da. What are you doing here?' Mary asked as she saw him.

'I was coming to see if you fancied something to eat.'

She laughed. 'Have you been reading my mind? I'm famished.'

'Not meeting anyone?'

'Just me. But if you're offering to pay . . .'

'Come on, then. I suppose I can treat you.'

A few smiles, some laughter, anything to take his mind off the cases. No talk of Annabelle today. He listened to her chatter brightly about her business, all the plans for her trip in July. She had her passport, all her currency.

'It's still more than two months away.'

Mary grinned. 'You know me. I like to be prepared. I'm trying to make sure nothing crops up at the last minute.'

'Do you have a list?' he teased, but she nodded.

'On my desk. Gladys is going to run things while I'm gone.' She took a sip of tea. 'There's a niggling part of me that wonders if I'm doing the right thing. Whether I should just let it go. I know I've changed a lot recently.'

A lot? Completely, he thought.

'If you're asking, I think you need to go. It'll lay everything to rest. If you don't, the what if of it will always be niggling at you . . . and there's Len's mother, too.'

'I know.' She nodded. 'I think she needs it more than me.'

'Of course. She's on her own now,' he said. The flu had taken her husband.

'Yes.' A smile. 'What's going on with your cases?'

A pity, Harper thought. But too much to hope they could put them aside during dinnertime. 'You don't want to know. I'm not even sure I do.'

'Just over a week and a half until you retire. Will they be done?'

He sat and thought. 'One of them, probably. The other . . .'

He let his words trail away, leaned closer and lowered his voice. 'Then there's the gang of shoplifters due to arrive tomorrow.'

Mary's eyes widened. 'Oh?'

He felt heartened as he walked to the town hall. They were almost done with the Model T gang. Close enough to the end that he felt he could taste it. The women descending on Leeds didn't worry him too much. They seemed more like an annoyance of midges in the summer. Something to be swatted away. Ricks had everything under control, and he was confident the sergeant would handle it all well.

But Charlotte Radcliffe was another matter.

'The papers to sign are on your desk,' Miss Sharp told him. 'Mr Dickinson asked if he could have a word, too.'

'Very good. Could we have tea for two?'

'Albert,' he said, when the man picked up the telephone. 'It's Tom Harper. You wanted to see me. Why don't you come down to the office?'

'I wanted to know what I'm likely to inherit in terms of these cases.' Dickinson looked jovial, happy to be taking over as chief constable, even if it would only be for a short time.

Harper ran through it all, watching the man nod. He seemed so easygoing that it was easy to forget he'd worked his way up from constable. He knew every single part of the job as completely as Harper did himself.

'These shoplifters worry me,' Dickinson said when he'd finished.

'Manchester contained them.'

'They're too organized.'

'Ricks seems to have everything covered.'

The man pressed his lips together. 'Do you mind if I work with him? I just have a bad feeling about this.'

'Be my guest.' Coppers needed to follow their instincts. It would help to have someone senior running everything. 'Just see the sergeant. He has all the details.'

*   *   *

A visit to the infirmary to see David Templeton. The man had already undergone two operations, and had at least two more ahead. At least he looked more comfortable than the day he'd been brought into the hospital.

'I just have a couple of things to ask you,' Harper said. 'How many guns does your gang have?'

The question seemed to take him by surprise. 'Four Webleys. One for each of us.'

'No rifles?'

'No.' He snorted. 'We saw enough of those damned things in the army.'

'Thank you.' He turned on his heel and left.

Late afternoon and the office felt warm. He heard Miss Sharp leave for the day. He wouldn't have this place much longer. Today things had crept up on him; retirement suddenly felt all too real and immediate. He'd miss being a copper. It had defined every day of his life for the last forty years. Setting all that aside was going to be difficult.

But he was ready. All that time, the physicality of the work, walking the beat and as a detective, had worn a heavy toll on his body. More than anything else, Annabelle needed him. He was lucky; they had enough money for the rest of her life to be comfortable. It was some small consolation. What about all the families without that cushion? How did they cope? But he knew the answer to that.

Finally he put on his hat, gathered up his raincoat and walked downstairs to the car.

'Millgarth,' he said to Bingham.

'We're close,' Walsh said. 'The problem is the more we narrow it down, the more careful we need to be.'

Wariness, not to alarm or tip them off.

'How certain are you?'

'Almost one hundred per cent, sir.'

'That plan we discussed this morning, is it ready to swing into action?'

'Yes, sir. We'll probably need two hours for everything to be ready.'

'Fine. I have an extra little wrinkle, something that might keep us safer. We'll discuss it in the morning.'

He felt drained as he leaned back in the car seat and felt the movement of the car. The next he knew, Bingham was speaking, telling him they were home.

'No strange vehicles around, sir.'

'Thank you. Early start tomorrow.' His body ached as he clambered out of the car. It wasn't so long since he'd been able to work all day and all night and not feel a thing. Time had caught up with him.

Annabelle was quiet. She stared down at her lap, eating and swallowing when he put food in her mouth. But the actions were purely mechanical; she wasn't even aware of them.

He talked to Mary as they sat in the parlour. Inconsequential things, stories from the paper. He hoped Annabelle might perk up and take part, but she remained silent. Her body was sitting in the chair, but her mind was lost, wandering far away.

It was a still morning, barely a breath of wind as he stood on Hawthorn Road in the early half-light.

'Where first, sir?' Bingham asked.

Harper thought for a moment. 'The railway station,' he said. 'After that, we'll go to Millgarth.'

Still too early for much traffic; a quarter of an hour and the car pulled up outside the station, with its smell of smoke and the sounds of whistles and brakes from the trains.

Ricks was there, supervising his squad of uniformed constables, three women Specials and two detectives in plain clothes. Albert Dickinson stood close by, listening and nodding his approval. After the sergeant finished his final instructions, most remained at the entrance to the platform where the London train would arrive. A pair drifted towards the main station entrance.

'Everything ready?' Harper asked.

'Yes, sir.' He was smiling, sounding confident, but Harper could see the nervousness. Ricks needed this to work. If it did, he'd be certain of promotion. If not . . . he'd never advance. He took out his pocket watch. 'Due in five minutes.'

Everyone looked ready, tense as the train pulled in and screeched to a halt a couple of yards from the buffers. The doors opened and people began to step down from the carriages. Porters hovered discreetly with their carts.

A bustle of people, but Ricks's squad was swift and sure, picking out women and escorting them away. Plenty of anger and protests, but everything was done quickly. Less than five minutes and it was all over. The platform was clear; most people hadn't even noticed a thing.

'How many did you find?'

'Eight as they came off the train, sir,' Ricks replied. He was beaming, relieved. 'Another three before they could leave the station.'

'How many do you think you missed?'

'Two, maybe. Perhaps three. The floor walkers in the stores should mop those up. But it was a good sweep to begin.'

'Very good indeed.' He'd been impressed at the way it worked.

'We'll meet every London train for the next couple of days and do the same.'

'Excellent work, Sergeant,' Harper said. 'Thank them all for me.'

'The lad has it all in hand, doesn't he?' Dickinson sounded impressed.

'He does.'

One thing had gone well, he thought. Perhaps it would be an omen for the rest of the day, he thought, then smiled to himself. Coppers were the most superstitious bunch he knew. Everything became a sign, an indication. But maybe it was true . . .

'We're absolutely certain where they are, sir,' Walsh said. He was grinning with pleasure, as if the work was already finished. He pointed at the map. 'This house here.' The last one on Bellbrooke Avenue, across from the Sunday school and church. If they could get out, it was no more than fifty yards to the reservoir and escape. Hard to capture them if they made it that far. But this pair wasn't likely to surrender.

'We'll evacuate about half the street,' Jackson said. 'If we're careful, we should be able to do that without alerting them. We'll have officers going into the church and school disguised as workmen. I've already had a word with the vicar.'

Harper could feel the knot forming in his belly. The urgency building, waiting for the release of action.

'What about the back, and cutting off the way out to open ground?'

It was in hand. Harper took out his watch. 'How long until everyone's in place?'

'Two hours, sir,' Jackson told him.

'Good.' He lifted the telephone receiver and asked for Carlton Barracks. 'Colonel, it's Chief Constable Harper. Can you send those men to Millgarth as soon as possible, please. In mufti.'

Ample time to go to the town hall and do a little work before it all began. To try to pretend it was a completely ordinary day. He signed letters and glanced at correspondence, keeping one eye on the clock. After an hour he put on his hat.

'I should be back this afternoon.'

Miss Sharp raised an eyebrow. 'Should be?'

'Yes.' He gave her a smile. 'Should be.'

The day seemed too pleasant for an encounter like this, Harper thought as he stood behind the car at the entrance to the reservoir, next to Walsh. Jackson was in the church with Hopkinson the marksman and a pair of army sharpshooters from the barracks.

He felt the weight of the Webley in his jacket pocket and the dryness of his throat. For the third time in two minutes, he checked his watch.

Harper knew he didn't need to be here. He could have left it to the men. But this gang had made it a very personal battle. They'd come to his home; they'd shot at him. He needed to be there for the finish. He owed himself the satisfaction. The final act of his time as a copper.

'Ready?' he asked, but it was just a word to fill the silence. The rest of the world seemed far away, all its noise muted and distant.

Walsh was pacing, eager to make an end to this. It had plagued him for too long. He needed to be here to see it to a close, too.

Suddenly the superintendent stopped and pulled out his gun. 'Something's happening.'

Harper cocked his head. Some faint noise at the very edge of his hearing. Angry, sharp, but he couldn't make out any detail. The assault on the house couldn't have begun yet; three blasts by Jackson on the whistle was the signal. He drew his weapon. Something had gone wrong.

He traded quick looks with Walsh as they moved behind the car, gun arms resting on the roof. The vehicle would offer some protection.

No shots yet.

A figure in uniform came sprinting down Bellbrooke Avenue, appearing in the gap between houses as he reached the open space around the reservoir.

Harper moved into the open, holding the Webley by his side, as the man ran up to them.

'What's going on there?'

It came out in small bursts as the constable tried to catch his breath. Hobson had opened the back door of the house and spotted men taking position. He and Booth had barricaded themselves inside. Jackson had sent the officer down to tell Walsh and Harper.

'If we try and ram our way in, it's going to be a massacre,' Walsh said. 'They'll just be able to pick us off from upstairs.'

'I'm not going to take that risk with my police officers.' He glanced at the man, standing and waiting for orders. Harper made a decision. 'We need to have them at the windows with their guns to make a target for the marksmen. This is what you're going to tell the inspector . . .'

'Are you sure, sir?' Bingham asked. 'This isn't the way to learn to drive.'

'I don't give a damn. It's what we have.' Harper gave him a strained smile. 'And before you ask, I'm not going to change my mind. I'm not going to take the chance of losing anyone else. Not after Endicott.' He glanced at his driver. 'I mean it. No objections. Not a word. There's open ground here. You have five minutes to show me the basics.'

'I don't like it, sir.'

Harper settled behind the wheel, feet testing the pedals. 'It's

only for a hundred yards, and it's in a straight line. All I need to
know is how to keep the bloody thing going and how to stop it.'

He saw Bingham glance at Walsh. They probably imagined
he'd gone mad. Had a death wish. But he was damned if he was
going to let any of his men do something that he could manage
himself. The men in that house would never expect this.

'Very good, sir.'

So simple that he'd mastered it in two minutes. If he concen-
trated, he could keep the car going in a straight line. Stopping
smoothly, in the right place, would take more effort.

'You're as ready as you're going to be, sir,' Bingham told him.
He took over, driving the car down to Harehills Lane, then a right
turn on to Bellbrooke Street. Women were out of their houses,
gossiping on the pavement. All of them wondering what was going
on. This wasn't a place that saw a motor car from one month to
the next. Right again, on to Bellbrooke Avenue, and he pulled over.

'I'm willing to drive the last part, too, sir,' Bingham offered.

'Thank you, but no,' Harper said with a weak grin. 'Why put
that lesson to waste?'

He felt the warmth of the day as he sat and gathered himself.
The engine was so soft he could barely hear it. Only a short
distance to go, but as he looked ahead, the cobbles seemed to
stretch out forever in front of him. Nothing on the street.

Christ Almighty, he was terrified. It wasn't too late to stop all
this. Find another idea. All it would take was a tiny amount of
pressure on a trigger and he'd be gone. No, it didn't matter how
much it scared him, he had to drive down this street. For a
moment he thought about Annabelle, then pushed her from his
mind. This was his duty. One of the last things he'd do as a
copper. Lure the pair to the window with their guns, targets for
the sharpshooter. The car would offer a little protection. He hoped.

Harper held up his hands. They were trembling. He tried to
swallow but couldn't. Time, he told himself. Get going before
you walk away.

He eased up the clutch as he brought the other foot down on
the accelerator. Caressing it, exactly as Bingham had instructed
him. The car jerked forward. He gripped the wheel, arms straight
as he guided the vehicle along.

No need to change gears, Bingham said. It was true; he wasn't moving fast enough. Close to the corner, he jammed one foot on the brake, the other pressing down hard on the clutch. Put the car into neutral, then set the handbrake. Exactly like the quick lesson.

He stopped right outside the door. Lowered the window. His body was rigid. Every second he expected to hear the whine of a bullet. But there was only silence. Just the width of the pavement separated him from the front door of the house.

In for a penny. Harper needed them in the window, where the marksmen could take their aim. He took a breath, hoping nobody would hear the fear in his voice.

'You know who I am,' he began. His voice stayed steady. Firm. 'You've left bags at my house. You've taken a shot at me. The police are all around here. I'm giving you a chance to surrender. I don't want anyone—'

The crack of the bullet was sharp and loud in the morning. A tinkle as a few tiny shards of glass fell and glittered in the light.

A volley of bullets that made him crouch on the seat, covering his head as if that might save him.

'Stay down, sir!' someone yelled. He hunched on the seat, cowering, trying to curl himself into nothing.

The shots were all coming from the church, a series of rounds from Hopkinson and the pair of army marksmen.

And then silence.

It wasn't real. An absence of all sound that seemed unearthly. The only thing in the air was the drifting stink of cordite.

Very warily, Harper raised his head.

He could pick out the noise of coppers running, arriving from around the corner.

'Back,' Harper shouted. 'Stay back.'

The front door of the house flew open. A man, blood on his face and down the front of his shirt. Raising a pistol. Arm steady, taking aim. Terror and fury on his face.

Nowhere to hide from the bullet. He stared at his killer, unable to speak.

This was how it ended, was it?

A single shot came, sending the man spinning backwards into the house. The Webley clattered to the pavement.

Harper realized he'd been holding his breath. He took hold of the steering wheel. It was the only thing he could do to stop his hands shaking. Lady Luck had given him a final kiss.

He heard the quick rasp of hobnails as someone dashed across the road. A pair of shots whined up into the sky to cover him.

Then Jackson was there, up against the corner of the house.

'This one's dead, sir. I saw the sniper hit him right between the eyes.'

'Sounds like I owe someone a pint.' He tried to make his voice light. It wasn't going to fool anyone. 'What about the other one inside?'

'We're fairly certain we got him. I'm going in to find out.' He waved an arm for the waiting coppers to follow.

'I'll follow.'

'No need, sir.' Another voice as Walsh appeared. 'You've done your bit. Stay there. I want to make sure these bastards are dead.'

The superintendent had earned that. Harper nodded.

'Very good.'

He cradled his gun as he watched them disappear through the open door, stepping over the body. Every second he expected to hear a shot.

Nothing.

Finally the two men came out, pistols back in their jacket pockets.

'It's all there if you want a look now, sir,' Walsh said. His voice sounded ancient, as if he'd aged decades in the house. He shook his head. 'The only thing left is all the paperwork.'

'Over.' After everything, it was almost impossible to believe. The superintendent drew in a breath. 'Finally.'

Walsh walked back towards the church, Jackson beside him. Harper opened the car door and stood, keeping his hands in his pockets to hide the trembling. The soles of his shoes crunched over the slivers of glass on the pavement.

The body in the doorway looked small, pale. The man stared up at the ceiling, but he'd never see anything again. Harper moved through the rooms. The house seemed unnaturally dark after the brightness outside. A bureau was smashed against the wall. A Welsh dresser blocked the back door.

Harper climbed the stairs. The iron smell of blood grew stronger.

The other man was sprawled back across the floor. A parody of sleep except for the small, neat holes in his skull. Harper stared down at him. Nothing remarkable about his face. Nothing to mark him as evil or a killer. But there never was. Even the men who committed the worst deeds looked as human as everyone else.

He should have felt more. Even his own fear was beginning to recede. Back downstairs, stopping to examine the other face. He wanted to summon up some sorrow. After all, they'd served bravely during the war. But try as he might, the only thing inside him was relief that this was finally over. They'd murdered a copper, killed a civilian and executed one of their own. Dead, but he couldn't find a scrap of sympathy for them.

It had ended the way they wanted. No courtroom, no explanations of who they'd become. Swift, ugly, final, but it was done.

Back out in the sunlight, Harper took a deep breath.

Bingham was inspecting the car's coachwork. 'Not a scratch on her,' he said with a wide grin. 'You did champion there, sir. I could probably get you up to snuff before your retirement, if you like.'

It punctured the gloom of the dying. Brought it all back to the everyday. He shook his head. 'I think I'm happier in the back, thank you. Let's go to the town hall.'

TWENTY-SIX

Harper sat with the door closed, a cup of tea growing cold on the desk. How long had the episode on Bellbrooke Avenue lasted? Probably no more than three minutes from the time he sat behind the wheel until he walked into the house. But it had passed with horrific slowness, the way these things always did.

Had it been that way for the soldiers when they went over the top in the trenches? he wondered. Or did time speed up as they waited for a German bullet? It was a question he'd never dare ask a man who'd been there, the same way as he'd keep today's experiences to himself.

Of course it had been reckless and stupid. But they'd reached an impasse. Either someone acted or they'd still be sitting out there, waiting for a chance to end things. Harper couldn't have ordered anyone else to drive and expose himself; the words wouldn't have come. The only solution was to do it himself.

A tap of the door and Miss Sharp entered with a handful of papers. She glanced disapprovingly at the full cup and placed everything on his desk.

'You only need to sign,' she said, then cocked her head. 'I hear you had a driving lesson today.'

He chuckled. 'I suppose you could call it that. Not sure I'll bother with another, mind you.'

'The men have been talking. They say it was a brave thing to do.'

'No,' he said. 'It was a desperate thing to do. A stupid thing.' He smiled. 'That's why it took a stupid man to think of it.'

'Get away with you. Do you want a fresh cup? It's not like you to leave it.'

True enough; it wasn't like him to sit and brood either. But he'd deliberately set two men up to be killed. They were murderers themselves, yet was there anything to be proud of in what he'd done?

If there was an answer, it wasn't going to come easily or quickly.

'No. Thank you, though.'

He skimmed through the documents, adding a flourish of ink on each before pushing them all aside and taking a pad of paper from his desk. Slowly, he began to write his report about what had happened during the morning. Just the facts, none of the fear or what he felt afterwards; they didn't matter.

Compacted into a few sentences, it didn't seem like much. One of many reports that coppers would write about the incident, each from their point of view.

He'd just finished, folded the sheets and placed them in his pocket to take to Millgarth, when Sergeant Ricks arrived.

'It looked like you were on top of things this morning,' Harper said. 'That was a very well executed operation.'

'Thank you, sir.' He lowered his head and blushed. 'We're still checking the London trains. We put the women on them to go home, they get off at Sheffield and come back here. We've had one return three times so far.'

'And each time they do, one or two slip through the net.'

'Exactly, sir.' Ricks gave an emphatic nod. 'The shops have caught a couple. We're winning, but they're doing their best to make it hard for us. Whoever's behind this gang has learned.'

'Then we'd better make sure we do, too. Adapt. Put your thinking cap on, Sergeant. I want a strategy to deal with all this in the morning.'

He knew it was highly organized crime that could take thousands of pounds out of Leeds and hurt some of the biggest shops. Yet somehow he found it hard to think of it as more than an annoyance, low-key. Wrong, but he couldn't shake it from his head.

By five he had a thumping headache that one of Miss Sharp's powders hadn't been able to shake. All he wanted was to go home and find some peace.

No such luck. Alderman Thompson arrived just as Harper put away the papers in his desk. Still not quite the man he'd been before he was attacked, but growing back into himself. Standing straighter, his voice more assertive.

'You haven't done it yet.'

'No. Not yet.'

'Why?'

'Yours isn't the only important case in Leeds.'

'I heard about the Model T boys. Everyone's saying you did a good thing there. But now it's over—'

Harper cut him off, his voice hard and flat. 'I went to see Miss Radcliffe yesterday. She wasn't at home. Today has been filled with other things. I'll go back tomorrow.'

'Just make sure you do.' He wanted to sound insistent, but Harper saw the begging look in his eyes.

'I already told you, Alderman. I'll do it.'

'Right.' And he was gone.

'Home,' he told Bingham with a long, weary sigh.

'Don't fancy driving yourself, sir?' The man grinned.

'I think I'm a damned sight less danger to the world sitting back here.'

*   *   *

For once he was glad of Annabelle's silence. He was lost in his own thoughts. No guilt, just sorrow at more loss after years when millions had died. The sheer waste of it all. But it was the end the gang had chosen. He needed to force all that from his head before it burrowed into his soul.

Chapel Allerton was quiet. Still a nip in the air as darkness came. The Co-op at the top of Hawthorn Road was closing for the night as he arrived to buy a quarter of tea, the lights inside winking out behind him as he left. Sheepscar would still have been bustling. Even the conversation from the Regent along the street was a polite burble. Out here, even the public houses were softer and well-mannered.

He sat and stroked Annabelle's hand, wondering if his cold fingers might stir her. Nothing. But she was here, she was breathing, and she'd come back to him in short bursts for a while yet. Wouldn't she?

Harper had barely had chance to settle in his office when Sergeant Ricks arrived, looking fresh and eager. A clean collar on his shirt, different tie, shaved and his hair neatly combed, he looked more like a man on the rise in a company than a copper.

He placed a folder on the desk. 'Full report on the events at the railway station yesterday and a plan for containing the shop-lifters, sir.'

'Very good. How much do the stores think they lost?'

'Very little, sir. They were on top of it, and only a few slipped through our net. More pickpocket reports than usual, which is probably due to these women. I don't see any way we can stop that.'

'Have any been arriving this morning?'

'On the first train. We've already taken four into custody. One made it out of the station, but a Special caught up with her.'

'How do we make sure the ones we send back to London go all the way there?'

Ricks gestured at the file. 'It's in—'

'Just tell me, Sergeant.'

'The express only makes a few stops. That's about the best we can manage, sir. We can't lock them in to compartments in case there's an accident.'

'Then it'll have to do.'

'Yes, sir.'

'You're doing excellent work on this.' He saw the young man puff himself up with pride.

'Thank you, sir. Mr Dickinson was happy, too.'

'As well he should be. I don't think anyone could do better. Let's see these women off, shall we?'

'Here,' Miss Sharp said, as she placed the papers to be signed in front of him. 'I thought I'd catch you before you wander off somewhere. You have that look in your eye.'

'Do I?'

She looked him in the eye. 'You know full well you do. No need to read any of them, nothing important will happen until after you've gone.'

He laughed. 'You know, in a strange way that's very comforting. I don't suppose there's any chance of a cup of tea?'

Most of the men had gone from the detectives' room at Millgarth, returned to their divisions around Leeds. Now the space felt empty and strangely quiet. Inspector Jackson and Sergeant Clough were writing up their reports, just the scratch of pens on paper and the striking of a match as one of them lit a cigarette.

For the first time in weeks, Walsh looked relaxed, the tension vanished from his face.

'Did you see this morning's papers?' Harper asked.

The superintendent nodded. 'We came out well. All very pleased that nobody was hurt apart from the two killers.'

'There wasn't any way to save them, was there?'

'What? Booth and Hobson?' The question seemed to catch him by surprise. 'Not without putting our own men at risk, sir. You said so yourself.'

He nodded. 'I know. But when I saw the bodies . . . I'm not sure I can explain it.' He'd known Walsh for well over two decades. They'd worked on many cases together over the years. This would be the final one. The man was one of the few who knew him well. 'We did the only thing we could. In the end, though, all I felt was sadness.' He looked up. 'Does that make sense?'

'If you ask me, we're better off with them dead, sir. They've tormented this city. They took a shot at you.'

'Believe me, I'm never likely to forget. Not that or the names of the men they killed. Maybe it's just too much blood.' He sighed. 'I'm glad I'm retiring. I think I've grown too old for all this.'

'At least we finished this one.'

'All except the reports.' He reached into his jacket and took out the sheets he'd written the day before. 'Here's mine.'

'I'll miss you, sir. I'm used to you always being there.'

'So am I. It'll be a shock. But,' he said as he stood, 'I'm not done yet. A couple of other things that need attention. I'm hoping to have it all wrapped up by the end of the month. No loose ends.' Harper gave a short laugh. 'Maybe it'll happen. And maybe pigs will fly, eh?'

There was still one glaring loose end. Charlotte Radcliffe. He telephoned for his car and sat back for the drive out to Shire Oak Road. A circus was setting up on the cinder moor, and plenty of small boys had gathered to watch.

On the other side of Headingley Lane, people paraded in the sunshine around Woodhouse Moor and the grass looked green and inviting. This week he'd buy plants to put in the ground at home. Keep his promise to Annabelle.

The street was quiet, with the kind of dry dustiness to the air that felt more like summer than spring. He pressed the doorbell. No answer again. Still, once again he hadn't telephoned first; she could easily be out. He tried the landlady in the ground-floor flat.

'I'm sure she was here this morning,' the woman answered with a tight, nervous smile. 'I thought I heard her on the stairs. I never look, mind, it's not my business. But I thought it was early for her.' She gave a smile that worried itself away before it fully arrived. 'She's not usually one for a morning, if you know what I mean.'

'I do. Has she had any visitors?'

'I don't know what you mean. She's a tenant, she has her privacy.' She straightened her back and stared at him. 'I don't check up on her.'

'No, of course.'

He didn't believe a word; the woman was reddening at her

own lie. But there was nothing he could do about it. 'I'll come back later and see if she's here.'

It worried him. Charlotte Radcliffe was a woman with the means to run off. With her brother gone, her set in tatters, there was little to keep her in Leeds. All too easy to disappear. He considered the best course as the car glided back towards Leeds.

'Do you know anywhere that sells plants?' he asked Bingham.

'Flowers, shrubs, like that you mean, sir?'

'Yes.'

The driver's face creased into a smile. 'I reckon I do, sir. My brother-in-law, he's a bit of a nurseryman. He has a lot in that line.'

'Are you on good terms?'

'He's all right, sir.'

'Fancy paying him a visit?'

Harper pulled out his watch as they left. Half an hour. He'd had an education as well as a shopping trip. More than that, he'd enjoyed the break. Thinking about things that grew, being told how to plant and care for them, had cleared death from his mind. As the car pulled up outside the railway station, he felt ready for the rest of the day.

Ricks was there, striding around and marshalling his men. A London train must have just arrived, with coppers gathered by the platform barrier to question the passengers. Some were taken away, a few sullen, others cursing a blue streak as they were dragged to the waiting room.

'Looks like a good haul.'

'Not bad, sir,' Ricks agreed with a smile. 'We have someone going through all the compartments in case any of them decided to hide. But I think we have all the shoplifters from this trip.' He pursed his mouth. 'Fewer than the earlier train. I wonder if they're realizing they can't win here.'

'Let's hope so. We have too many men tied up on this. Those women Specials we recruited, are they doing a good job?'

The man's eyes lit up. 'Couldn't be better, sir. Most of them worked the Voluntary Patrol during the war, so they already knew what to do. It's all been going smoothly. Mr Dickinson was here earlier; he seemed happy with them. I tell you, sir, we should probably have more women police constables.'

'Take it up with my successor, Sergeant. He might have more luck than I did. One policewoman isn't enough.' He stared around the station, the thick smell of coal and soot rasping against the back of his throat. A reminder of the way all of Leeds had been when he started on the beat. 'Carry on. Keep me informed.'

A stroll back up to the town hall, still brooding over the best way to deal with Charlotte Radcliffe. He had no evidence to directly connect her to a crime; she'd been careful to keep all that at arm's length. She'd lost her brother and the official verdict was suicide; that meant she'd be grieving. No judge was likely to issue a search warrant for her flat.

He'd managed to pierce her defences when he'd questioned her before. But she'd recovered her poise. Why did he think he'd have any more success the next time?

It didn't matter; he had to try. She might be willing to part with the letters. They'd caused far more damage than she'd ever anticipated. He could give the damned things back to Thompson and be done with it. Let him live with his folly. Maybe he'd learned from it.

Then Chief Constable Tom Harper could close out his career with a clean slate. That was the real reason, and he knew it.

A visit to round out the afternoon. To Burley and a chance to see Ash.

'He'll be glad you've popped by,' Nancy Ash said as she opened the door. 'He's been pining for company.'

'How is he?'

'Improving,' she told him. 'A nurse comes out every other day. He has some colour back.'

He heard the word she didn't say. 'But?'

'He needs something to keep his mind occupied. I try, but he's not one for reading. Never has been.'

'I'm here for advice.'

She chuckled. 'Oh, he's full of that. He'll advise you on everything if you ask, will Fred. You go on through, I'll bring you some tea.'

It was a warm day, but an invalid's fire burned in the grate again. Ash wore his shirt and tie, a heavy cardigan buttoned over the top of it. As soon as he saw Harper, he began to beam.

'Sit yourself down, sir. It's grand to see you.'

He looked much healthier than he had in hospital, with some life in his eyes, almost as if he was ready to return to work.

'Staying out of trouble?'

'I am. My Nancy won't let me anywhere near it. I hear you took care of that gang.'

At least the news was still reaching him, Harper thought. Keeping abreast would make him feel he was still part of things.

'We did.' He gave the bare details.

'It sounds as if that young lad Ricks is keeping a lid on that invasion of shoplifters.'

He smiled. 'He's impressive. Future chief constable material.'

Ash nodded. 'One thing left, isn't there?'

'Miss Radcliffe.' It didn't take long to bring him up to date. 'We're never going to be able to charge her. But I'd like to see the alderman has his letters.'

'Then it sounds as if your only choice is to confront her.'

'You've met her. What do you think my chances of success would be?'

'Probably fifty-fifty,' Ash answered after a minute. 'We both know the whole thing slipped out of her control.'

'It started out as fun and turned very dark.'

'Exactly, sir.' Another nod. 'Her brother and his best friend have gone. Someone else tried to kill himself. Any gloss is long gone. She might be glad to be rid of it all.'

'Might,' Harper said.

'We both know she's an odd duck, sir. Much of it might depend on her mood or the way the wind's blowing at the time. Give her the chance to close the book on it all. She might be grateful.' He gave a small laugh. 'Not that she'd ever show it, of course.'

'No. I can't imagine that.'

The talk drifted to other, inconsequential things. After three-quarters of an hour, Harper rose and they shook hands.

'That's exactly the tonic he needed,' Nancy said. 'You for retirement soon, isn't it?'

'Days away.'

'Don't be a stranger. You've known each other too long.' She nodded towards the car. 'I took your driver a cup of tea. He looked parched out there.'

TWENTY-SEVEN

Sergeant Ricks's report sat on top of the pile of papers to sign. Almost nine o'clock, another pleasant morning, and he could sense the hours ticking away to retirement.

The police had done an excellent job of containing the shop-lifters. The invasion. Most of those who escaped the net had been caught in the shops. A few were certainly still operating, Ricks wrote. At least he was honest about that, Harper thought. He'd learn to shade the truth as he rose through the ranks.

Soon it would all be over, and the women hadn't managed to do much damage to the businesses in Leeds. Before he left the job, he'd put a commendation in Ricks's file. The man had earned it.

Harper picked up the telephone and spoke to Sissons in the intelligence section. 'Do you have an hour or so?'

His mouth twitched into a smile. 'Something to do with Miss Radcliffe, sir?'

'What else?'

'We're short-handed here, with Ricks and his case.'

'I'll have you back soon enough.'

He had Bingham park the car farther along Shire Oak Road as they put together a plan. Simple, something that gave her a way to end things without losing face.

'If we try and corner her, we'll get nowhere, sir.'

'I agree. You've met her, you know,' he added on reflection. 'This might seem more believable if it came from you.'

'Very good, sir.'

'Right.' Harper grasped the door handle. 'Shall we?'

The gravel on the drive crunched under their feet. Third time lucky, he thought as he rang the bell.

No answer.

He tried again, and a third time. Finally he tried the landlady.

'I don't pry, I never have, I told you that yesterday. I did hear her moving around earlier. There are a couple of floorboards up there that creak. And I heard someone climb the stairs, but I didn't hear anybody leaving.

Nobody leaving. He felt it in the pit of his belly. Something was very wrong. He glanced over at Sissons. The superintendent's face was like stone.

'We need to go up there.' He heard the urgency in his voice.

'I don't know. It's her flat.'

'This is police business. Can you come upstairs with us and bring your keys in case you need to unlock the door for us?'

'What?' Her eyes opened wide. 'Do you think . . .'

'We don't know,' Sissons told her. 'We're simply trying to take care of possibilities. It's probably nothing. Could be a problem with the doorbell.'

Words to try and assure her. But both policemen knew the truth. Something was waiting up there.

He felt the prickle of fear as they climbed the stairs. Everything in the house was clean, the wood brightly polished and smelling of lavender and beeswax. A stained-glass window on the landing shone reds and blues and yellows across the walls.

Harper knocked on the door of Miss Radcliffe's flat, straining his ears to try and pick out any sound inside. He glanced at Sissons; the superintendent shook his head. He brought his fist down on the wood for a second time. Still nothing.

'You're certain you heard her and someone else up here earlier?'

'Yes.' The landlady's voice seemed to catch in her throat and her face was pale. 'I'm positive I never heard either of them leave.'

'Then I believe we have a situation of interest to the police. If the door doesn't open I'll need you to unlock it.'

He grabbed the knob and twisted it. It gave under his hand and he pushed it open.

'Miss Radcliffe?' he called into the room. 'Charlotte?'

But there was only silence. He took a pace inside, then another. The heavy curtains were closed, the living room a large gloomy space. He heard Sissons speak gently to the landlady.

'It's probably best if you go back downstairs. We'll take care of things from here.'

She moved slowly away, caught between curiosity and horror. Once she'd gone, Harper drew back the curtains and let the light flood in. A pair of empty glasses on the table, two ashtrays piled with cigarette butts. No sign of any struggle.

The kitchen looked pristine, as if she'd never done any cooking in there. A glance and he came out again, shaking his head.

A toilet with sink off the living room. The towel hung, rumpled. He felt it; damp.

'Bedroom,' Harper said. Without even thinking, he kept his voice low.

They were in there, on the bed. Charlotte Radcliffe lay on her back, eyes open as she stared up at the ceiling. She was dressed, not a mark on her that he could see. Her skin was pale. Harper placed his fingertips against her neck. The flesh was cold, and there wasn't the faintest hint of a pulse.

'Cyanide.' Sissons spoke into the stillness of the room. 'That's what it looks like to me, sir.'

Harper nodded. The man beside her was every bit as dead, but his passing hadn't been as peaceful. He had hold of her hand, but his lips were drawn back in an horrific rictus grin. A mask, not a face.

Robert Wilton still had a bandage on his left wrist.

'Sir?' Sissons asked.

'In a minute.'

'We need the coroner here.'

'Yes. Ring them. Don't use the phone here. Downstairs. The landlady should have one.'

The door closed. It was impossible to take his eyes off the pair on the bed. Grotesque, awful, but something compelled him to keep looking and try to understand how it had happened. Robert Wilton had felt guilty enough over his friend to try killing himself. Perhaps he imagined that coming here and doing this would make amends. His mind had twisted in on itself. Maybe the thought that murdering the woman behind the deaths would balance the scales.

Had he caused this? Harper thought back over the things he'd said to Wilton in their last conversation. If this was how the man had tried to find peace, it hadn't worked. The expression on his face was torment. Regret? Too late to ever know.

His eyes were damp. Harper rubbed them before a tear could form. Never, not in his wildest thoughts, had he imagined something like this. He wanted Charlotte Radcliffe to pay, but not like this. He stood, shallow breaths and prayers.

Four bodies in three days. Christ Almighty, an extreme way to bow out of a job. Not what he'd have chosen, not what he wanted.

Was it? Had he given Wilton a nudge, a hint, the way Charlotte had done about her brother or Ben Rogers?

He didn't know. The only certainty was that the guilt would come to choke him.

Harper took in the empty air of death and roused himself. The letters were here somewhere. Time to find them while he could.

It didn't take five minutes. They were buried at the bottom of a drawer under some silk underwear, still in their envelopes, neatly bound with a piece of ribbon. He recognized Thompson's scrawl on the address. A collection of love letters. Harper slid them into his inside pocket, out of sight.

Sissons returned. 'On their way, sir. I told the landlady what happened, then I made her a cup of tea. I think she's in shock.'

'I'm sure she is. I'd never expected this, either.'

Charlotte Radcliffe had seemed to be one of those people who glided through life. Someone who caused things to happen, initiated them with a hint or a word, then stayed completely untouched by them.

But it had caught up with her. She looked peaceful, as if death had crept up on her before she had chance to fight against it.

And Wilton? Had he waited until she was dead, until he was certain, before he took his own poison? It would probably be in the glasses in the other room. Had he decided later that he'd made a mistake? At least he'd died holding the hand of a woman he'd once loved. The one who pulled the strings of all her men.

'There's nothing more for us here, sir.'

He sighed. 'No, I don't suppose there is. Nothing for anyone. Not now.'

Too much death, all of it too close, he thought as the car sped back to town. The sun was bright, people looked cheery as he passed, but Harper didn't notice. The black cloud hung over him.

Standing on Great George Street, Sissons looked uncomfortable. 'I'll be needing a statement from you later, sir.'

'Of course.' It was the superintendent's case, after all. He'd simply stood aside this morning and allowed Harper to take the lead and do what he needed. 'Thank you.' He attempted a smile, but knew it wasn't really there. 'At least you know where to find me. For now, anyway.'

A man passed on the other side of the road with a gauze mask tied around his face. Someone determined to stay alive. Harper sighed. Here he was, surrounded by death. Drowning in it.

The stairs just seemed to go up and up, taking an age to reach the top. He was weary, stopping to hold on to the marble balustrade and look down as he caught his breath.

Thompson was still working in his office, surrounded by a blizzard of papers. He glanced up, grunted, and pointed to a chair before returning to his place in a document. Only when he'd finished and set it aside did he give Harper his attention.

'You look like a man who could use a stiff drink.'

'Maybe so.' He reached in his jacket, took out the packet of letters and tossed them on to the desk.

The alderman's eyes grew wide. He tugged on the ribbon, then riffled through the stack. 'Thank you. I mean that. Where were they?'

'In a drawer in her bedroom.'

He pursed his lips. 'She just handed them over? You didn't arrest her?'

'For what?' Harper could hear the sorrow that filled his voice. 'No. Even if I wanted to, I couldn't.'

'Why?'

'Because she's dead, Alderman. Lying on her bed, poisoned. The man who did it was right next to her. He'd killed himself, too. He tried once before, a week ago, and he didn't succeed. This time he finished the job.'

Harper wanted to see how his words affected the man.

The colour left Thompson's face. He dropped the bundle as if it was burning him.

'I had no idea,' he said after a long time. 'I . . .' He couldn't find the words to finish the sentence. 'I'm sorry.'

'Charles Radcliffe. Ben Rogers. Robert Wilton. Charlotte Radcliffe. You're going to be carrying a lot of weight on your shoulders. I hope they're broad enough.'

A little fire came into the man's eyes. 'I didn't start this. They did. You said so yourself, just the other week.'

He had, that was true. But today he had no charity in his soul. No forgiveness. 'I did, and they all carried their share of the blame. But what was it all about?' He shifted his gaze to the letters. 'Those. You wrote them. You were the one who had your fling with her.'

'I know. Believe me, I know.'

At the door, Harper turned back.

'Tell me something: was she worth it all?'

Thompson cocked his head and gave a small, faraway smile. 'At the time, I thought she was. There were moments when I believe I'd have walked through fire for her.' He snorted. 'It passed as soon as I received the first blackmail letter.' He placed a hand on the envelopes. 'Thank you for returning these. No one will ever see them again.'

'It's the last favour you'll ever have from me. No more debts.'

'No,' the alderman agreed. 'None.'

It was done. But as long as Harper was alive, it would never be over. Charlotte and Wilton would join the parade of his dead, behind Booth and Hobson and all the others from his time on the force.

Still, as he unlocked the front door on Hawthorn Road, Harper felt all the tensions and anger begin to drain away. There was sorrow enough inside these four walls, but it was familiar and he was with the people he loved.

'She spoke a little this morning,' Julia said. 'Just two or three sentences. Everything ordinary.'

'What happened after that?' he asked as she settled beside his wife. She didn't stir.

'She withdrew. As if someone had touched a switch. I helped her eat, I've taken her to the toilet.'

'I'll sit with her.'

He read stories from the newspaper. Light, amusing pieces she might enjoy. She never heard, of course, but they helped to purge the day from his mind.

Mary cooked after she arrived home. At the table he fed Annabelle, watching her eat.

He washed the pots, then they settled with a jigsaw and records on the gramophone. Annabelle didn't stir; even the music couldn't reach her.

Before bed, he made his circuit of the house, checking the doors and windows were locked. All the usual routines. So ordinary, so mundane, so comforting.

The thoughts came in the darkness as he knew they would. They turned into dangerous dreams, tormenting and rebuking him.

At least his wife had slept peacefully, Harper thought as he rose on Saturday morning. While he felt as if he'd barely rested, she hadn't stirred during the night. No more than a snuffle and an occasional snore. He glanced over at her as he dressed.

He loved her as she was now, but when he looked, he saw the woman with the smile and the wink, the quick comment, the passion and the intelligence that had made him fall in love. That was who she would always be to him.

His final Saturday on the job. He'd thought of it for so long that it was hard to believe it had arrived. Tomorrow he'd put those plants he'd bought in the ground. After that, five more days and it would all be over. All that time as a copper, gone.

'You look like you have a lot on your mind.' Mary sat next to him as he ate breakfast, feeling the teapot to check it was still warm, then pouring a cup.

'It's been quite a week.'

'Those robbers? Everyone said the police did the right thing.'

'Them, and other things.'

'The *Evening Post* called you a hero.'

He chuckled and shook his head. 'I just wanted it to be over, that's all.'

'Clearing the books?'

'Something like that.'

'Is there going to be a big leaving do on Friday?'

'I don't know. Nobody's said anything. I hope it's quiet.'

She stood and kissed him on the top of his head. 'I'd better get moving. Don't want the business disappearing under me.'

A clear morning, the sun shining, already warm. No need for a raincoat. He'd enjoy the spring while it was here.

He wrote his report on the deaths they'd found yesterday. Nothing more than facts, and not all of them; no mention of Thompson's letters. Everything was blunt, in the plain, dry language coppers used that kept clear of all feelings.

'I'll be closing the case as soon as the post-mortems are complete, sir,' Sissons said as he handed over his report. 'I can't imagine any problems.'

'No,' Harper agreed slowly. 'Neither can I.'

Better to let the truth lie sleeping. No one would ever know.

Ricks arrived, grinning, almost bouncing as he stood.

'It looks like we've broken the back of it all, sir. Only five arrived this morning, and we stopped all of them. They'll be on their way home in an hour.' He beamed with pride. 'The word I've had is that they've decided to cut their losses here and move on to Nottingham and Derby.'

'I'm glad to hear that. You've done very well with this.'

'Thank you, sir. My best estimate is that there are still three of the women here. We're working with the stores and doing everything we can to find them.'

'Looks as if it'll all be over soon.'

'Thank you, sir.'

At least one of the cases had gone smoothly. Tidy up the loose ends with the shoplifters and everything would be closed. He'd be able to leave with a clean slate. Apart from signing some papers, there was nothing more for him to do. A final meeting with the Watch Committee on Monday; that was the only important thing ahead before retirement.

It was a curious feeling, to eke out the morning and feel the minutes slipping away. He was grateful when twelve arrived and Miss Sharp slipped her head around the door to wish him a good weekend.

Harper patted one of the stone lions as he went down the steps in front of the town hall. Plenty of traffic on the Headrow. On Commercial Street the pavements were packed with pedestrians.

He felt an impulse to buy something for Annabelle. They'd been caught up in her illness for too long, maybe a present would help her. Something bright and colourful. Something to give her pleasure when she noticed it. The idea made him smile as he glanced in jewellers' windows, hoping for something to catch his imagination.

It was a copper's eye, all those years of experience that made him notice. Just ahead of him, a woman's hand snaking out to reach into someone else's handbag and lightly draw out the purse.

Harper quickened his pace, catching up with the woman as she tried to disappear into the crowd. He put a hand round her arm and called out, 'Pickpocket! Someone get the police.'

She turned to face him. Pure fury in her eyes. The sunlight glinted on something in her hand. A pair of scissors.

All he could do was watch in horror as she stabbed him. No overcoat, jacket open. He felt the point slice into his skin. Harper put his hand over the wound, as if that might stop it. But the blood kept flowing. Someone was screaming. He saw the trickle of deep red over his fingers, feeling the horror grow. Oh Jesus, he thought. No. It couldn't end like this. So ordinary. After everything, it was all down to a pickpocket with a pair of bloody scissors.

TWENTY-EIGHT

He walked, an army of shadows behind him. He could feel them there, keeping pace, silent and urging him on. It was a long journey, a slow, steady exhausting climb up a hill.

Finally, he opened his eyes, blinking at the sudden brightness all around him. The ones who'd been there had vanished, leaving him alone. He was in a bed, he knew that. Too tired to even raise his head.

'You're back with us, then. Very good.' The woman was smiling down at him. Her face was familiar. So was her uniform. He breathed, tasted the harsh carbolic at the back of his throat. Harper coughed, and in the space of a heartbeat, his mind began to work and everything fell into place: he was in a bed in the infirmary. The woman was Sister Carter.

Annabelle. She must be frantic. Panic started to rise in his chest.

'What . . .' He tried to speak, but his mouth was too dry to make the words.

'Do you remember?' she asked. He stared at her, thinking it would come to him. But after a moment he gave a small shake of his head. Nothing. Just a blank. He'd been walking in the middle of town and now he was here.

'A woman stabbed you.'

His eyes widened. Her words pulled back a curtain and he remembered. The way he tried to staunch the wound with his hand. Harper began to raise his arm, to see if the blood was still there. But the effort was too great.

'The surgeons did a good job on you, Mr Harper,' Sister Carter told him. 'Just as well, too. We've had half the senior police officers in Leeds here, and your daughter reading the Riot Act.'

He smiled. He could imagine Mary buttonholing the staff and demanding information.

'My wife.' The words came out as a croak.

'Your daughter is looking after her. She said you'd be desperate to know that, and everything is fine.'

'Yes.' Thank God for Mary. She was on top of everything. The fear started to ebb away.

'You're going to survive. The doctor will tell you more in the morning, but there's nothing to worry about.' She squeezed his hand. 'Right now you need to sleep and start your recovery.'

His body was so heavy as his eyelids closed.

Harper woke in daylight. It came through a window, the paleness of early sun. He lay, watching it, letting his thoughts drift. It was all there now. The pickpocket. His hand on her arm. The sharp pain of the scissors in his belly. For a moment he was tempted to try and look. No, he decided; best not.

He must have dozed again. The next thing he knew a doctor

was bending at his bedside, two others beside him. The sheets were pulled back and he was examining the wound. Pointing out a few things to the people with him. Acting like God. A nurse hurriedly scribbled in his chart, trying to keep pace.

'You're a lucky man, Chief Constable,' the man said, straightening up. 'Before the war a wound like that might have killed you. We know a great deal more now. Learned it in the battlefield stations and the hospitals in France and at home. Half an inch to the right and you'd have had some awful damage. As it is, you'll be as good as new in time.'

'How long?' He croaked out the words.

'Impossible to say.' He waved the question away, as if it was too unimportant to concern him.

The doctor moved on, the others trailing behind. He was in a private room; Harper hadn't noticed that before. He tried to push himself up, to sit. After thirty seconds he was panting with the effort. Sister Carter bustled in.

'Don't you dare,' she scolded. A glance at his notes, hanging on the end of the bed. Then her hands were lifting him, as if he was a doll that weighed nothing, until he was propped up against the pillow.

'Better?' she asked with a smile.

'Thank you. What time is it?'

'Just after eight o'clock on Sunday morning.'

She put a glass of water in his hand. He swirled it around his mouth before he swallowed. Nothing had ever tasted so good, so sweet. Almost twenty hours since he'd been stabbed. A lifetime, but no time at all.

Sitting helped. He felt less of an invalid. There was pain, more of it as he tried to shift position; enough to make him gasp. But he was alive. He was here. He was going to be fine. The doctor had said so himself.

Mary was the first visitor. Standing, smiling, as if he was a view to be savoured.

'God, you terrified me, Da.'

Then her arms were gently around his neck and he felt her tears against his face.

'It didn't do much for me, either.'

She snuffled and sniffled, pulling away to wipe her eyes with a handkerchief.

'The doctor says you're going to recover,' she told him.

'Let's hope he's right.' He took a breath. 'Your mother?'

'She's still quiet most of the time. Last night she asked Julia where you were, then she forgot about it.'

There were a few times when Annabelle's illness could be a blessing, he thought.

'I don't know how long I'll be in here.'

'As long as you need to be.' Her eyes flashed. 'I had a word with that nurse, Sister Carter. She's going to let me know. You'd better do what she says, Da.'

He tried to laugh. Even in hospital, his life was ruled by women.

Walsh came next, sitting by the side of the bed.

'How are you feeling, sir?'

'Better for being alive.'

'We caught the one who did it. One of the women Specials was following her when you stepped in.'

He could see it now, the fingers slipping into the handbag and taking the purse. His arm reaching to grab the woman.

'The pickpocket was one of that London group,' Walsh continued. 'We're charging her with attempted murder.'

He nodded. Typical of his luck to find one of them.

'Thank the Special for me, please.' He gestured at the bed. 'I'm not too mobile at the moment.'

'Probably not home until the end of the week, sir. That's what they told me. And that's *only* if you're doing well.' He grinned. 'It's an extreme way to get out of your leaving do.'

Trust a copper to make him smile. 'At least you won't have to chip in for a present. Has Mr Dickinson taken over?'

'Yes, sir. Looks like you've retired now.'

Not how he'd planned things, but it could have been much worse. He was alive. He'd mend.

'I suppose you want my statement on what happened.'

The offer seemed to take Walsh by surprise. 'Are you sure? There's no rush.'

'Let's get it out of the way.'

* * *

Monday brought Dickinson. Acting Chief Constable Dickinson now.

'Settling in?' Harper asked.

'More or less.' He looked abashed, uncomfortable. 'I'm sorry it all ended this way.'

'In a blaze of stupidity, you mean?'

'You were doing your duty.'

'For all the good it brought me.'

A parade of visitors. Sissons, Inspector Jackson, all the divisional heads. Alderman Thompson, staying a few minutes and saying little. Ash, looking around warily, as if they might not let him leave again.

'Matching pair of stomach wounds, sir,' he said. He'd been shot in the belly three years earlier.

'I wasn't trying to copy you,' Harper said with a smile.

'I could send my Nancy over to keep you on the straight and narrow once you're out of here.'

'I think my daughter will take care of that.'

'Always like to offer, sir.' He winked and they began to laugh.

And every evening Mary appeared, staying until visiting time was over. She talked about cancelling her trip to the battlefield, but he insisted she go.

'I'll be back to normal by then. Julia's in the house if there are any problems.'

Finally she agreed. Maybe that would be an end to it.

Every day he felt a little stronger, but the doctor refused to discharge him for over a week. He was chafing to be home, to begin this new life of retirement and see if it was any better than being a copper.

Mary was supposed to be waiting to ferry him home in her Model T. He'd wanted to walk out of the hospital, to prove something to himself. A few hesitant steps across the room showed he still had a long path to being fit again. Safer to settle for Sister Carter pushing him in a wheelchair.

No Mary outside. Instead it was Bingham, helping him into the back seat.

'Should you be doing this?' Harper asked as they pulled away. 'I'm not the chief any more.'

The driver gave a sly grin. 'What they don't know won't hurt them, sir. Besides, this way I can take you on a detour.'

Millgarth. As they approached, he believed he could smell the way it was inside, those years of wear and sweat and fear. Bingham pulled up outside and tapped the horn. In seconds the men began to emerge. Both the night and day watches. Every beat must be deserted, Harper thought. God only knew what crimes were being committed right now.

Finally Walsh emerged and stood everyone to attention. They all saluted. Sitting in the car, all he could do was return it, feeling moved in a way he'd never known before.

'You'd better drive on,' he said, glancing back to see them all still standing there. 'How long did it take to organize that?'

'Hardly any time at all, sir. They were happy to turn out for you. It would be the same at every station.'

All for him, he thought, and shook his head.

On Hawthorn Road, Mary bustled out of the house. But Bingham was the one to help him out of the car. As Harper rested his weight on a walking stick, they stood facing each other.

'Thank you,' Harper said. 'For everything.'

'It's been a pleasure sir.' He stuck out his hand and the men shook. 'Just make sure you have a long retirement now.'

'I'll try.'

Inside, he stood for a moment, soaking in the feeling of home. This would be it now. No more going to work each morning. His life was here. With Mary and Julia supporting him, he shuffled through to the parlour. His heart rose as he saw Annabelle there. Her head didn't turn as he said hello. She simply stared at nothing.

'She was bright first thing this morning,' Mary told him.

'It doesn't matter.' He leaned over and kissed the top of her head, drawing in the scent of her body that he'd known for so long. That was home. 'It doesn't matter at all.'

He had the quiet life forced upon him. For the first few days he stayed in bed, grateful to simply be home again. Then sitting in the parlour with Annabelle, moving round the house in an invalid's hobble. At rare times his wife was there, alert and aware. When she asked why he was home in the day, Harper simply said, 'I've finally retired.'

She nodded slowly, then looked at him. 'We've grown old, haven't we, Tom?'

'I suppose we have.'

'Was it all worth it?'

No need to ask what she meant by it. Or perhaps it wasn't important.

He kissed her. 'Of course it was. Every bit of it.'

As time passed, he began to walk a little more easily. But the recovery was slow.

'Takes longer to spring back,' the doctor told him. 'It'll never be the same. Your body took a hammering in all those years you were a policeman.'

Each day he felt a little better, a tiny bit stronger. But the plants he'd bought in April withered in their pots; no chance of putting them in the ground in his condition. There was always next year, he decided. He'd be able to do it then.

Mary left on her trip to France, and the house seemed unbalanced without her energy and eagerness. When she returned, she was sombre, reflective. Harper wasn't surprised. Even without the bodies, death had been all around her on the Somme. It would be impossible not to sense it.

'The guide took us through everything,' she said. She'd been at home for a week, glad to dive back into the routine of work, not to have to spend all day thinking about what she'd seen.

'How bad was it?' he asked. Not that there could be anything good about it.

They were sitting at the table, working on an old jigsaw of the Houses of Parliament. Annabelle was comfortable, another quiet night in her chair.

'Not like anything I could imagine,' Mary told him quietly. 'I don't know how they lived in those trenches.' She was silent for a long moment. 'The strangest thing, though, is that grass is already growing back over no man's land. There are bodies under there. Len's, probably.'

'How did his mother take it?'

'The same as me. At first it seemed impossible. I felt like we'd entered hell, Da. I swear I never heard a single bird when we were around the trenches. By the end of the day we were crying. It was all we could do.'

'What about afterwards?'

She shook her head with sorrow. 'I don't think any of us talked much on the train home.'

He took hold of his daughter's hand. 'Are you glad you went?'

A long exhalation of breath. 'I think so. I'll probably be trying to understand it for years. I'm not sure you can make sense of so many deaths. But I've seen it. I know it'll sound daft, but I feel I've made my peace with it now.'

'It sounds like it was exactly what you needed.' The car, the clothes, the trip. There would be bumps along the way, and the past would always be there, but it could no longer own her.

The envelope was a pure, brilliant white and heavy for something so thin. Harper opened it and took out the paper. Embossed, official and grand. He'd been put forward for the honour of Member of the Order of the British Empire in recognition of his services to policing. Would he reply and tell them he accepted the award?

He refolded the letter and returned it to the envelope. Thompson's doing, he was certain of that. The reward for returning the letters. Even in retirement, the man couldn't let him be.

There would be ample time to decide later.

By the start of autumn he was able to push Annabelle around Chapel Allerton in her wheelchair. The leaves were beginning to turn, he could feel the freshness in the air. It was as if summer had vanished, slipped through his fingers without him realizing.

How many more years, he wondered as he took her through the park.

EPILOGUE

Leeds, 1924

H arper sat and stared out of the car window while Mary drove. The leaves were falling, there was the smell of coal fires in the air when he walked. Soon enough another year would be over.

She changed gears as they climbed the steep hill of Harehills Lane. Mary was a calm, assured woman behind the wheel. In everything, he thought. His daughter was in her thirties now, unmarried, content with her life. Her business was flourishing, she was successful, wealthy by anyone's definition.

Left on to Kimberley Road, then down to the cemetery. No need for conversation. As they walked along the path, Mary took his hand and gently squeezed it. He gave her a brief smile.

The way to the grave was imprinted on his mind. He came here every month, winter or summer, making the journey on the tram. He was retired, what else was he going to do with his time? But that wasn't the whole truth. He needed his visits to this place.

Today was the anniversary of her death. October the twenty-ninth. Two years in the ground.

They stood side by side facing the headstone and the words carved in the granite.

Annabelle Harper
1859-1922
Beloved wife and mother

Short, simple. Decades from now it would mean nothing to anyone. But it said everything they felt. Harper bowed his head. Not to pray but to remember.

The final year had been hard. A few things managed to touch Annabelle. The photograph she'd made him pose for in full detective uniform of top hat and frock coat had her laughing. A record on the gramophone. A scent in the air when he took her out in the wheelchair. But it happened so rarely, as if she was curling in on herself, preparing to leave.

At least the end was peaceful. In the middle of the night, her body seemed to buck twice in the bed. The movement woke him. He turned over and put his fingertips against her neck, hoping against hope that it had been nothing. A bad dream, some sort of spasm.

But she was already gone. No pulse, no breath.

Peaceful. Instant. In her own home. The thoughts flickered through his mind. She'd been next to him, not alone.

He stood and dressed in the darkness, the way he'd done so often when he was still working. Now it seemed strange as he fumbled for his clothes. The world had tipped off its axis. He could feel silent tears coursing down his cheeks as he climbed the stairs and tapped on Mary's door.

She opened it, dressing gown clutched around her, hair down, panic in her eyes.

'What is it?'

'Your mother.'

He didn't have to say more. They held each other for a long time, then he began all the business around death.

He'd felt relieved, and then guilty for it. Now, after so many visits here, he still wasn't sure what was better, this or having her as she'd been.

Selfish. This way Annabelle had peace. Release from it all.

He placed the flowers he'd brought in a stone vase planted in the ground and filled it from a milk bottle of water. Pulled a few weeds until the grave was pristine.

'She loves us, you know, Da.'

'I do.'

'More than anything.'

Silence on the drive home. They still shared the house on Hawthorn Road. Julia the nurse had left after the funeral, gone to a new post in Ilkley.

Harper paid a woman to cook and clean for them. She came Monday to Friday, and on the weekends it was just the two of them. Mary was old enough to have the vote now, but she'd become more active with the suffragettes again. Perhaps it was a way of filling empty time.

He'd planted flowers in the garden the spring after his retirement. By then his body had been strong enough to dig. Annabelle had lived long enough to see her rose bush bloom. Full, white Yorkshire roses. What she'd always wanted. He'd picked one, stripped off the thorns and placed it in her hands. Her expression never changed.

He made a pot of tea and turned on the radio, hearing the hums and crackles as it warmed up. The BBC had become good company, a sound to fill the rooms.

He turned his head, thinking he'd heard something, and for just a moment he believed he saw Annabelle sitting in her chair, smiling and winking at him.

What Became of Them

Frederick Ash enjoyed a quiet retirement. Harper would occasionally visit and they'd stroll on Woodhouse Moor, reliving past cases. He took up crown green bowling, becoming a regular at his club, enjoying the sport even if he didn't play it well. He had a second heart attack in 1927 and died in hospital. His wife, Nancy, passed away two years later.

Superintendent Dominic Walsh never rose in rank. He remained the head of A Division at Millgarth until his retirement in 1933. He died in 1938 after a short illness. His son joined the force and ended up as a uniformed inspector during the Second World War.

Superintendent Sissons was head of the Intelligence Division until 1933, when he was recruited by the War Office to lead a programme linking intelligence units from all the major police forces. He served until 1945 and then retired, living quietly in Knaresborough with his wife until his death in 1960.

Sergeant Ricks progressed through the ranks and became the chief constable of Leeds City Police shortly before World War II began. After leading the force through the war and the brutal winter of 1947, he took early retirement to become a farmer with a smallholding outside York.

Alderman Ernest Thompson surprised everyone by choosing not to stand for re-election to the council in 1921. Instead, he enjoyed a quiet retirement, refusing speaking engagements. He died of cancer in 1930.

Mary Harper never married. She handed over complete control of her secretarial school to Gladys Naylor, the woman who'd been running it, and focused on the secretarial agency. Both

continued to prosper. Her interest in politics grew stronger during
the Depression. She joined the Labour Party and accompanied the
Jarrow marchers from Leeds to Wakefield as they passed on their
way to London. That same month, she took part in the demonstration against Oswald Mosley and his Blackshirts on Holbeck
Moor. In 1945 she was elected as councillor for Chapel Allerton
ward, holding the seat for eight years. She retired from the council
and business in 1953, sold the house on Hawthorn Road and
moved to a flat in Moortown, becoming an avid motorist, touring
Britain. She died in 1979 and was buried in Harehills Cemetery
next to her parents.

Tom Harper MBE found that retirement left him with too much
time on his hands. In 1926, after long discussions with his
daughter, he ran for Leeds City Council as an independent in
Chapel Allerton ward and won. For the next ten years he threw
himself into council business, days filled with meetings and
engagements. Finally, at the age of 76, he stood down. Two years
later he died peacefully in his chair in the parlour as the radio
played. According to his wishes, he was buried beside his wife
in Harehills Cemetery.

ACKNOWLEDGEMENTS

I t's hard to say goodbye to Tom and Annabelle, Mary, and all the others. They're not simply characters on a page to me, they're family. I care deeply about them. Hard as the decision to end the series was, I know it was the right thing to do, and leave each one of them with a gentle hug.

Now there will be no more for me to write about them. There had been a great deal, though, more than three-quarters of a million words, which seems staggering. In retrospect, I realize that these are not only crime novels, but also the story of a family over thirty years, and – in some very small way – the story of Leeds. I'm proud of all of that.

While I might have initially put them on the computer screen, I'm certainly not the only one involved in bringing them to the page you hold. All the people at Severn House who have believed in the Harpers: Sara Porter, my editor there, Piers Tilbury, who's produced all the stunning covers, and everyone else up to Joanne Grant, the publisher. I've been working with them for thirteen years, and it's been a pleasure that I hope will continue for much longer. Lynne Patrick, who's done the detailed edits on all my books, knows my work and me so well. We've become good friends over the years, and I trust her judgement implicitly.

And none of this would be possible (or worthwhile) without the love and support of Penny Lomas. That's more important than I think even she knows. Thank you, all of you.